Being born, bred and bored in Essex for 45 years has provided Jonathan Durden with ample fuel for this dark tale, as have his 30 years in the advertising industry.

In 1990, Jonathan co-founded the media group PHD, leaving as its UK President in 2007, when it boasted a £5 billion turnover across 44 countries and a strong reputation for creativity.

He has been a columnist for the *Daily Telegraph*, the *Guardian*, *Media Week* and *Marketing Week*, but is best known as a housemate in the TV reality series *Big Brother* from 2007. (He walked out to attend the funeral of his 104-year-old grandmother.)

Currently, Jonathan is a partner in the successful advertising agency MCBD and is a co-owner of the production company Good TV.

Jonathan is 50 and has two children.

Essex, Drugs and Rock'n'Roll is his first novel.

D1189320

ESSEX,
DRUGS &
ROCK'N'ROLL

ESSEX, DRUGS & ROCK'N'ROLL

A novel by
Jonathan Durden

First published in 2008
by Adelita Ltd
www.adelita.co.uk

ISBN: 978-0-9552017-2-1

Printed and bound in Great Britain

This book is dedicated to life.

So thank you for having me here, and for blessing me with such an amazing family and wonderful friends to share it with.

A special thank you goes to Adam Phillips, without whose editing genius and calm nature this novel might have been more a work of friction than fiction.

I hope you enjoy reading it.

PROLOGUE

There is a phrase out there to impart wisdom in any situation and draw the sting out of life. These truisms have no author. They spring loosely to mind, the exact words varying for want of an authentic version, quoted and misquoted by generations.

'Youth is wasted on the young.' The battle cry of those in the first, second or final flush of ageing.

'Life is a journey.' The sad prop of every loser suffering a thwarted promotion or failed relationship. And the slogan from a Nissan Micra ad.

Just when we feel alone and abandoned, washed up on the bank of life, up springs, 'There are plenty more fish in the sea' to plop us back in the warm water, and see us swimming happily on our way without a backward glance.

This way, we can survive the consequences of our own failures or lack of vision or plain bad luck and surface-skim over it all like a cowboy plasterer. The peaks flattened, the troughs raised slightly, the status quo maintained.

It is painful to dig deeper, and we are not encouraged to do so. Instead we live life in a linear fashion. Like a long relay race, passing the baton from day to day, events planned ahead under the delusion that we can make plans at all.

It's the curse of mankind to be born without any retained memories or wisdom from previous generations. A blank floppy on to which society can write its code of practice.

Laws and the 'jam tomorrow' philosophies of religion keep us safe from ourselves by channelling our hopes and fears down designated lanes.

Yet, by and large, people accept this situation, content to measure success and happiness by modest victories. Cash put away for a pension. The mortgage paid off and the kids whisked off to Disneyland before they're too old. Most of all, not to be alone, even if the alternative is miserable. Better to sit down when the music stops, in a game of musical chairs, than be the one left standing at the end.

Well, that's fine and dandy. But what if there were another way? To have the luxury of being able to revisit those things we mucked up, finish all that unfinished business, put right all those injustices. To die without needing to come back and haunt anyone or anywhere.

To be liberated by a series of revelations and be transformed. To be lifted high above for a helicopter view, we would see our familiar, predictable world in all its rich variety. To see life no longer as a linear process but as an intricate tapestry. Multiple experiences happening in the same instant, every second becoming more delicious and precious.

To lose all sense of fear or consequence. To be on a rocket-powered runaway rollercoaster, fuelled by anger and joy, with no worries about what comes next. To grab the past and the future by the scruff of the neck, and make them both dance to your tune in the present.

Now that's living. And there's no reassuring platitude for that one – as Mark Cohen is about to find out.

CHAPTER ONE

Armageddon Day, 21st February 2004

To the outside world, the large Edwardian house in the tree-lined suburb of South Woodford in Essex looks very attractive. Without doubt the home of a successful family, with a BMW 7 series, bricked driveway and impressive curtain pelmets just visible from the roadside. In Essex, such things are observed more acutely than anywhere else on the planet.

Essex is *OK!* magazine made flesh. Where spray-tanned terracotta women enjoy marriage to city trader rascals on the manicured estates of neo-Georgian mansions. And a Jimmy Choo stiletto stepping from a white Mercedes 500SL parked outside the David Lloyd leisure centre (followed of course by an ankle with chain and Japanese tattoo) is the ultimate measure of success.

However, this house is more classic and less showy than the wedding-cake piles standing close by, untainted by the Essex taste for adding pillars and Tudor beams to every structure. Behind those tasteful curtains, anyone would suppose there lurked an ordered, idyllic household. This is the home of the Cohens. Mark, Grace, seventeen-year-old daughter Poppy, and twin boys Samuel and Max aged twelve.

If anyone were walking past, it would seem quiet, as no lights are on. Despite the fact that it's midweek and nine o'clock on a dark, drizzly evening, only Mark is home. He is sitting on the floor of the lounge at the rear of the house, still in his Boss suit, Thomas Pink shirt and Churchill brogues. He has been there for some time, alone in the gloom, with a single low-wattage floor lamp for company.

The walls are lined with painted shelves, filled not with books but photo albums. Hundreds of them all lined up, row after row like neat little soldiers, looking down at Mark silently.

Two hours he's remained there, brooding, staring into his lap, the cogs turning in his head. Turning over the events of just a few hours ago, when he returned to the cosy scene of his eighteen-year marriage.

He had parked the BMW in his customary fashion, driving up the driveway far too fast after an extravagant late-swing turn which made the tyres squeal bitterly. He ended the ritual by halting two inches from the double garage door and revving the powerful engine in a final flourish, just in case neighbouring Chigwell had missed his arrival.

Hoping that someone, anyone, had witnessed this minor circus, he was gratified to see a small boy aged about ten on a BMX bike staring at him from the road. Even though it was dark, Mark kept his sunglasses on as he got out, knowing the gesture was pathetic, but powerless to his Essex roots.

'Nice car mate,' the boy said, taking Mark by surprise, given how shy he had been even at twice this kid's age.

'Thanks son, it's a BMW.'

'I know,' said the oiky kid. 'My granddad's got one like it, but his is the V8 Alpina version. Pisses on your one.'

That's Essex for you, thought Mark. The kids know the brake horse power of every BMW variant, and are trained to use the data for a competitive advantage over everyone else.

Crushed by a ten-year-old, Mark forced a weak smile as he turned to push the key into the front door, noting for the first time that no welcoming light shone through the stained-glass panel he'd fallen in love with all those years ago.

He opened the door to an icy silence. Not that he had exchanged an enthusiastic greeting with his partner in recent memory. But part of him thought that, as he had been abroad for a couple of weeks, on business for the ad agency, maybe this time it would be different.

He dropped his bag on the floor with a thump, and headed for the kitchen in search of Grace. Or Poppy perhaps, though he knew she often stayed with friends even during the week. The boys were packed off to boarding school, as Poppy had been, and only came home during the holidays. The kitchen was in darkness too. But something was moving in it. Mark could just make out a soft buzzing noise from somewhere nearby.

'Hello?' he said, breaking the silence. No one replied.

'Any chance of some movement?' Still nothing.

Muttering 'Sod you too' less bravely under his breath, he set about finding the source of the buzzing. He opened the cupboards, but found only the crockery they had eaten from for eighteen years, bought for virtually nothing from the now-defunct Reject Shop on Tottenham Court Road when Mark and Grace had been happy and the choice of the first coffee cup had seemed important.

I always hated that stuff, he thought. It's cheap, chipped and crap, just like Grace. He immediately took it back, realising that the bile rising in his throat had nothing to do with Grace.

Buzzing, buzzing, but where from?

He opened the larder and was immediately assaulted by bluebottles. Big, fat, juicy flies, with an unnaturally loud buzzing. He started to scream and two of them flew into his mouth, one disappearing straight down his throat, the other swimming under his tongue.

Bent double and retching, he spat the Olympic swimmer on to the floor and crushed it with his foot. The other was lost forever to his digestive system. He felt sick, momentarily gripped by a boyhood fear of becoming the host for a colony of insects which would eventually break out of his body in gory Technicolor.

'Aaaaaaaaaaaahhhhhhhhhhhhooooooooooaahhh...'

He groped for the light switch and flicked it on. Suddenly the horror got worse. He could sense movement in the larder. Not the movement of a person or an animal, but movement nonetheless.

The vegetable baskets, normally home to potatoes, carrots and cabbage, were lined with what looked like tar with lumps in it. Peering more closely, Mark saw hundreds of plump maggots wriggling and writhing, crawling up the walls and spilling out across the floor. The stench was incredible.

Mark was overwhelmed with repulsion. One of the reasons he had married was to avoid cat litter, bodily fluids and anything rotting. Screaming continuously without even realising it, he headed for the bin in the utility room. Opening the lid, he saw that its pungent contents were moving too, as a second colony of maggots made its bid for freedom.

'For God's sake,' Mark said, frantically rooting for the bottle of bleach. It was funny that he wanted to find Domestos. Yes, he was an advertising executive for the fashionable BC agency, but Domestos had a far deeper hold over him than his career-long appreciation of the household cleaner market.

When he was a child, the good people at Unilever would run

their Domestos TV commercials ten times a day, tattooing their message under the eyelids of an entire generation of impressionable youth in between *Magpie* and *The Man From Uncle*.

And now, in Mark's hour of need, all that investment finally paid off. 'It kills 99 per cent of all known germs, dead. Yes, D-E-A-D!' he shrieked in triumph, as he popped the spout of the blue bottle of salvation and sprayed everything in sight.

He was soon awash in it, as the poor, unsuspecting maggots dissolved into a slimy grey ooze. He then flung the windows open as wide as they would go, chucking vegetable baskets, shelves, bins, towels and crockery out on to the back garden lawn.

Mark had only been home twenty minutes and he was a gibbering wreck. His Boss suit looked as if it had been tie-dyed, thanks to the liberal application of bleach. His brogues were no longer shiny black, but encrusted with the grey sludge of melted maggots. A few escapees clung to his hair, but he was too wound up to notice. He headed for the stairs and a showdown with the cause of this domestic version of the Somme.

Grace. Bloody Grace.

His hand on the wooden ball of the bannister, he performed one of his signature swing turns to catapult himself up the steps, as though back in the BMW. He did not wait to see her before letting rip with the words he had been rehearsing somewhere in the depths of his brain since this horrible evening had started.

'You are a lazy, selfish disgrace to humanity. You don't care about me, or our kids, or anything except that bottle of Scotch and finding ever more ingenious ways to hurt me, you worthless piece of shite...'

By the time he reached the bedroom door, he was actually enjoying his own rhetoric. He was now Churchill, or Aragorn from *The Lord of the Rings* on the eve of battle. And he knew that Grace could not defend herself, fearing confrontation more than almost anything else.

He knew this but, fuelled by self-righteous indignation, he would let her have it all. He barged the door open so hard that it bounced back off the wall, leaving a knob-shaped dent in the plaster as a memento of the moment.

What Mark saw stopped him dead in his tracks.

Grace was a beautiful black woman. Slim, with short-cropped hair and an elegant sense of style. She had full, expressive eyebrows above light hazel eyes and beautiful hands and feet with perfect short nails which were usually painted a deep aubergine colour. Her dimples were deep when she smiled, which used to be all the time.

Mark had thought she was the sexiest and most exotic creature he had ever seen. But things had changed, first gradually and then in recent years in a landslide.

She had not bothered with herself for so long, yet even at her worst, when most 'ill', Mark would be melted by that face. A face he would never tire of, never stop desiring, no matter what. Until now.

Around the bed were dozens of cigarette butts. Full-flavoured Marlboro red tops, overflowing the ashtrays or left to burn out on the carpet in an I-dare-you-to-burn-the-house-down kind of Russian roulette. Half bottles of whisky lay empty on the window sill and the filthy, ash-covered duvet, alongside cold toast. The smell of vomit rose from a waste paper bin by the bed.

The small hump under the duvet might have been pillows, except for the foot hanging over the edge of the mattress from a skeletal leg. Mark saw its frailty for the first time, as though previously blind to how tiny she had become.

He was utterly terrified, the anger draining away from him as the thought that she might be dead seeped into its place.

He took the corner of the duvet nearest to where he assumed

her head to be, and peeled it back slowly with a dread he had never felt before in his life. Until this moment, that life had been one of self-imposed numbness and blind optimism.

'Help me...' she said, a dry whisper crackling from an empty husk. Twenty minutes later, the ambulance arrived and the tiny, bird-like figure was taken away. Mark sat on the floor crying, before realising he needed to find out where his daughter was. He went to the kitchen to get the phone but saw the answerphone light was blinking on and off. Perhaps it was Poppy phoning to say she was at a friend's house, he thought.

Mark pressed play and a woman's voice came out of the speaker: 'This is a call for Grace Cohen. You called to check on your daughter to see if she was out of danger but we have heard nothing from you since. Poppy is asking for you...'

Mark's mind raced as he tried to comprehend what he was hearing. Out of danger? Asking for Grace? What the hell was going on? With a feeling of dread growing deep in his gut, Mark replayed the message and frantically scribbled down the number the caller had left.

He punched it in, unsure of exactly where he was calling, blurting out in panic when the phone was answered. In his agitated state, he didn't register the name of the hospital but did find out that Poppy had been taken in the day before. Without any hints or warning signs, she had tried to take her own life.

Apparently she had rounded up whatever pills she could find, and decided to swallow as many as possible. Thankfully, she had been treated in time and was now in a stable condition. Mark was denied access by the hospital, as the circumstances surrounding what had happened were unclear, and was told to call again in the morning to arrange a visit.

With Grace in the hospital, unconscious, Mark was left alone to be tortured by his apparent insignificance to these events whilst away on business. Why hadn't anyone even let him know? Okay, he was overseas and, as usual, had left no word of where he was. But not a single word from anyone? A carrier pigeon would have done.

He was stunned, as if he had accidentally driven the BMW not just through the garage door, but through the lounge, garden and back fence too. How had it come to this? He turned to his photo albums, which chronicled so many moments of their lives. Photographs were soon scattered on the floor around him.

For as long as he could remember, he had carried a small camera in his pocket. A sort of talisman that he would turn over in the palm of his hand for comfort in times of stress, without even realising he was doing it.

He had taken a snapshot of the wasted foot dangling from the bed, and the ambulance as it sped away into the night. He printed off the two macabre images from the digital Pentax and filed them into the next vacant slots in the latest photo album.

By now, Mark had been in the darkened lounge for some considerable time. He leaned back against the base of the sofa and noticed something that resembled a narrow coil of rope on the floor beside him. Lifting the skirt of the sofa, he found the body of a large rat.

By this time, he felt nothing could shock him. He stared into the creature's shiny, dead, black eyes, and saw his own reflection. His face was distorted, all nose and cheekbones, like a caricature of himself.

Suddenly he stirred, as though a piece had just fallen into place in some mystical puzzle. He went in search of pen and paper. Although he would have found it hard to express how he felt in spoken words, he was suddenly driven to write something down.

Back on the floor, seated bolt upright at the coffee table, he stared at the blank sheet in front of him with no idea of what he was about to write. But it flowed as soon as the pen touched the page. It began with a question directed at himself: 'If I were to die this very night, what reason would I have to come back and haunt the world?'

In a way this was the most fundamental thought he had ever expressed, or would ever express.

Surprisingly, the words had come from him easily, and he was in awe of just how selfish they sounded, given that those he loved most in the world were presently in such anguish and pain. He should have been moved to go to their aid before anything else.

At the least he could have jumped in the car and driven to Samuel and Max's school. But no. He did not feel that way at all. Both of the women in his life had sought death without his knowledge or understanding or permission, and his only reaction was a powerful sense of his own mortality mixed with a strange, freakish elation.

As yet he barely grasped the significance of these feelings, but his new path was set. It struck him this was like one of those cheesy pacts where some fool sells their soul to the devil. I mean, even Homer Simpson had done so for a doughnut! He smiled at the darkened room and experienced the beginnings of a revelation which allowed him to be honest with himself for the first time in his life.

CHAPTER TWO

Bar Mitzvah Boy

Growing up, Mark was a slim, good-looking Jewish boy, with large, dark, saucer-shaped eyes and a complexion which, when tanned, could see him mistaken for almost any nationality except Swedish. He lived in the taxi-driving hub of the Jewish world. All the exotic, successful Jews lived north: not in Scotland, but Stanmore, where they taught Chigwell a thing or two about pillared homes.

But Mark's home was not like anyone else's he knew. It certainly didn't have pillars. A 1930s bay-windowed semi, it sported rubbish joinery and a shoddy porch built on the cheap by a half-blind builder named Glen.

Inside, it had books which had actually been read, crammed on to bookcases in most rooms of the house. Some of the books had Nazi swastikas on their spines, as his father, Sidney, was a Zionist and a self-taught expert on communism and the Holocaust. Instead of going with his dad to watch Spurs like most of his taxi-family friends, Mark would be taken begrudgingly to dusty libraries in order to browse musty books on Poland, Trotsky and the Russian Revolution.

However, his father did impart one passion to him – photography. Sid had caught the bug while in Palestine in 1948 as a volunteer in the 7th Brigade, fighting to establish the state of Israel. With no uniform and only decrepit old weapons to defend himself with, he took shelter behind his Box Brownie, recording those extraordinary times.

Mark's happiest times as a child were spent with his dad in the park, taking shots of strange trees and skyscapes, then comparing results when the films came back from Boots. For a father-son relationship constipated by blocked feelings and clumsy words, observing the world together through a camera was the perfect therapy.

Mark's mother, Mavis, was a home-maker devoted to her only son and to keeping the peace. A pretty woman, she was pencil-thin with a large nose that dominated her narrow face. Mark looked very little like her.

The one thing in her life that gave her total pleasure was her son. Mavis was a natural mum, but she had been told before she was married that she could not bear children, having suffered 'women's problems' since she was a teenager. Mark was her miracle child.

When Mark was nine, his school invited pupils' dads to come and talk to the class about their jobs and experiences in life. Mark was horrified at the prospect.

The father of his closest friend Barry began by addressing the class on his life in the furniture business. Needless to say, Barry was lined up to follow him into the world of teak nests of tables and Slumberland beds. Maurice bored the class with a twenty-minute description of how a sideboard is made, charting the progress of dowels and glue in mind-numbing detail.

At the end, Barry glanced over at Mark and made the wanker sign towards his dad, and Mark giggled. He loved Barry because he was a little bit evil, something Mark himself never was.

He attributed this to their very different mums. Mavis was always hugging her little treasure and cooking varied and exotic food for him. While other kids took jam or crab paste sandwiches to school, Mark had smoked salmon with black pepper or salt beef and mustard. Barry's mum, Shirley, gave him a packet of digestives.

Shirley looked like a glamour puss, only slightly gone to seed. She had a myna that could mimic her voice with creepy accuracy. The bird would shriek 'Barry! Make me a cup of tea... now!' at the slightest encouragement.

Cups of tea aside, Shirley disliked having Barry at home as he cluttered up the house and reminded her of his father, Maurice, of whom he was a scale replica. She was a cleaning fanatic, and was once seen hoovering leaves from the lawn in her bikini, an image which Mark found highly erotic and which left a permanent mark on him. In later life, he often secretly fancied his girlfriends' mothers more than his girlfriends.

When it came to Sid's turn to address the class, Mark wished he could die. Sid stood there in his sky-blue safari suit and little Polish peaked cap, which was embarrassing enough, but his manner was deadly serious: 'During the Holocaust, millions including children were sent to the gas chambers, the fillings ripped from their mouths before the gas taps were turned on,' he began. The class was rapidly reduced to tears, and its teacher, Mr Bates, unsure of the connection to Sid's current job as export manager for Percy Daltons Famous Peanut Company, politely asked him to leave.

Denise, the girl who sat next to Mark, was so traumatised that she soiled herself. After that, Mark was known as 'Skid Mark' or simply 'Skid', being the indirect cause of the great poo scandal of 1970. He sometimes wondered whether his driving style in the BMW was an attempt to glamorise the childhood nickname.

A few years later, when the boys were twelve, they gathered at Barry's house one evening to talk about the girls they fancied.

'I love that new girl, Sammy. She's supposed to be a right slapper, too.'

'Who?' asked Mark, who knew exactly whom he meant but wanted more details.

'You know, Skid, the blonde with the long legs and no knickers in class seven."

A voice piped up from across the kitchen: 'No knickers in class seven,' like a perfect echo. The myna had not lost its touch. Mark knew class seven, as it had the only black girl in the school.

'Grace's class,' he inadvertently muttered out loud.

'Jesus, don't tell me you fancy her. She wears a bloody vest! And I thought you took your coffee with milk.'

'Coffee with milk!' shrieked the bird at the top of its lungs, mimicking Barry's voice.

At which Shirley called back, 'Barry, make me a cup of tea. You know I hate coffee, you worthless lump!'

Barry threw a tea bag into a cup and, before pouring on the boiling water, dredged up an enormous ball of phlegm and spat it in. 'Here you are, bitch,' he muttered, taking it into the sitting room to a chorus of 'bitch, bitch, bitch' from the myna, which by now was just plain showing off.

Barry was not worried about whom he upset, and Mark worshipped him for it. But, even with Barry as his mentor, he could not pluck up the nerve to so much as speak to Grace for eight more years. Needless to say, Barry spoke to Sammy every time he saw her, but she urged him to 'Bug off, fat boy'. God, Barry loved that girl. She was just like his mother!

Mark's Bar Mitzvah year was miserable. As if it weren't bad enough to be dragged to dusty libraries by his dad, on Thursdays he had a philosophy class with the new rabbi and a Hebrew class on Sunday, to prepare for the ordeal to come.

'You'll make us proud, son,' Sid would say, but always with a hint of doubt, which Mark took to mean that he believed the opposite.

All too quickly the day of the Bar Mitzvah had arrived. Dressed in his new three-piece suit and salmon-coloured kipper tie, Mark sat staring out of the modern synagogue, which had all the ambience of a fridge-freezer, while lightning flashed and thunder raged outside as if God were issuing some kind of warning and doing his level best to drown out the voice of the earnest young Israeli rabbi.

Fancy becoming a man just in time for the end of the world, Mark thought. Then it was his turn to stand on stage and read his Bar Mitzvah piece from the scrolls in Hebrew. The storm ceased abruptly and an eerie light shone through the windows, illuminating Mark with an almost ethereal quality. And something odd occurred to him – he liked it.

Not the Hebrew bit, but the fact that he was the centre of attention. His voice grew clearer, he slowed his reading, relishing the use of dramatic silences to make points in a foreign language with no idea of their meaning. The drama was intoxicating and, perhaps courtesy of the God-given lighting, the congregation seem to hang on to his every word.

It was power of the best kind and he was feeling it for the first time. Dreams of great oratory, serious acting or becoming a stand-up comedian entered his head. A strange image of himself as a shepherd with a bazooka, surrounded by hundreds of sheep, crossed his mind.

And then, all too soon, it was over. He sat down to the kisses of his mum, a smile from Sid, and the wanker sign from Barry.

Next came the party, which was held in the synagogue. It was unusually informal for those days, a disco with a finger buffet substituting for the more typical nine courses and long speeches. Sid was the photographer, preferring to take unposed shots, another departure from convention.

Mark's friends were invited but Grace wasn't, which upset him a little as he had not yet been able to utter a single sensible word to her, far less introduce her to his family, so there was no hope of his mum inviting her on the off-chance. Hidden in his inside pocket, he carried a photo of Grace taken at school a year before without her knowledge, while she was talking to Denise in the fields at the back of the gym.

Denise (she of the great poo scandal) was at the party and was still close friends with Grace. That was as close as Mark could get, and he would pump her mercilessly for snippets of information.

Denise was a tiny girl, barely 5 ft in height. She looked like Woodstock from the *Peanuts* cartoon, with short, spiky hair and small, twinkly eyes. She loved gossip and knew everything about everybody. She had a sixth sense about people that Mark valued, and they shared an almost unhealthy love of Grace.

Fat Dave was there too, a classmate who made Barry look undernourished. He had once been a gentle giant, with a huge grin full of higgledy-piggledy teeth. Uncomfortable with his own size, he had been bullied until one day a particularly small boy chose the wrong time and place to provoke him. Dave hit him full force, nearly killing the poor sap. After that, Dave developed a remarkable tolerance for pain – provided he was inflicting it on other people.

Finding himself standing beside Dave at the Bar Mitzvah, Barry struggled to come up with something to say to him. Dave's equally fat younger brother was with him, as he would otherwise have had to be left unattended at home.

'All right, Fat Dave? Who's this fat ginger wanker then?' asked Barry.

Barry was not frightened of anyone, and could be rude to the wrong people without a moment's hesitation. Given Fat Dave's size, the remark was highly reckless, though the 'fat ginger wanker' himself posed no threat to Barry's welfare as he was also short.

'Bazza, this is my younger brother, "Fat Kevin". So just zip it,' Dave replied. Kevin was deeply hurt by Barry's remarks, as he knew he was both ginger and fat and didn't need to be reminded of it. But he said nothing, instead taking it to heart in silence.

'Anyway, Mark done well didn't he?' Grunted Dave.

'For Skid, he did great,' replied Barry. 'How's tricks then? Any women in your life?'

'Fuck off, Baz.' Even Barry was not foolish enough to pursue this line of questioning any further.

If Barry had been eavesdropping on Denise and Mark's conversation at that precise moment, he would have realised why Dave was being quite so touchy – unrequited love It seemed that Dave shared Mark's crush on Grace, and had been seen hanging around her house, hoping to catch a glimpse of her getting undressed through her bedroom window.

Mark was outraged, but despite this competition he took another seven years to pluck up the courage to speak to Grace.

The next couple of years were as difficult as they are for

any young boy – exams, sports teams and the mysteries of girls, with the added handicap of acne outbreaks at the worst possible pre-date moments. And hair became a major preoccupation of the young Cohen. Sid, his father, had gone bald at age seventeen. Bloody seventeen! The bastard!

And then, came a memorable Yom Kippur – the holiest day in the Jewish calendar, the Day of Atonement where one fasts all day and goes to synagogue. Because the Jewish community was so large in Gants Hill, the venue chosen for this ceremony was the cavernous 1930s Odeon cinema. The entire youth of the area would gather in Valentines Park in their best finery to smoke cigarettes and make bitchy comments about each other's outfits all afternoon.

Mark was there with Barry, together with other mates from the club. Then something extraordinary happened – a girl of sixteen, wearing jeans with a sharpened steel comb in her back pocket, sauntered straight up to Mark. Her name was Chrissie, a heavy hint that she was not Jewish.

'All right, Jew boy?' she asked. 'What you doing with this sad bunch of losers?'

'I'm only here out of pity for them. They're all part of the Ugly Potato-Faced Youth Club of Great Britain,' retorted Mark with uncharacteristic nerve, 'and I'm its President.'

Chrissie grabbed his hand and led him out into the middle of the grass in front of the throng of kids. She lay down and tugged him to the ground roughly. As soon as his crushed velvet-clad bum hit the turf, her tongue penetrated his mouth and executed a reef knot with his tonsils.

Utterly lost to this turn of events, he pushed a hand down the front of her jeans and into her knickers. She opened her thighs obligingly and for the first time in his life he felt the wetness of female excitement. What a way to atone for the sins of the year, he thought, ejaculating into his pants almost instantly.

Mark never saw Chrissie again, but this brief encounter forever etched the joys of the flesh into his young and impressionable mind. Twenty-nine seconds on a lawn can change the course of a life.

Nonetheless, things fell back into a familiar pattern for a while, resulting in an okay set of exam results. More worthy of Asti Spumante than champagne, except of course for Mavis, who was as boundlessly proud of her son as ever.

Then Kerry Goldstein burst on to the scene. She was beautiful and feisty; square-jawed and nearly 6 ft tall, she had an athletic build, with swimmer's shoulders and, Mark suspected, a glorious left hook.

Kerry was Mark's first real relationship. He had met her at the local club and had to compete with Barry for the chance to speak to her.

Her life was even more complicated than Mark's. She was beaten at home by her overbearing father, Malcolm, and there was always an atmosphere when Mark walked in. He was quiet and respectful and completely out of his depth, as he had no experience of such domestic problems. No wonder she spent so much of her life underwater, Mark mused.

Nonetheless, once her family were in bed, they would embark on fervent speed sex and he found that she could kiss for hours without taking a breath. 'Must be because her lungs are so over-developed,' Mark once theorised to Barry.

Within three months they had become a couple and been on holiday together to the Canary Islands. On their return, Mavis was thumbing through bridal magazines and treating Kerry like the daughter she never had. Kerry clearly loved this, spending her evenings with Mavis instead of at the swimming baths, even when Mark was not home.

Mark actually had a job by now. He had applied to an advertising agency the year before, after Kerry nagged him to get off his arse and do something other than watch *Countdown*. Advertising was the best thing he could think of, given how much he loved TV shows.

The three years he had spent with Kerry had gone by in a heartbeat. Mavis had given Kerry her own front door key, and Sid was spending more and more time abroad exporting nuts to the Eastern bloc, to avoid listening to the women talk about recipes, feelings and family issues. Mark could see his whole future laid out in front of him.

The warning bells were louder than wedding bells, and he finally spoke his mind. Sitting on a bench in the sun in the local park, he just blurted it all out.

'Kerry, I can't do this anymore.'

'Do what? Feed the ducks?'

This is not going well, he thought.

'Er, no, I mean I want to have a break. I need some space. It's for your own good, really. I'm not good enough for you. You've sacrificed your swimming for me, and I'm not worth it. Don't hate me, I'm sure this is only a short break.'

Spineless twat, he thought.

The tears came, and soon she was crying.

'Spineless twat!' shouted Kerry.

She slapped him with that long-anticipated left hook and stomped away into the distance.

That was on Tuesday. By Thursday, Mark was waving goodbye to a sobbing Mavis with his suitcase in his hand, and moving into an old cottage a mile away with Barry. God, life is good, Mark thought as he banged on the door.

'You're early. Wait a second, mate,' called Barry from his bedroom window.

The front door was opened by Kerry, wearing a dressing gown. Barry's dressing gown. Her 'lungs' were on full display, and a beaming triumphant grin filled her face. Mark stepped inside, dropped his bag and closed the door behind him, struggling to decide how he felt about the turn of events.

'Well, you deserved it, you spineless twat,' said Barry, not entirely helpfully.

CHAPTER THREE

Armageddon Day, Part II, 21st February 2004

Mark felt strangely elated, given the total devastation all around him. He had written the question 'If I were to die this very night, what reason would I have to come back and haunt the world?' on a blank sheet of paper in front of him. Before continuing, he did two things.

First, he queued two CDs on the hi-fi. Muse, followed by Beethoven's *Symphony No. 6 in F Major*. The first track gave him a spiritual lift, while the second he would have chosen for his funeral, which seemed appropriate given his state of mind. He pressed the repeat button so the two would play in a continuous loop – until the end of time as far as he was concerned.

Next, he grabbed his digital camera and took a shot of himself in the large mirror above the fireplace. Perhaps to see if he had suddenly sprouted horns. Or maybe just to record what he felt in his marrow was a pivotal moment in his life.

Without the proof, it might fade away and be lost forever.

The house was dark and still. It felt like a religious experience in some far-flung temple, thousands of miles from his troubles and pain. Mark was strangely focused – something was burning itself on to the paper without thought, almost without him needing to pick up the pen. Three headings appeared on the page, in a script he barely recognised as his own handwriting. They read:

Redemption
Unfinished Business
Make My Mark

Far from sure what he meant by these less-than-specific words, he nonetheless sat back in awe at their completeness. They felt right and that was enough, at least for now. The startling revelation for him was not the list itself, but the fact that intuitively he knew something else about it – that, if life were like the film *Kill Bill*, he would now be driven to deal with each item on the list in the order in which they were written. All neat and tidy – but that would be dull. Worse than that, it would be predictable and, worst of all, just a repeat of his approach to life up until now.

Revelations are all about fundamental change, not the repetition of mistakes in the hope that next time the outcome may be different. A linear life is fine if you're immortal, with an unlimited amount of time at your disposal. But Mark felt as though he had just sat and had tea with the angel of death.

His wife and precious first-born wanted to die. Without any doubt or phoney melodrama, he knew that was their wish. So to hell with waiting for anything, he had to do the three things listed simultaneously. As it said at the top of the document, he could die that very evening, so why wait?

He stood up and shouted at the top of his lungs: 'Bring it on. Bring it all on, you bastards!'

He had no idea why these words exploded from his mouth at that moment. But he felt better for the outburst. It startled Mr and Mrs Robinson, his next-door neighbours, who peeked from behind their net curtains before retreating to the safety of *Coronation Street*. How could they know that they had just overheard a man's life changing forever?

Feeling drained but strangely soothed, Mark drifted off to sleep, his eyes losing focus on the page. The last thing he saw was the first word on the list, 'Redemption'. Then he began dreaming about Grace and Poppy. And Sammy…

CHAPTER FOUR

Playing Happy Families

Sammy, or Samantha Moore, was born and raised in Newbury Park in Essex.

Her father, a mechanic, emigrated to Australia, having divorced Sammy's mother Dianne in favour of his young receptionist. Dianne had fled to Gants Hill (all of three miles away) with her young daughter and taken a job as a dinner lady.

Sammy and her mum looked more like sisters. Both were blonde, with huge, wide mouths filled with beautiful teeth and circled by bright lipstick. Sammy enjoyed the theatre of dressing up, and looked like a hooker when out of school.

By the time she got to her eighteenth birthday, Sammy had come off the rails after her boyfriend of the day broke off their pre-, pre-engagement party. She stopped eating, started drinking and began to hang around with a fast and dangerous crowd. Then, one night, a red 1972 Corvette pulled up beside her outside the Epping Forest Club in nearby Abridge. The notorious (and notoriously wealthy) Derek Peterson had taken a shine to her.

If Danny DeVito had ever successfully mated with a Bee Gee, Derek would have been the result. Short, fat and bald, he wore white suits and high-neck shirts with vast, brightly coloured lapels. His belt buckle was custom-made and had 'Bite Me' inscribed on it in giant gold letters, while his underpants bore the legend 'Beware, long vehicle'. Luckily for Derek, this lie was lost on most of his women, who couldn't read.

He had amassed a substantial fortune thanks to his 'distribution business' which unbeknown to the authorities, specialised mainly in shipping anything distasteful or illegal. Because of his enduring success, Derek owned the biggest house in the best part of Chingford. It looked like Buckingham Palace with extra pillars, and was usually lit up like Caesar's Palace in Las Vegas.

And that is where Sammy ended up most nights, snorting cocaine and taking part in orgies in 'ornate' rooms filled with ageing medallion men who looked like rejected extras from *The Godfather* – the cream of Essex con men, porn publishers and sex-movie producers, together with a few prominent local restaurant owners. Most of the girls were strippers and models, or still at school. Another was a junior doctor, and there was a student writing about her experiences as part of a university thesis. A mother-and-daughter combo were perennially popular.

Rashly, Sammy shared her stories of those wild nights with her church-going friend and closest confidante, Grace. They were then relayed to Barry via Grace's friend Denise, who was the queen of gossip. If Barry was turned on by Sammy before, he was absolutely bewitched now – she was far more exciting than the manufacture of fake pine wardrobes.

Barry had been working for his dad Maurice for some time now and, to put it mildly, he absolutely loathed everything about it, especially the public. When the phone rang, he would answer with the line, 'Regal Furniture, what the fuck do you want?' And that was when he was at his most diplomatic. It became a cult place to go and be insulted.

Inevitably, Barry lived for the evenings and, when he was not in the cottage with Mark, he was out in search of people from Sammy's crowd. The Kerry incident was long forgotten between the two best friends. If anything, it had helped Mark to get over his own guilt, though he would never admit it.

Their life together fell into a version of *The Odd Couple*. Mark played the Felix role and did the shopping and cooking, while Barry was the messy, macho Oscar, though he showed an out-of-character interest in the laundry and ironing (an attention to hygiene which he probably inherited from his mother).

The cottage itself was a small, two-up, two-down Victorian home for Hobbits, with the front door opening straight into the lounge from the street. It had no heating or bath, and mushrooms grew in the shower tray in the bathroom next to the tiny, cold kitchen. But they had waterbeds and a wonderful hi-fi, and enough drugs to keep a Colombian drugs baron happy. Bath towels were tacked across the front window to ensure privacy, giving the place the ambience of a Moroccan opium den.

One evening, Denise came over to catch up over a bowl of homemade chilli. She became utterly bored by Mark and Barry going on endlessly about Grace and Sammy.

'Barry, if you shut up right now about Sammy, and Mark if you stop your pathetic Grace-worshipping, I will organise a date for you both with them. Deal or no deal?'

'Deal, deal and deal,' they squealed in delight.

The following day, Saturday, was filled with frantic preparations. Denise had phoned at approximately 10.30am. 'You lucky bastards, it's on!' she exclaimed. 'Can't think why, but they're actually looking forward to it.'

Mark went to the supermarket and bought fillet steaks, white rice, onions, cream and various spices, plus red wine and chocolate-fudge flavour ice cream. Barry took the sheets, towels and their best boxers to the local launderette. He also squeezed the three spots on his bum and trimmed his horn-like toe nails.

It was now eight in the evening and the cottage looked as good as it ever had since Barry bought it the previous year. There were candles everywhere, and they had borrowed a fan-heater from his mum.

They paced the cottage impatiently, having finally agreed on the right music for the seduction scene. They settled on the old standby for moments such as this – Barry White.

There was a tap on the door, and the two girls walked in. With stroganoff bubbling on the stove and the wine breathing, the two couples paired off immediately.

The evening was flying along when, after a while spent pushing her food around the plate, Grace confided that she was vegetarian. And that red wine gave her a migraine. Mark laughed with her through gritted teeth, and they held hands for the first time. 'Do you remember me from Staples Road School? I was in the year above you.'

'Of course I do,' said Grace, 'but we never talked did we?'

Mark could think of nothing witty to say, so just replied 'No'. He picked up his camera and took some pictures of her face, which he had always known he would never tire of seeing for the rest of his life. This magical moment was only slightly marred by the sound of the tide ebbing and flowing upstairs, as Barry penetrated Sammy hard and fast on the waterbed.

Grace finally succumbed to Mark's charms the following evening in his freezing bedroom, between sheets damp with condensation. Steam came from their mouths and it looked like they were smoking before the post-coital cigarettes were even lit. They lay in bed fully clothed except for their shoes, giggling at the cold but fired with the excitement of a new relationship.

When they finally got naked, she was like an angel to Mark. Satin skin, small, perfect breasts with tiny rosebud nipples and a fragrant scent which, if he could bottle and market it, would have made them both millionaires.

So much can be discovered from a single kiss. The two of them were on fire, kissing long, deep and slow, a kiss that had no need to go any further. They smiled, then resumed the oral exploration for a long, long time.

Within the first hour, Mark had said 'I love you' and he really meant it too, for the first time in his life. He was basking in overwhelming emotions, without feeling the need to deflect them or run for the hills. Yet another first. What a night this was.

From that time on, the two couples were inseparable, eating, drinking, laughing, snorting, confiding and shutting out the rest of the world with glee. Poor Denise was becoming really annoyed: 'I've just lost my four best friends in one go. That's the last bloody time I match-make anyone.'

This turned out to be untrue, as Denise later went on to set up one of the most successful online dating agencies in Britain.

The four virtually lived together in that tiny cottage for months. Finally, like squirrels emerging into the daylight after a particularly long hibernation, Mark and Grace went to her house so that he could be introduced to her parents, 'Mr and Mrs Christmas'.

That should go down well with his father, thought Mark, as

he walked up the path to the tiny bungalow.

'Mum, this is Mark. Mark Cohen.'

A black woman aged around forty stood on the doorstep. She was not fat, but plump in a voluptuous, curvy way, with bosoms that had clearly skipped Grace's generation. Mark's gaze fixed on them.

'Pleased to meet you,' Mrs Christmas said politely, adding, 'Have you never seen a pair of breasts before?'

Mark went bright red, but recovered quickly. 'No, Mrs Christmas, we Jews are bottle-fed in Gants Hill.'

After that they got on famously.

Mark enjoyed the Christmases' hospitality, and their warmth reminded him of his own family. Except that jerk chicken beat the crap out of boiled fish balls.

They would play cards and he discovered that Mrs Christmas, or Gene as she preferred to be called, was a natural at poker. Texas Hold'em was her favourite variation, and he would regularly lose £2 a night to her, which endeared him to her further. Given the games were for coppers, these were spectacular losses but he took it in good spirit.

Mr Christmas, or Harry, was a short, wiry man with a full head of grey hair and a crumpled, prune-like face. A quiet chap, he worked hard as a painter and decorator, though you wouldn't have guessed it from the state of the wallpaper in 53 Hillsdale Gardens.

These days, Grace worked as a secretary to a legal firm. She was quiet at work, only occasionally going out for a drink with her colleagues on Friday night. She had secret hopes and dreams, but was insecure about herself for no apparent reason.

Her older sister Mary came over from their native Barbados quite often, and provided Mark with some insight into this mystery.

Mary was just as beautiful as Grace, but with her mother's breasts, and was a strong and driven personality. She was training to be a doctor and clearly Mr Christmas worshipped her. He even rose to his full height of 5 ft 4 in and offered her his armchair and newspaper when she entered the room. Growing up with a role model like Mary would undermine anyone's confidence, thought Mark, and, for once, he was pleased to be an only child.

At no other time did Mr Christmas seem to notice either his wife, who ran over him like a lawn mower over a dandelion, or Grace, who just kept herself to herself. Instead, Mark often found himself engaged in heart-to-heart conversations, sometimes about the use of vinyl wallpapers but mostly about Harry's other consuming passion, West Ham United.

Mark scoured the *Exchange and Mart* and asked around at the advertising agency where he now worked, Bond Craze, in search of West Ham memorabilia. He had been promoted and was now able to call himself a professional, which made Mavis proud and surprised Sid, though he was secretly proud too. As an executive on the Smith and Nephew account, there was very little Mark did not know about the value of width-ways expansion in the sanitary protection market.

On the face of it, this was not a huge help in locating footballs signed by the West Ham team. But it happened that his counterpart at the client end went to school with the son of one of their board of directors. In just three weeks, Mark had a shirt signed by the entire team, personally addressed to Grace's father with the heading, 'Have a Harry Christmas from the boys at Upton Park'.

That Christmas, Mark's present made Harry cry for the first time in a decade, and he was officially proclaimed one of the family. Gene rang Mavis to wish her happy Chanukah.

The wedding deal was secretly struck between the mothers there and then. Grace kissed him under the tree and pinched his bum for luck, so Mark wouldn't have argued much about it, even if he had known.

Life in the cottage between the four of them was better than good: in fact it was idyllic. And then something unforeseen happened. 23rd January.

Grace was out that evening, staying up north, and Mark had been with God himself, Andrew Bond, the creative guru and founder of the agency, who had chaired a planning meeting with Mark and ten other colleagues. Mark had spoken, giving his opinion on why women aged between eighteen and twenty might be prepared to consider the new applicator for a tampon's lubricated range.

What possessed one man to engage with another man about a product which neither was physiologically equipped to use, Mark did not know. But he had received a 'Well done' and 'How interesting' from God himself. This was the biggest high of his career to date.

He had returned to the cottage after a few Jack Daniels with his co-workers. Jack Daniels was becoming a good friend to Mark, as he could blame him for almost anything. 'It was Jack's fault,' was his new catchphrase if he were late, loud or insulting.

He was being all three that evening and, as he could not show off to Grace, sought out Barry instead, who had been in the warehouse all day and was exhausted, as Maurice, his father, and half the staff were off work with the flu.

'Yeah, yeah, yeah, Skid, I don't care about your tales of gin and tonic or how you did sod all for the planet again today. Do me a favour and put your ego in a small plastic bag, tie a knot in it, apply some lubrication and shove it up your arse.'

Barry had lost none of his salesman's smooth talk.

Mark laughed, but was still needed someone to brag to. Just as Barry went for a shower in the newly redecorated bathroom (courtesy of Harry Christmas), Sammy walked in.

'Thank goodness you're here,' squealed Mark from upstairs, where he was getting changed.

'Wow, what a greeting,' she replied. 'Barry hasn't done that since I turned up wearing nothing but a thong and some body oil.'

Mark laughed awkwardly. He quickly pulled on some pants and a towelling robe and went downstairs to fill her in on his triumph that day. As he finished the by-now much-embellished story, Barry returned in his over-washed, sludgy grey bath robe.

He said 'Hi babe' to Sammy, turned on the TV and slumped into the huge armchair that no one else was allowed to sit in. Sammy went and sat on his lap, but he wasn't in the mood, still smarting from having to single-handedly lug a three-piece suite up the stairs of a tower block where the lift was broken.

So she retreated back to Mark, who was sitting with a vacant smile on his face, his words to God playing like a tape loop in his head. He made room for her on the sofa. 'What you up for drink-wise, Sam? I'm going to carry on with Jack, and coke of both sorts. Sod if it's Monday, I don't care. I'm immortal tonight. I am a Godette.'

'That sounds female to me, and mine's vodka with ice since you're asking. And put out a nice thick line for me too, if you're feeling generous.'

'You want one, Baz?' asked Mark.

No response. Barry was already in a deep coma, his thighs parted to reveal his hairy undercarriage.

'Well, that's put me off eating anyway. Plus I may never be able to have a tortoise as a pet,' said Mark.

'I'll drink to that,' said Sammy.

Soon Barry was snoring like a chainsaw through a megaphone.

Sammy and Mark had been drinking heavily for two hours and had polished off a gram of the Colombian nasty. Sammy, who liked to have her skin stroked like a kitten, was lying across Mark's lap, talking in fast-forward mode.

Mark had been stroking her arm for about twenty minutes by this time, and now graduated to her ankle, Sammy not even pausing for breath in her account of her day, week, month and year. Then he began stroking arm and ankle at the same time, using both hands.

Next he moved to her midriff, followed by her lower back when she rolled over. What a body, what a girl. He had always found those wild stories of orgies and excess a turn-on.

'Sammy,' he whispered, 'I've an erection that is so rigid and pulsing purple that, if I dropped my pants right now, aircraft would land here in Woodford. Please move a little so I can adjust him.'

She smiled and shifted a bit as he'd asked, then looked over at Barry. Mark did the same. Barry broke wind in his sleep. Dribble was running from his open, snoring mouth on to his dressing gown.

Faced with this horror, Sammy kissed Mark full on the lips and pushed her hand down to release the air traffic control tower trapped in his pants. Mark pushed his trembling palms under her T-shirt, cupping her breasts and tweaking her large, erect nipples. So different from Grace, he mused briefly.

They engaged in frantic tonsil hockey for a full minute, until she slowly slid down over his chest towards his penis. Mark could feel her breath tantalisingly close to his erection; that single moment of anticipation was the most electrifying he'd ever experienced. The spell was broken abruptly by Barry as he coughed and murmured to his mother in his sleep, 'Cup of tea, bitch?'

The couple leapt to their feet – Sammy didn't look at Mark, and he didn't look at her; instead he hastily rearranged his undercarriage to try and hide the protruding 'evidence' of their liaison while Sammy rushed over to Barry. Desperately, she woke him and dragged him up to their bed.

The banging and thumping that ensued would have rivalled the construction of the Channel Tunnel. Mark was left with a hard-on, a memory, a huge fear of being found out, and considerable confusion. He tip-toed to his empty, freezing bed and wanked for Britain with only one girl on his mind. Sammy.

The next morning Barry came down to Mark as he was eating Frosties on the couch and exclaimed, 'What happened last night? I got bloody raped!'

'Stop complaining, Baz, sounds amazing,' replied Mark.

Not a word was said between Barry and Mark about that evening again. And Sammy and Mark ignored it for decades too.

CHAPTER FIVE

Father of Mercy

It was the day after Armageddon Day, 22nd February 2004.

Mark had spent the night sleeping fitfully on the floor of the lounge, with only the dead rat for company.

He woke finding himself surrounded by great drifts of loose photographs taken from the various albums he had yanked off the shelves and thumbed through frantically in the small hours, looking for answers.

No answers had been forthcoming, except for the three items on his list. Those words were the first thing he saw as he opened his eyes blearily, then recoiled as he realised that he had been hugging the fat, furry rat to his face like a comfort blanket during the night.

Hmmm, bubonic plague and a list of mystical commandments. The day's barely a minute old and already it's shaping up to be something special, he thought. Then he began churning the list over in his head:

'Redemption, Unfinished Business, Make My Mark...'

He repeated it over and over until it was permanently locked in his brain, as instinctively as breathing or swallowing.

'Well, no time like the present,' he prompted himself, taking another picture of the chaos in the room for posterity, and grabbing ratty by the tail. He stepped outside and drop-kicked the corpse over the garden fence before heading upstairs to wash his hands, take a shower, and shave. It was a relief to finally get out of the bleach-streaked suit and kick off the ruined Churchill shoes.

It was 7.26am according to the digital alarm clock in 'his' bedroom, which was located down the hall from where he had found Grace, in 'her' bedroom.

Mark had been banished to what was previously the au pair's room, as Grace had said his snoring was intolerable. He suspected this was in part true, although he knew the real reason was far worse and more insulting.

She didn't want him anymore. He repulsed her. It was pure and brutally simple – she could not bear to touch or be touched by him, to kiss him or have him anywhere near the anaesthetised fortress that she had slowly constructed around herself.

He shaved using a bladed razor without a single suicidal thought crossing his mind, then had a long, steaming hot power shower in his en suite.

It was now 8.41am.

'Time to contact the outside world,' he muttered out loud, feeling in control of himself, at least on the surface, for the first time since he had arrived home the previous evening.

He rang the hospital that Grace had been taken. Ringing doctors and hospitals and anything else to do with family health was traditionally Grace's area of responsibility. She was so capable and calm, or rather had been so capable and calm in the past.

Mark had been excused from such duties practically from day one of their relationship, when they agreed that he was completely inept at handling that sort of thing. He had hugged her with gratitude, since dealing with medical emergencies (along with cleaning up bodily fluids) filled him with an urgent desire to rush to the nearest airport and book a one-way flight to Gdansk, Bolivia or Alaska.

Well, look at me now, he thought to himself, as he dialled the number.

'King George's Hospital,' answered a woman's voice, 'how may I help you?'

Mark explained that his wife Grace Cohen had been admitted the previous evening.

He was transferred to Dr Evans' office, where he spoke to a woman called Pat, his 'Medical Administrator'. She confirmed that Grace was out of danger, but little else, other than that she could offer him a ten-minute window in Dr Evans' busy schedule later that morning. Mark thanked her and agreed to be there at midday.

Next to get more information on Poppy. He looked at the number he'd written on the piece of paper the night before and realised that it was the number he'd just dialled.

'King George's Hospital, how may I help you?'

'Hello, it's me again,' Mark began awkwardly.

He went on to explain that his daughter Poppy Cohen had been admitted the previous evening, and that he wanted to speak to the consultant and to see his daughter as soon as possible. The outcome was identical to his previous call. He was transferred to Pat in Dr Evans' office again.

'Hello, Pat, I feel like I know you well already.'

'Who is this, please?' said the puzzled Pat.

'Oh, sorry, it's Mark Cohen.'

'Hello, Mr Cohen, is there a problem with the twelve o'clock appointment? As I explained, Dr Evans is very busy and I'm not sure when he can...'

'No, no, Pat,' he interrupted. 'It's my daughter, Poppy Cohen. She was dmitted a couple of days earlier.' He explained that he had just returned from abroad, and that he wished to speak to her consultant and visit her as soon as possible.

'They're falling like flies round there aren't they?' she giggled, dropping her former sensitivity like a hot brick. 'My, you're keeping us gainfully employed, Mr Cohen.'

'Err, I suppose so,' said Mark. 'I'm going for a family discount. Do you do air miles for loyal customers?' he added, joining in with the strange mirth which somehow seemed highly infectious.

'Ha, ha,' she chuckled. 'Okay Mr Cohen, why don't we add it on the end of the other appointment? And feel free to ring me back if anyone else in the family feels a little under the weather.'

Mark wasn't sure how he felt about the hospital's light-hearted attitude to his family misery, but clearly today was going to be a surreal experience. With that in mind, he made himself a lukewarm cup of instant coffee and, instead of using sugar he impulsively tipped a teaspoon of cocaine into the cup, and stirred it in before taking a sip.

'Disgustingly bitter!' He groaned and nearly poured the contents of the mug down the sink. 'Still, at about £60 a gram...'

He gulped the drink down in one, picked up the phone and rang the school where the boys, Samuel and Max, were, he hoped, blissfully unaware of recent events back in Woodford.

'Hello, St Edmund's College, how may I help you?'

'Hi. This is Mark Cohen, father of the twins Samuel and

Max. I need to speak to their house mistress and to arrange to drop by to talk about some family issues with the boys.'

The helpful voice transferred Mark to Mrs Ballcock.

I bet she doesn't get much stick for a name like that, in a school full of boys like mine, he thought, remembering his own teacher Harold Bates, or Master Bates as he was inevitably known.

'Ballcock here, how may I help?'

Mark explained the situation in polished fashion, having had so much practice recently, and was in full flow when Mrs Ballcock interrupted him.

'Mr Cohen, do you know my sister, Pat Ballcock? She works at King George's. I just put the phone down on her and, before you ask, we don't do air miles either.'

Surreal, Mark thought. The Cohens' role on this earth was evidently to provide moments of tragic-comic relief to the overworked administrative community of Great Britain.

Nonetheless, he arranged to go to Hertfordshire, to one of the oldest Catholic schools in the country, that same afternoon. He could start to take up the slack, to be there as a father to the boys, in a way that his career had so often precluded in the past. And he felt good about that, at least.

The children loved their father, he knew that. And he loved them so much too, but somehow he had been watching from the crowd when it came to their growing up. Always in the office or at meetings, rather than present for parents' evenings and sports days, or a walk in the woods as a family.

And, all along, it had been a conscious decision to avoid those things.

Mark had known he would regret it. He had visualised regretting it on board his sixty-foot yacht with its crew of seven Swedish babes. Of course, he had arranged the Disney trips, the minimum standard for any parent of young kids. But it was always about when he was ready for them, not when they needed him to be there. In the fantasy universe of Mark, he was the sun, his family the planets and moons orbiting around him.

But, Christ, that was what Grace had bloody well asked for, he argued with himself. She hated being a bloody legal secretary, earning the equivalent of what the lawyers spent annually on biscuits. And let's not forget that her mum, Gene was there too, as well as his mother, Mavis. Grace was not alone.

So how come he had been left to pick up these bloody pieces? These thoughts were followed by another, more immediately pressing question: what would he do about the pitch he was supposed to be running for Vertec's flagship detergent brand, Primo, at BC, where he was now Deputy Chairman and had people who relied on him (or listened to him at least)?

The office! He hadn't called them. It hadn't even occurred to him. The office seemed in a different orbit from the huge issues he was now dealing with. Yet the germ of an idea struck him at that moment. An idea which suddenly made Primo quite important in achieving two of the three objectives on his list. The Make My Mark and Redemption bits.

Hmm, he thought, this could work.

But for now he parked this emerging plotline and called the office, to speak to his trusty PA, Ellie Durdzinski. In truth she was anything but trusty – beautiful as a magnificent racehorse, loud and funny, but constantly putting his diary through the blender. It was like having Barry around the office, but with glorious tits.

She would have him turning up for lunch at The Ivy when his guest had cancelled the month before, leaving him to make the walk of shame, the sad rejected diner publicly let down by his guest, in front of every peer in the advertising industry.

Competitors from other agencies would heckle him. 'You poor fellow, must be the aftershave! Why don't you fire that Ellie? Enough is enough, big man.'

It seemed she was more famous in the business than he was these days. Even Mac, the maître d' at The Ivy, would say, 'Not again, Mark, you should fire that Ellie. Great legs, though, I can see your problem...'

'Cheers Mac,' Mark had replied. 'See you tomorrow, and keep me a table for one just to save time.'

She's bored because she's too smart for the job, he would tell himself. More likely she was just crap, but they laughed together and he could not imagine life without Ellie to smoke and drink with, and to cover for him.

One thing was for sure. He needed her a great deal at this moment. He dialled her on his mobile, strutting around the lounge before setting off for the hospital.

'Ellie? Is that you?'

'No, it's the bloody tooth fairy. Who do you think it is, you big cock?'

'Nice of you to notice.' He couldn't resist that, as the incident on the fire escape during the Christmas party of 2002 flitted across his mind.

'Don't get big-headed, you know my eyesight is rubbish. Hung like a hamster you are!' Ellie retorted.

'Listen, Ellie, this is serious,' Mark interrupted, and went on to outline his domestic situation and its impact on his schedule for the day, the following week and possibly the whole year ahead.

'But one bridge at a time,' he said. 'I need someone to do the client briefing for me with Vertec today.'

'Fuck, fuck, fucky-doodley fuck-fuck,' she replied, adding one last 'fuck'. They had clearly worked together too long. But she concluded with, 'Okay, mission understood. Keep your various chins up, lovely, don't worry about a thing.'

Reassured if not entirely convinced, Mark grabbed the long, soft black leather coat that made him feel cool, and jumped in the BMW. It started with a roar and he sped off towards King George's Hospital.

On the way, he used the speakerphone to call Barry.

'Hi, Baz, I'm just back from the States.'

'Cool, Skid. Have fun out there with all those power women? I hear they outnumber the single straight men six to one, and that a British accent makes even a gargoyle like you seem like George Clooney with elephantitis of the genitals.'

'Yeah right, Baz, but listen. I haven't got long to speak, 'cause I'm on the way to the hospital.' Silence on the other end, then Mark continued, 'It's Grace and Poppy.'

'Oh my God! A car accident?'

'No, Baz, just listen. When I got back, the house was filthy. Like rat-infested medieval dungeon filthy. I found Grace in bed, drunk and drugged out of her mind. Like nearly dead. Scared the shit out of me. Then I found out Poppy had taken an overdose the day before. I think Grace must have found her and just wanted to die.'

'Wow, mon brave,' said Barry, 'I'm thinking of you. I'll tell Sammy, she'll want to know, and probably want to go and see Grace. Anything I can do, just ask. I'm there for you, Skid. Do you want me to tell Denise as well?'

'Yes, good idea, but please tell her not to put it on the net or take a double-page spread in the *Jewish Chronicle*. Ciao, I'm at King George's now.'

Barry had married Sammy in a registry office just a month before Mark and Grace tied the knot, eighteen years ago. They did not have children, as Sammy was unable to, and their hedonistic lifestyle meant they rarely regretted it.

Back then, Grace and Mark had asked them to be the legal guardians of any kids they might have in the future. Barry thought this was hysterical, given Sammy's domestic ineptitude, but after a bottle of vodka it 'seemed like a good idea at the time' and they had all agreed. A will was drawn up the next day by Sid's solicitor and signed over a chicken madras in the Ajunta curry house, South Woodford. Everyone then promptly forgot about it.

This was probably no bad thing, as Barry and Sammy had got seriously into the S&M scene, filling their leisure time with fetish clubs, sex toys and the theatrical dressing up which Sammy had loved since she was young. Derek Peterson, the king of sleaze from Sammy's pre-Barry days, was still a friend to them both, the gates of his chateau now sporting the name 'Wattapenis Palace' in ornate ironwork.

Fat Dave now worked for Derek, and had virtually been adopted by him as a stepson. Apparently Dave had done a huge favour for Derek in shady circumstances, and Derek had been grateful to the point of truly trusting someone for the first time ever. As a result, Fat Dave was set for life, given a role as Derek's minder and commander in Del's unofficial army of east London, and dressed to impress in head-to-toe Boss.

Grace was more M&S than S&M, and their different lifestyles had seen her and Sammy drift apart over the years. There was still love between the two girls, but not enough to sustain the daily closeness of their youth. Somehow, time had been kinder to Mark and Barry's friendship. Or maybe time had a wry sense of humour.

Mark executed one of his trademark skidding late turns into a parking space reserved for consultants, but no one bothered him as it was a 7 series and he might have been a doctor. Having announced himself and been directed to Dr Evans' office, he finally met Pat Ballcock.

Pat was in her mid-fifties, slim with a big, back-combed nest of ash blonde hair, and steel-rimmed glasses perched on a large, red nose. Her smile was lovely, reflecting her happy disposition, which reminded Mark a lot of Mavis. He liked her immediately.

'Hi, Pat, I'm Mark Cohen, here about my air miles.'

'Oh, hello, my sister rang me back to say she had spoken to you. My, you are having a day of it Mr Cohen. But you're in luck for once, the doctor can see you right away, if you'll come this way please.'

It was a tiny cubicle of a room with plastic cafeteria-style chairs, littered with charts, papers and discarded plastic coffee cups. A broken clock hung on the wall beside a 1987 poster for an Austrian ski resort. Mark noted this oddity in case a future gift was on the cards. He also noted that he wouldn't accept this office as a storage room for his old files, far less as the anteroom of a revered consultant. A criminal lack of respect by the NHS, he thought.

After a few moments of poring over medical notes, Dr Evans looked up at Mark from under his unkempt, bushy eyebrows. He resembled a distinguished army colonel, and had such an air of authority, humanity and confidence that Mark immediately felt he would do anything this man said, without question or complaint, even though he was yet to utter a word.

Right at this moment, the feeling was humbling but hugely welcome.

'Hello, Mr Cohen. Good to meet you. Let's get on with the business in hand.'

He paused briefly, then continued: 'Poppy is a very unhappy young girl, and I'm concerned about her because she is so deeply depressed. Have you noticed this in her for a long time? Does it run in the family?'

'Well, not really, although, as you know, her mother has been having a tough time recently.'

'Yes, Mr Cohen. It must be hard on you. How are you doing?'

'I'm okay, but this is all news to me, Doctor, so let's talk about Poppy first. What is happening, and what's going to happen?'

'We got to her quickly and pumped her stomach out, so there should be no permanent damage. We're observing her at present and have her on Prozac, which will kick in after a few weeks. Meantime, she needs more immediate help. With your permission, we'd like to make enquiries about placing her at a rehab clinic as an in-patient. We don't think she should be sent back home any time soon. Are you aware Poppy has been self-harming?'

'What?' said Mark, trying to process information through the hammer blows of each new shock. 'But she was doing well at school not so long ago, and was planning her gap year. What self-harm? I haven't seen her undressed, and I have been away a lot. But her mother never said anything to me.'

'Well, Mr Cohen, Grace has been having her own issues and may have been an absent parent for quite a time. She is much more damaged than Poppy, and you may have to face the fact that she is both mentally and physically a very ill lady. We have a lot of tests to run, to try and get a grip on things she's been doing to herself for a very long time.'

The doctor concluded: 'Be warned that your daughter does know about your wife's admission to this hospital. Poppy demanded to know where her mother was when she failed to appear by her bedside.'

With the 'meeting' over, Mark went back out to his car

before visiting Poppy. He sat alone in the car park and the tears came. No longer was he feeling the elation of his new 'demonic' list, or the selfish power-trip of possibilities. Just the realisation of his utter failure, and the fear. He was scared out of his mind.

He wept until the snot rolled down his face, hanging from his chin like the stringy cheese from a good French onion soup. His eyes were swollen and red, and he looked like he had been hit with a dozen raw eggs thrown by Mike Tyson. More than anything, he wanted to go and visit his best friend, Jack Daniels, for perhaps a month or three.

Still, he had made a vow to himself to follow the three objectives on his mystical list.

First on that list was Redemption and, whatever else it meant, he knew now that this entailed behaving like a real father for the first time. Poppy was in there, and she needed to know someone was there for her, and that was going to be her dad. He was going to step up to the plate.

He dug out his Gucci shades, the largest he had in the car, to cover his puffy red eyes, mopped up the mucus, blew his nose and prepared to 'Face the Music and Dance'.

Always knew Nat King Cole would be perfect for something, he thought, rolling the digital Pentax around in his pocket as he walked towards the ward.

He headed down the row of beds, past colourful murals and toys – this was a children's ward, Poppy being just under eighteen. He spotted her through the narrow gap between the curtains drawn around her bed.

'Hi, darling girl,' he said, popping his head through the curtains. 'I'm so pleased to see you, my lovely.'

Poppy lay there in her jeans, staring up at the ceiling. She turned to look at her daddy, holding her arms out wide to him in a way he couldn't remember her doing since she was a toddler.

They hugged and squeezed and made each other's shoulders wet without a word being spoken. Then he found a chair and sat beside her gently holding hands.

She had a drip, a bedside table with grotty plastic water jug, and not much else.

After a long time he said, 'So what happened, princess?'

'Can't talk right now, daddy. I'm so tired.'

She did look tired, but still seemed gorgeous to her father. Braided hair down to her shoulders, coffee-coloured skin, hazel eyes with short, sparse eyelashes, and freckles all over her face. A pierced nose, ears and tongue for Goth measure.

For the first time, he noticed her arms in the short-sleeved shirt and he gasped. They were covered in angry red gouges and slashes, like a pair of carved totem poles. He didn't cry, though he felt wounded inside.

'At least you were disciplined enough to make a pattern,' he joked weakly.

'It's not funny,' she said, covering the scars.

'Sorry, darling, it's just my way of dealing with things.'

'Or not dealing with them,' she said with soft venom.

'I know, you're right,' Mark said, drawing breath. 'Listen, sweetheart. Dr Evans is talking about therapy for you. Can I come too? I think I may have to join you, if you can bear it. I'm not trying to crowd you, but this may be one journey where I need you as much as you need me. Like two survivors of a shipwreck, clinging to the same bit of driftwood. I love you, darling, and this is going to be a hard road. I'm up for it, are you?'

They stared at each other for a moment, then Mark went on:

'I'm going to see mum in a minute. I'll come back and see you tomorrow, or maybe you could call me tonight on the mobile?'

'Sure, dad. I'm going to sleep for a bit.'

Mark left, reeling, shell-shocked but happy because this was the most adult conversation he had managed with his daughter in her entire seventeen years.

And then came Grace.

If anything, Mark was more agitated about this encounter, as he did not know what to expect after the doctor's warning of her fragility. A vegetable? An angry lunatic? His mind raced through the possibilities and he was uncomfortable with all of them.

Ironically she was in the Princess Grace Ward, as if they had been expecting her when it was named. It was similar to Poppy's, but without the cartoons on the walls. Instead of children there were many older folk, confused, vacant, some dribbling in the desolation of their damaged eighties.

Grace was always wonderful with old people, and Mark loved her for it. But this was different. He feared she might be right at home with them in her present state of mind. If this were permanent, he was already dreading the Sunday visits.

He could picture Grace sat in a wheelchair with a chequered blanket, unable to recognise him or her own children. He would be spoon feeding her mush which dripped from her mouth like a baby, and wiping her arse in the toilet, while she giggled for no reason in a world of her own.

But when he turned the corner, he saw Grace sitting up in bed talking brightly to a young nurse, and he was let off the hook for a moment. And that's all it took.

He wanted to throw his arms around her and comfort her forever, but now there was a reason not to do so. All the pressure that had built up in his head was deflated, because she looked so much better than he had imagined.

What rotten luck. If she had seemed more lost, more needy, Mark might have been able to open the valve and spill his emotions, and they may have lived happily ever after. The devil might have been thwarted, at least for a while.

Instead he sauntered up and sat next to her and said simply, 'Hi.'

She turned and said 'Hi' right back at him.

All that bottled-up emotion, for so little communication. And so many questions were still bouncing around inside his skull. Why did you just check out on me emotionally? Why did you reject me? Why didn't you tell me how you felt? Why did you abandon our daughter? Why don't you love our boys enough? Why do you drink? Why have you done this to me? Why did you marry me?

But nothing.

A lump came to his throat and he fought back the tears, but not for long. Once the dam was breached he couldn't stop, and he had to leave to get some air.

Mark did not go back in, as he observed through the window that Grace had resumed her animated conversation with the nurse and seemed quite happy.

He climbed in the car and set off for the boys' school in Hertfordshire. The radio was set to Virgin fm, 105.8, and was blasting out the 1980s Simple Minds hit, 'Don't You (Forget About Me)'. He had to pull into a lay-by for another messy crying session.

'God, I'm unravelling here. Get a grip, Mark,' he said to himself out loud, then pulled out of the lay-by and pushed pedal to metal, taking the car to 127 mph and counting along the A10.

Barry rang: 'Hello you. Listen, Sammy's driving me nuts. After your ordeal today how about coming to a titty bar tonight? Drown our sorrows with Jack D and the biggest jugs in Essex.' Mark could have kissed him, and felt better for the first time in two days.

He drove up the mile-long gravel driveway to St Edmund's

College with a smile on his face. It was a magnificent school, resembling a gothic cathedral set in a hundred acres of sports fields, with countryside as far as the eye could see. The gravel was perfect for dramatic skids and Mark naturally went for it. Too much in fact, as he slid right into an ancient oak tree that had been quietly minding its business for more than a century.

Mark got out and examined the damage to the car, blushing furiously, then walked to the office pretending to be the invisible man. He asked to see Miss Ballcock, the house mistress.

She arrived looking like a slightly fatter version of her sister Pat, only her nose was crimson rather than red and she did not wear glasses.

'Bonjour, Mr Cohen.' (She taught French.) 'So good to meet you finally. Très bon in fact. You missed the parents' evening and the firework party last year?'

'Yes, business can be demanding sometimes,' Mark said, blushing again. 'Can I see my boys please? It's a family crisis, and I want them to hear it from me.'

Within minutes, he could hear the shuffling of loafers approaching the office. That's Samuel and Max, thought Mark. Can tell them a mile off. Boys love to scuff and ruin their shoes as quickly as possible.

'Daddy!' they both shrieked, and jumped into a three-way family hug without any self-consciousness in front of everyone.

Samuel and Max were affectionate, tactile boys, popular with everyone from babies to pensioners. Identical twins with dusky complexions and shocks of curly chestnut hair, they had brush-thick eyelashes which Poppy had always envied and cheeks which dimpled when they smiled, which was often.

They were both physically strong and played for the school rugby team. Indeed, the only noticeable difference between them was that Max had a crooked nose, broken by a tackle from the St Albans prop forward. Samuel had put that kid in hospital after his brother was injured. They defended each other like that all the time, and the same loyalty extended to their sister.

Without going into detail, Mark told the boys that Poppy and their mother were ill and staying in hospital for a while. He said they would be fine, and that he would talk to the boys each and every night to keep them informed. He also suggested that in the next half term it might be cool if the three of them went away for a long weekend, a boys' trip. Maybe Uncle Barry would come too. He felt the pill needed sugar-coating.

'Wow!' said Max.

'Thanks dad!' said Samuel.

They finished by casually telling Mark that Poppy had rung them already, that their mum was an alcoholic, and that their sister was depressed and had done something stupid by overdosing on drugs. Mark looked at his boys and never again made the mistake of underestimating them.

Later that night in Secrets lap-dancing club, Mark forgot his troubles, wallowing in the ample 36DD bosoms of a dancer called Bev and a haze of bourbon. Barry was enjoying a blowjob in the booth next door and shouted to his mate, 'Hope this is helping, Skid. It's doing wonders for me. Can I borrow that Pentax for a minute please?'

Mark was far too distracted and merry to feel anything much, which was probably for the best. He was also deaf to Barry's request, sounds muffled by the soothing warmth of Bev's cleavage.

He nodded off in Barry's old E-type as it headed back to Woodford at two in the morning. Never did a bed, even in his spare room, seem so warm and welcoming.

CHAPTER SIX

Amazing Grace

When Grace was sixteen she was a timid girl, despite being very pretty. Each evening she would sit in front of the dressing-table mirror in her box room at home, trying through sheer willpower to give herself bigger bosoms.

'Why is it mum and Mary have got tits like overblown Zeppelins, and I'm still wearing Aertex vests? I'm an asexual boy-girl creature, a flippin' eunuch,' she had said to Denise on many occasions.

'You're bloody lucky,' said Den. 'I'd look at home on *Sesame Street* or in *The Simpsons*.' It was true, she did have a touch of the glove puppet or cartoon about her.

With willpower alone proving inadequate, Grace would perform bust exercises and apply various creams and lotions to her underwhelming chest in the privacy of her room. However, this privacy was compromised by the fact that her dressing table sat in the bay window of the Christmas family bungalow.

Under the circumstances, it would have been wise for Grace to draw her curtains while performing the nightly topless ritual, or at least to turn off the big light. But she did not.

Fat Dave, who had nurtured an almost obsessive crush on Grace since they were thirteen, would loiter on the corner, skulk under hedges, or simply walk back and forth along the pavement in all weathers, hoping for a glimpse of the youngest Christmas's bare chest.

Grace was blissfully unaware of this, though she would have been flattered, if very creeped-out, had she known how long it had been going on. She was not used to drawing much attention.

Life in the Christmas household revolved around the titans of the family – mother Gene, and eldest daughter Mary. Daily disputes would see the two square up like sea lions for a barging contest, with the old grandma throwing her weight in whenever she visited, turning it into a tag-team match in which Gene and 'Ma' took turns to try and subdue Mary, young pretender to the title of loud-mouth, opinion-about-everything queen bitch of the Caribbean.

Grace would withdraw from all of this and lose herself in her art. Alone in her room, she painted watercolours of places far, far away, hiding her work in a portfolio in the bottom of her wardrobe. Even her best friends had no idea of this talent and passion.

As ever, Grace could not risk being laughed at.

Her natural ally in the household should have been her father, Harry, but he yearned for the quiet life, an impossible ambition with Gene, Mary and Ma about. Much like the wallpaper he hung for a living, he went largely unnoticed in his own home. But, instead of bonding with the equally quiet Grace, he sought refuge in work and his beloved West Ham on Saturdays.

So Grace was left to wither on the vine through lack of interest. But, as her paintings would have shown, were anyone allowed to see them, Grace had dreams. Dreams of travel and of changing the world, not by gaining money or power, but by helping people. Most of all, Grace loved children and was looking forward to having her own, maybe three or four.

But Grace's goody-goody ideals sounded wet even to Grace herself, so she chose to hang around with the Sammys and Denises among her peers, girls who were dark and a little dangerous. She hoped to appear more interesting by association, hiding her natural goodness under their bushel.

Grace's introduction to sex was unusual, and came as a direct result of this association with wild child Sammy.

Sammy had invited her to visit Derek Peterson's manor in Chingford for drinks one evening. Grace was fascinated by the prospect, as she had a playfully wicked streak just waiting for a chance to surface from under all that goodness. The fact that Mary would never have accepted such an invitation added fuel to her little pilot light of wickedness.

The girls were giggling as they piled out of the mauve Datsun Violet mini cab on the long driveway to Derek's mansion, having consumed large amounts of Cider Bomb, the perfect tipple for loosening inhibitions. It was about 10pm, and the Las Vegas lights were blazing, showcasing the scale of the place to the two impressed and happy young nymphs.

Sammy pulled the rope bell cord, which dangled under a canopy supported by ten or more stone pillars which rose to a dizzying height of about 25 ft.

'Who does this Derek think he is?' asked Grace rather too loudly. 'Lady Penelope?' At that moment, a butler with a striking resemblance to Parker opened the huge door and said languidly, 'As a matter of fact, he does.'

It was what you might call a casual household. The staff were all stoned, walking round with massive roaches hanging from their mouths, or drinking and taking cocaine with the guests. They still tried to serve people, though, and regularly succeeded in spilling finger food and booze over the large suede sofas and expensive rugs in the many lounges.

The guests were of all ages and shapes. One man named Rex was at least seventy, with a Bobby Charlton comb-over, open shirt and deep crinkled-walnut tan. He wore Elvis-style sunglasses and had a young boy perched on each knee. Despite appearances, he was interesting to talk to and kind to Grace, watching out for her and patiently explaining what was happening when Sammy disappeared with Derek for a 'chat'.

When Rex and his boys left the party early in his red Bentley (flashy and trashy, thought Grace), everyone shouted 'Elvis has left the building' in unison. They all loved Rex, and this was a ritual.

Left alone, Grace drifted from room to room, taking in the sights. There was a cage hanging from the ceiling with a girl tied up inside, naked except for a leather gimp mask. Various men were squeezing their hands inside the cage, and inside the girl. Orderly queues waited outside the bedrooms, some with their ears pressed eagerly to the thin walls.

In the centre of the biggest lounge was a large, doughnut-shaped couch sunk into the floor, with at least twenty naked bodies writhing on it. Small drifts of white powder were laid out on most of the glass surfaces, reminding Grace of the way in which Gene would put out boxes of After Eight mints for her coffee evenings. She giggled to herself at that homely thought.

She was having a lovely time, which was a real surprise to her. She had been made to feel comfortable and safe and not threatened at all. So much so, that she did not hesitate to accept a pill she was offered by an older woman called Christine, whose fellow exotic dancer happened to be her teenage daughter.

Grace swallowed it down with neat vodka and went off looking in some of the other rooms. She bumped into Derek as he was leaving his private study.

His appreciative head-to-toe scan suggested he was pleased to see her, which was confirmed by the small bulge Grace noticed in his camp velvet trousers. Sammy was standing just behind him and signalled to Grace, wiggling her pinky finger in a downwards droop and mouthing the words, 'Got a cock like a dormouse.'

Grace stifled a laugh, feeling happy, heady and floating. She barely noticed Derek grasping her hand in his sweaty, stubby little paw, leading her into the study with Sammy.

What followed was not unpleasant, but mainly because Grace wasn't really present. She hovered above it all as her body was touched intimately by her best friend and a deeply unattractive old man. It was surreal to say the least.

Derek was not twisted or violent, but tender, caring and considerate. It was simply that she had little choice in the matter, and afterwards could not even say if she had had an orgasm or not. As she collected her knickers and shoes to go, Sammy gave her a cuddle and said, 'That was wild wasn't it? My God, talk about unplanned.'

Grace was confused, and felt soiled, if not actually violated. There was a hint of betrayal in the way her friend had exploited her, failing to defend her even as well as a perfect stranger like Rex. It was never spoken of again.

CHAPTER SEVEN

Sex and the City

Mark woke the morning after his visits to the hospital and school – and of course the titty bar with Barry – this time without a rat in his face. Instead, he had an elephant standing on his head. The hangover confirmed that the titties had been accompanied by copious drinking, even if Mark couldn't remember it.

'Bloody Jack, it's your damn fault again,' he muttered, quivering on the brink of a diarrhoeic eruption in his own bed. Not daring to break wind, he ran with a peculiar ambling gait to the nearby toilet.

'Ah, wow, that's so good,' he said with near-religious fervour, as the horn section from the the chariot race score in *Ben Hur* trumpeted from his arse.

He wallowed in the pungent stench for a moment, accepting it as a self-inflicted punishment for the excesses of the night before, and reflecting that a good shit is right up there with a good fuck as far as male pleasures are concerned.

He did not ponder the mysteries of the male psyche any further, however, as at this point he noticed that in his hurry to avoid Armageddon under the duvet he had neglected to close the door to his en suite, and Vicki had entered.

Vicki, their cleaning lady, was an illegal immigrant from the Philippines with little command of the English language and even less command of bathroom etiquette. She was standing next to him with a blue plastic toilet brush ready to be deployed on the bowl that Mark had so enjoyed pebble-dashing moments before. In her other hand was a bottle of Toilet Duck, also awaiting some serious front-line action. She looked vaguely like the Statue of Liberty.

Mark chuckled at this image and in a kindly tone ordered, 'Vicki, go away. Now. Now please, Vicki. Out now, darling.'

She looked deeply disappointed. She realised the chances of Mark cleaning up his own detritus were slim, and as a professional she knew that, if the brown carnage was allowed to set, removing it would be harder than shifting three-day-old porridge from a forgotten breakfast bowl.

Vicki was the post-modern version of a 'treasure', and Grace had increased her hours some months ago to include every day except Sunday. Vicki was so grateful (and so nervous of customs and immigration) that she would put up with anything, even Mark, and still say thank you very much with a smile.

However, she had not been around for the past few weeks, as she had been holidaying in exotic Huddersfield and Bridlington with a cousin, her first holiday in the UK. And now she returned to discover Grace's room looking like a tip and half the contents of the kitchen residing in the garden.

What must she make of us, Mark wondered.

After a shower, he got dressed and wrote a list of calls to

make and people to see that day.

1) Speak to Poppy, if not actually go and visit her.
2) See Grace.
3) Check in with the boys. Not possible to call until evening when the school day and study periods are over. Maybe text?
4) Call Dr Evans, or at least Pat Ballcock, re Poppy and Grace.
5) Tell Mavis.
6) Face Gene.
7) Ring the office. Ellie then Patrick (his boss).
8) Call and thank Barry for last night.

Then he came up with something just for him. Something he had thought about for half his life, since it began more than twenty years ago on that fateful evening in the cottage. Someone who came under Unfinished Business – Sammy. She was his evening task. After only a day, he had already started to address the contents of his list. He was proud of this change of pace in himself. In the spirit of Redemption, he had started on the long road to being a proper father to his children. Early days, but a first step had been taken.

The Primo washing detergent pitch and the idea it spawned yesterday might well help him with two other items, Make My Mark and another aspect of Redemption – but this evening's call to Sammy fell under the banner of Unfinished Business.

That's a full day in anyone's book, he thought, with a particularly tantalising evening to round it off. A smile crossed his face at the prospect; then he remembered all the things he had to do first. 'No time like the present,' he said to himself briskly.

As Mark left the house, he could hear Vicki singing to herself upstairs while she scrubbed the residue of his previous day from the toilet bowl: 'Happy talk, keep talkin' happy talk, talk about things you'd like to do...'

He decided to return to King George's Hospital to see Poppy first. Chastened by his accident at the school, he avoided any tyre-squealing antics, drove there calmly and arrived at the hospital more quickly than usual.

I'm a changed man. Mature, measured and more in control, he reflected smugly.

'Hi, lovely,' he hailed as he approached the curtained area of the children's ward where Poppy was.

'Oh, hi dad,' came the less than enthusiastic greeting. 'Sorry, I'm not in the mood for chatting, daddy.'

'Why not?' said Mark, somewhat put out. 'I take the day off and drive down here, now you're not in the mood?'

'That's right. Why, you got a problem? You disappear for the first seventeen years of my life, pop back for five minutes yesterday, and now you think I have to fit in around you? No wonder mum climbed into bed with all those men.'

Mark felt sick. 'What m, m, men?' he stuttered. 'Not more revelations, I can't take it.'

'Oh, you know them, dad,' she spat out cruelly, staring down at one of her mutilated arms so she did not have to look him in the eye. 'One of them is your best friend, actually.'

Mark really did feel sick now. Barry? Barry had screwed Grace? He could imagine it. She lying naked under crisp sheets, flashing her come-on eyes. He dropping his threadbare pants, peeling back the cover to reveal her pert rosebud breasts. Cupping one in his hand, kissing it while she gasps...

Oh my God, Mark screamed inside his head, a tear springing from the corner of his eye and making a bid for freedom down his cheek.

'How long?' he managed to ask.

'Oh,' replied Poppy, 'about four years seriously, perhaps longer.'

'Bastard, that utter bastard. I will tear his black, shrivelled heart out through his arse, then extract each bollock individually through his nostrils!'

Mark shouted this at full volume across the hospital. Even the oldest, most comatose patients in the next ward woke up. Nothing this dramatic had occurred since Mr Abrahams had caused a minor riot by switching the communal TV from *Watercolour Challenge* to *Home and Away*.

Mark stood quaking, his spittle settling in a fine vapour on the curtain around Poppy's bed, as nurses ran to see what the commotion was about. Poppy herself was laughing.

Mark was escorted off the premises and returned to his BMW. Pat had been paged and met him in the car park. 'Mr Cohen,' she began, 'Dr Evans thinks it may be better for all concerned if you don't visit Poppy or Grace for a week or two, or longer if you can't calm down. We may need to look at that family discount you spoke about and get you some therapy, too. Meantime, go home and do some yoga, Mr Cohen. Believe me, you'll live longer…'

Mark could not think of anything to say by way of explanation. As Pat walked away, he took the Pentax out of his pocket and recorded the moment – thrown out of a facility designed to welcome even the humblest dregs of society, an embarrassment to the charming Pat, the admirable Dr Evans, and his own family.

He started the car, executed a defiant 360-degree skid and shot out of the gates like a bullet from a Magnum. So much for the new and mature Mark. The good news was that his to-do list was now much shorter as a result of this fiasco, while the evening's task of contacting Sammy had just become even more urgent.

He sent a text to the boys while waiting at traffic lights,

saying hi and reassuring them that everyone was well and happy. He got a text back almost immediately from Max, who was sitting bored in a maths class.

Ok da. Poppy say u went nuts n u call'd unc baz a bastard. See ya. Sam n max. X

'Bloody kids,' Mark grumbled.

Once back at home, he reviewed the to-do list.

1) Seeing Poppy was ticked off, even if it had not gone exactly as he had planned. This morning's rose-coloured vision of himself as a perfect parent had taken a knock. If they ever let him back into the hospital, he must try harder he thought, recalling old school reports.

2) See Grace. Hmm. As noted, King George's had given him a red card in the first ten minutes of the first half, so this one was out for the time being. Now he knew how Eric Cantona must have felt when he kicked that idiot fan at Crystal Palace.

3) Text the boys. Phew, done, though they knew more than Mark wanted them to. Come to think of it, they probably knew more than him full stop. Out-foxed by two twelve-year-olds locked away in Hertfordshire – a depressing thought.

4) Call Dr Evans. The doc now had him down as a nutter, and Pat had switched to 'official warning' mode. Perfect.

5) Tell Mavis and...

6) ...face Gene. Okay, he could still do these that afternoon.

7) Ring the office. Absolutely, no problem.

8) Call and thank Barry for last night. Yeah, right. Thank you, Barry, for screwing my wife for the past four years. Thank you so very much.

Which brought him to the addendum. Sammy.

Dealing with this had become an even more burning desire now. He could feel the horns straining impatiently to break through the skin covering his cranium, as his devilish side woke again. Stirred by Barry? Well, thanks for that at least, Baz.

But the evening, or ideally the dead of night, was best for what he wanted to say to Sammy, so patience served his purpose. He had spent two decades rehearsing the speech, and could wait a few hours more for some payback.

In the meantime, he must complete tasks 5, 6 and 7. The first of these struck him like a cold shower, dowsing his spiteful ardour: he had to tell his lovely mother Mavis what had happened.

He picked up the phone and rang his parents, expecting his mother to answer. Instead, it was his dad who picked up. 'Hello, who is it?' he said, after a lot of rings. Far from the swashbuckling front-line war photographer and global activist of old, these days Sid needed two days' notice just to turn on the hot-water immersion.

'Hi, dad. How are you?'

'I'm the same,' said Sid, and Mark thought, 'If only, dad, if only.'

'I'll get your mother.'

'Hello, my little treasure,' Mavis said in her usual ray-of-sunshine way, and for a moment the world was okay again for her little boy.

He went on to relate what had happened to Grace and Poppy. He did not soften the blow, as Mavis was very tough despite appearances. Like the Terminator, her vulnerable organic exterior masked a near-indestructible steel core. Half a century with Sid had made her that way.

When he finished, she said, 'Darling, I love Grace like a daughter, you know that. However, she's a mess and I worry about her effect on you and the kids. Do you want me to come over for a few weeks to cook and be there for you all, so you and Grace can have some space to work it out together?'

Mark was speechless, and in danger of getting tearful again. It was all he seemed to be doing lately. He choked out an answer.

'You're amazing, mum, but leave this to me. I'll call the minute I'm drowning, but I feel stronger just knowing you're there. God bless.'

'God bless, son. Your dad sends a kiss too.' In fact, Mark knew Sid was oblivious to everything, because he could hear the TV commentary in the background.

He decided to call the office before going to speak to Gene at the bungalow. His PA Ellie picked up straight away.

'Hiya, babe. How is it there? Any news or instructions, oh light of my life and comfort of my declining years?'

'Let's get this straight,' Mark said. 'You're saying when your tits are so low that you step on them, that's when I'm eligible to be your man?'

'You got it in one.'

'Well, thanks very much. It's under control here, if you define control as skiing downhill blindfolded with a rocket strapped to your back, heading for a stockpile of explosives.'

'No change there then, boss,' she giggled.

'Ha ha. Did the Primo briefing go okay yesterday?'

'No, it didn't. Patrick and Julia insisted it was put back until you were around. I pleaded with them and pointed out you were a cocaine-using, womanising, small-cocked cretin, but to no avail.'

'Well, that's good, because I want to see them too. I have a plan. Tell Julia I'll be in the office at 8am, and I expect her to be there. Tell Patrick I expect him to be there whenever he chooses, and that I'm shit scared of him.'

'It's amazing you ever see the light of day, what with being buried so far up his back passage. Though I imagine it has a comfy suede lining, doesn't it? See you tomorrow. The meeting with the client is at 2pm, so Mac will have to do without you at The Ivy.'

'He knows to cross out any bookings with my name on as a matter of course.'

'Idiot,' said Ellie. 'Love you. Say hi to those boys of yours.'

'No chance, pram robber. See you in the morning, and thank you, darling.'

Next, Mark set out for the home of the Christmas-in-laws. Mary was back in Barbados, and Harry would probably be up a ladder somewhere working, so it was no surprise when Gene answered the door, wiping her hands after some cooking or cleaning. She looked voluptuous in an older-woman-in-a-navy-blue-velvet-track-suit sort of way, with wonderful glowing skin and large twinkling eyes.

She lit up when she saw Mark. 'Hello, stranger,' she gushed. 'To what do I owe this pleasure? Pleasure's in such short supply when you get to my age.'

Mark smiled and kissed her cheek and went in, accepting the offer of tea.

'Listen, Gene, have you spoken to Grace in the last few days?'

'Booby?' She looked puzzled. 'No darling, not for a few days at least. Maybe a week. The way she's been lately, I was quite relieved. Can't get a word of sense out of her, and she's so angry with me all the time. She can't just chat anymore. Always in a rush for me to hang up.'

She glanced up at Mark: 'That look on your face is really worrying me. What's happened?'

He told her the whole story of Grace and Poppy, not stopping for thirty minutes, by which time the tea had gone cold and tears were streaming down both their faces.

Gene settled beside Mark on the sofa, hugged him to her colossal bosoms, and rocked his head saying 'Shhhh, shhhh, shhhh' over and over, as if she were calming a baby after a nightmare in the middle of the night. And in truth that was not far from how he felt at this moment.

He hugged the back of Gene's neck with his hand, squeezing it as he felt another wave of tears about to wash over him. She reacted as if someone had massaged her, an electric shock running down her back, making her shiver.

'My poor baby...'

Somehow Mark knew she meant him and not Grace. The situation was becoming freaky. Surreal, delightful, wicked. Unfinished Business in fact. Mark had developed keen senses over the years and, when it came to the details of human behaviour, body language and tell-tale signs, he was at the top of his game. And right now he was sensing a heady cocktail of turbulent feelings in Gene, like lava bubbling inside a volcano just before it erupts.

And he loved it. No doubts and no worries. It was wicked pleasure on every level, and so unexpected – even he would not have had the nerve to plan this. Mental note to self: be more ambitious. No pain, no gain and all that bollocks.

He went with the flow, even taking the lead by gently stroking her neck, then licking and nuzzling it. By this point, Gene was groaning and cupping her breast. She pulled up her track suit top to reveal a bra of industrial proportions.

Mark had seen less impressively engineered suspension bridges. He wrestled briefly with the complex front-locking system which maintained the structure's integrity. Then, like his own integrity, it gave up the struggle and her bosoms spilled out.

The largest, darkest, most swollen nipple he had seen in his entire forty years was now just an inch from his nose. To his surprise, she had a circle of barbed wire tattooed around the areola. You wanton minx of a mother-in-law, he smiled to himself.

The erection in his pants was beyond hard. His penis was so full of blood diverted from elsewhere in his body that his other organs must have been gasping for oxygen.

He sucked the nearest breast, licking and rubbing it with his tongue while tweaking the other with his free hand. From this extreme close-up perspective, it was like a scene from *Gulliver's Travels*, his hands seeming ridiculously small alongside her supersize tits.

Then came the kiss, his mother-in-law's tongue plunging deep into his waiting mouth. It was getting so crazy by this point that he was beginning to wish they were in a hotel, rather than gasping and grasping at each other among the sofa cushions, on the coffee table and over the rug of 53 Hillsdale Gardens.

The sound of a key rattling in the front door lock cut through their passion like one of Harry's Stanley knives. Suddenly they were a pair of babysitting teenagers, caught in a mid-kissing session when the parents return home earlier than expected.

By the time Harry entered the lounge everything looked normal, and Mark and Gene were as far apart as it was possible to be without going to separate rooms.

Mark stood up to leave, saying he had to check up on the kids. Still shaking, Gene saw him to the door. They stared into each other's eyes, and she said, 'That was always on the cards.'

'That's an unfortunate expression, Gene, given you always slaughter me at poker,' Mark replied.

They giggled and it broke the tension. They squeezed hands, and she shut the door softly behind him.

Inside his car, Mark was about to ring Barry to tell him about his mad, bad afternoon. 'Damn that fat bastard,' he said, missing him already, but seething at the same time.

He drove home and called Samuel and Max, who were more worried about the forthcoming rugby match at school than family crises. He sent a text to Poppy, who was apparently still in no mood to communicate – with or without technology.

He ordered an Indian takeaway and settled on the sofa. The television was crap, but Manchester United was playing Fulham on Sky Sports. Having eaten, he picked up his mobile and, with his anger towards Barry feeling as intense as the vindaloo he had just suffered, he texted Sammy.

Hi Sammy. Mark here. I know I have never texted you before, but I have kept a secret for 20 years and I can no longer live with it, as it's eating me alive. Can I be honest with you? Love M x x x.

He pressed the send button and sat staring at his phone.

Time passed. At Old Trafford, Ryan Giggs shot at goal and narrowly missed.

A little envelope appeared in the corner of his phone. The game was on, and it wasn't football. This was going to be a long night.

Mark left the little envelope flashing and took a photo of the scene, himself included, to commemorate this surreal day. Then he turned off the television, opened the Jack, and read her reply. If Grace could see him now, or earlier in the arms of her mother, and if looks could kill, Mark would be stone cold dead before he could even touch the keypad of his phone.

Sammy said in her text: *Hiya! This is a first.*

(A day of firsts, it seems, thought Mark mischievously.)

What do you mean by a secret?

Mark tapped a quick reply: *I mean a secret about how I feel, which has been buzzing around in my head for two decades, but I worry about telling you.*

Sammy responded: *Sounds like you are going to tell me, so bloody get on with it!*

Mark took a deep breath and started to type: *Ok. Do you remember that night on the sofa at the cottage 20 years ago? Baz was asleep in his chair and we kissed. You came so close to me. Then you took HIM up to bed and screwed his brains out, leaving me to dream about you all night. Well, that's continued every single night since. I want to finish that unfinished business. I want you. M x x x.*

He pressed send and immediately realised the enormity of what he had just done. It was a written confession of his misdemeanour then, and of his adulterous intentions now, with his best friend's wife. Would it be used by Sammy to blackmail him at some future date? Or would it be discovered by fat bastard Barry as he was being nosey one evening?

He realised he had passed control of his reputation to Sammy, and she had absolute power now, at least until she replied.

The anticipation was thrilling. Dire consequences loomed, but he was way past being anything but excitement by then.

Minutes passed. Then more minutes. Nothing. Had he sent it to bloody fat bastard Barry instead? Now nervous, Mark checked immediately but, no, happily it was Sammy's number.

Then the glorious little envelope turned up. Like a masochist, he did not open the text immediately but took a gulp of magic brown fluid from his Tennessee pal Jack, snorted a line of the white stuff big enough to mark out a lane on the M25, and lit a cigar. Then he pushed the button.

Sammy's text was five pages long which is why it took so long to arrive. It simply said: *Wow wow wow wow wow wow wow wow wow wow…* and so on for page after page.

Mark sat back, took a drag of his cigar, and said calmly to himself, 'Gotcha.'

CHAPTER EIGHT

Fun in the Filth

That bastard elephant was back.

Mark woke to the ring of his alarm that he'd set for 6.45am. They'd been texting each other until 4.29am. He'd eventually begged to be allowed to sleep, as he had a heavy work day ahead, including meetings with his boss, Patrick Craze, and the equally terrifying Julia Hardy-Roberts, Head of Global Account Management. The latter he had rashly scheduled for 8am.

Most of the afternoon would be dedicated to the Vertec people, who spent north of £100 million on advertising in the UK alone. Mark was running the pitch for Primo.

He had worked at BC for twenty years and was now Deputy Chairman. Mavis adored this impressive-sounding title, but in reality it meant little. You were senior, paid a fortune, but marginalised. It brought dignity without any real power.

For Mark it was a long-service gong, the culture of BC

being surprisingly humane when compared to most other companies in the sector. But that was like comparing a serpent's pit with Dante's Inferno. Everything is relative.

Mark was popular and useful, not young enough to be a star, nor famous enough to be successor material to God, Andrew Bond, or the Devil, Patrick Craze. Although the agency was called Bond Craze, many referred to it as Before Christ. It resembled the battle between good and evil to outsiders, although in reality, of course, both protagonists had their kindly and wicked sides. They were a balanced partnership, with defined public roles along the lines of good cop/bad cop.

Mark was a lightweight in such company, and suffered the further disadvantage that his bosses remembered him as a young nobody in the junior ranks, when they were already at the zenith of achievement. After years of sickening success they had since redefined 'zenith', and Mark had no chance of ever catching them. He had done well, but Deputy Chairman (or Deputy Dawg, as Barry called it astutely) was as far as he was ever going at BC.

Mark had gulped a slug of cough syrup before going to bed, to counter the insomniac effects of the copious cocaine and alcohol abuse which had accompanied his texting marathon. He stirred sluggishly under the duvet, just enough for a fart to escape. But, as the memory of the previous day's weird and exhilarating events seeped back into his mind, he could feel a massive high on its way.

His head was pounding and he felt sick, but as he got out of bed and staggered naked to the bathroom, still half asleep, he was tingling with anticipation and a sense of latent power. It was a big day ahead, and he new it.

'Morning, Vicki,' he said breezily, lifting the toilet seat to piss like a dray horse. She was on her knees cleaning the floor, her face level with his crotch, the treasured bottle of bleach in her hand.

'Morning, sir,' she beamed. 'Do you know where bleach from bottle went, sir?'

'As a matter of fact I do, but I can't really engage in a conversation right now, Vicki,' he replied, shaking his penis heartily over the toilet bowl.

Had Mark asked Vicki to wipe his cock clean of stray urine, he suspected she would have obliged cheerfully. He didn't ask. Instead, he threw up all over the floor she had just finished polishing.

'Oh dear, sir.'

'Sorry,' Mark muttered. He wiped his mouth, and felt much better.

Next he shaved, quickly realising that his co-ordination had not yet kicked in for the day. He managed to remove areas of skin from his chin with near-surgical precision, while leaving a verdant patch of stubble on his neck and another just under his nose. He left the bathroom with bits of tissue paper glued to his face by seeping red dots of blood, and quickly got dressed.

He could hear Vicki singing a cover version of 'Oh Happy Day' as she mopped up his vomit from the marble floor. Poor cow, he thought patronisingly, as he pulled on his Kenzo suit and black suede Gucci shoes.

He smiled at himself in the hallway mirror before setting off for the office, and thought he looked a little like he had been mugged. But by then he couldn't do anything about it, and he didn't care a jot. He felt good.

His plot for the day was already forming. To say he was excited at the prospect would be an understatement. He felt like a kid in a toy shop armed with his own Amex card.

He jumped in the car and flew out of the drive.

Some twenty minutes later, the BMW was waiting behind a stationary bus on the Bow flyover, Pink Floyd's 'Shine On You Crazy Diamond' blasting from the CD player. 'Bring it on. Bring it all on, you bastards!' Mark shouted loudly, with an elation that had never struck him before, least of all when stuck in traffic at 7.30am. Other drivers glanced warily at his extravagant dance-like gestures behind the wheel.

Soon after, Mark breezed through heavy rotating doors into the atrium-calm of one of the UK's leading advertising agencies, BC. Truthfully, he was more at home here than in his marital nest. It was the world he knew, a place where he could leave all his emotional baggage in the boot of the BMW. But today his dark side had been fired up, and he didn't feel at home in quite the same way.

He was going to have fun today, without fear. Even of Patrick Craze.

'Watcha, Cherry,' he said to the receptionist who had been behind the desk since the formation of the company. 'You look fabulous today.'

Cherry was a wild, sexy, ex-hippy grandmother, confident in her professional abilities and disposed to take crap from no one. She tried to work out whether Mark's compliment was crap or not. Too late, as he was already in the lift by the time she replied neutrally, 'Thank you.'

Mark had always wanted to have Cherry, but had never had the nerve to say so, nor to tell her that he found her as beautiful as a big, feline predator in the jungle. He decided to add her to his list, if they both lived long enough. Gene had rekindled his long-established interest in older women but, as he was now forty, that meant some of them were just plain old. Cherry was maybe fifty-five, though far sexier than most girls half her age.

He wondered if these feelings of sexual euphoria were a sign of madness or just plain old lust, or even a form of positive energy which could be channelled into the important job at hand – Redemption.

Before he could decide, the elevator arrived at the eighth floor. Mark entered his office. It was located in the Tower of Power (as the staff called it) on the penthouse floor, but was not a corner office like Patrick's or Andrew's.

Mark jumped into his leather swivel chair at 7.58am, with no sign of Ellie or his latte. No matter – right on cue, Julia Hardy-Roberts, Head of Global Account Management, strode in.

Julia was thirty-eight and single, and so sharp you could cut yourself on her intellect. She was a stunner, with short, bobbed auburn hair flicked elegantly behind one ear and a wardrobe which avoided the power-dressing clichés of women in advertising. Instead she wore loose, almost see-through dresses in muted shades of cream, green and apricot, and shoes from the King's Road which cost the same as Mark's annual cocaine supply.

The ensemble was completed by a Tiffany silver bangle and a delicate, white-faced Rolex circa 1929, no doubt bought for her by an ageing French mogul or besotted London puppy. Julia did not need anyone to buy anything for her, but this independence acted like an aphrodisiac to the many men who buzzed around her.

'Like shit-flies on a dung heap,' Mark reflected.

'A delightful welcome, thank you Mark. You don't look so hot yourself today,' said Julia with a gorgeously knowing smile.

Maybe this ice maiden defrosts her icebox at the weekend, he thought, taking care not to blurt this out loud too.

She lit up a cigarette even though this was a non-smoking building, took a deep drag, and sat on his desk. 'You look like you've spent a week at a Roman orgy. Before we do anything, why don't I pop out to get the coffees while you go and shave one more time in Patrick's en suite. He won't be in for three minutes. Do it just for me, sweetie. That is, for me, for Patrick, for Vertec and lastly, if you have any time left, do it for your career which is in intensive care at the moment. Ciao. See you in ten minutes.'

As she turned, he saw her magnificent hind quarters moving under the hypnotic sheen of some very sheer material, and groaned to himself. It was the best bum in the agency, if not the universe.

Mark had tried to have a fling with Julia a couple of years ago. At least, he had gone so far as to make some vague suggestion that they meet at the Sanderson Hotel's Long Bar. She had flirted, but had not shown up. Her private life was very private. Mark had no idea what she did at weekends and he lost his nerve after that first rejection. He decided now to file her under the heading Unfinished Business.

What a woman, he thought. She would be an additional point on the agenda of his presentation today. Wild Cherry in reception would have to wait for another time.

He grabbed the electric shaver he kept in his desk for emergencies, and made the long walk to the other side of the building and the en suite. When he returned, Patrick had arrived, and Julia was back with coffee for three, and a pear which made up her combined breakfast and lunch.

Mark was now more focused, having used the break to master the whirlwind of thoughts inside his head.

'Good morning, Mark,' said Patrick. He was wearing an immaculate silver suit, cream shirt-and-tie combo with an over-large Beckham-style knot, and Italian brown suede loafers. Hugo Boss socks suggested this was a dress-down day.

Patrick was fifty-nine years old, slim, and well over 6 ft tall. He had a full head of fashionably spiky, white hair, cool, frameless Scandinavian glasses, and perfect capped teeth which he flashed with a practised smile. His accent retained a slight hint of his Newcastle roots, though it was Sussex and Lamborghinis all the way these days, and had been for more than thirty years.

Mark recalled a story that he felt captured Patrick's snake-like personality perfectly when he'd heard it circulating round the office. A couple of years ago, Patrick had been invited to a Lamborghini dealership to view the new Murciélago model, and was shown a bright yellow version with black leather interior. Patrick new exactly what he wanted and always chose the cream leather option.

'Sir, this is the finest car in the world at the moment,' the enthusiastic young salesman had gushed, 'and the black interior is so much more subtle than sir's Diablo model. After all, it's the car that's the star, and everyone will be looking at that, not the driver!'

Patrick stepped out of the Murciélago, fixed the salesman with his finest snake-eyed stare, and intoned, 'If I didn't want people to look at me, I wouldn't buy a Lamborghini. Get me a cream interior, sonny.'

Then on his way out of the showroom, Patrick casually asked the salesman to help him reverse his Diablo out of a narrow space on the forecourt.

'Stand behind please and just tell me how much space I have to the car next to me...'

Obediently, the young man made tentative hand signals, demonstrating that only a few inches separated both vehicles. He also mentioned that a particular vehicle, an Audi A2, was his car.

'Be careful please,' he joked nervously, 'it's my first-ever company car...'

Patrick nodded his head sympathetically before putting his foot down, veering into the little car, carving a deep gash down the side of the Audi and coming to a halt once he'd managed to roll right over the poor boy's foot.

After summoning the managing director and blaming the accident on the kid, Patrick insisted that he be fired for 'his incompetence', that his own car be repaired for nothing and that he receive an eight per cent discount on the new Murciélago, which he would order (featuring the cream leather interior, naturally). All of these requests were met instantly. That is the Devil for you.

At BC, three more different people could not have gathered together for a common cause. But today, Patrick, Julia and Mark were going into battle against AFT, the agency which currently had the Primo account. They were the enemy, not Vertec. Clients are only enemies if they fire you. If they leave for another agency, they become 'clunts', a term Ellie had coined with a much-celebrated typo.

Well, that wasn't going to happen today.

The advertising business is built not on rock, but wet tissue paper. It is an industry where ideas and the ability to sell them are paramount. Not that any old idea will do: it needs to answer a brief and address specific marketing issues. That takes specialised skills, drawn from various people in different departments by persons known as account handlers.

Julia and Mark were both account handlers or, more simply, 'suits' like Craze. At BC, only the God-like Andrew Bond was blessed with the multiple skills of planning, creativity and selling, although it was his creativity which made him world-famous. Mark would have killed to have that strand of talent, and it was probably why he had been drawn to Grace so strongly from such a young age. She was one of the naturals in the tribe of creativity.

But Mark was now determined to show that he too possessed these skills because, at last, he had the confidence to deploy them. He would regale his boss and his colleagues with powers of theatre and sheer nerve he had forgotten since that stormy Bar Mitzvah day, when he had stood centre stage for the first time.

He outlined his take on Primo, and how they could harness something that AFT would never dream of in a million years. He was winging it, as he had prepared nothing except his own agenda for the day. Truth be told, he did not care about the pitch or BC or his job at all any more. He felt liberated and, ironically, as a result, could see clearly what needed to be done for Primo, unclouded by company politics and similar nonsense.

Was this vision ambitious? Yes. Was it inspirational? Definitely. Would it win? AFT need not bother to turn up. Was it going to be fun? Oh yes, definitely fun.

Patrick and Julia said nothing while Mark spoke, but were suitably impressed by the power of his rhetoric, which lasted for a thirty off-the-cuff minutes. The gist of his argument was this: 'We're not selling soap powder, or the product's functional performance. We're selling the joys of filth.

'It's about dynamic tension. Coca-Cola is the corporation that teaches "the world to sing", and features cuddly

Christmas ads with Santa – it's like the 1950s reinvented for the Noughties. On the other hand, Tango is a fruit-based drink from a company of lunatics who slap you around the face when you least expect it and are on first-name terms with the Advertising Standards Authority.'

'The two brands are clearly coming from polar opposites,' stated Mark. 'That's why I believe Pepsi isn't working. They're saying it's like Coke, only not for everyone. Being exclusive is, by its very nature, smaller than being inclusive. And, for a soft drink (rather than, say, an upmarket car), that is lethal.

'Primo needs to take a wider view. Not just to be different, but to distance itself from the competition in an inclusive way.'

Mark continued: 'Our canvas is not confined to other cleaning products, but the stuff of life itself. We were born in the primeval slime of the swamps, and now spend hours in chemists buying cotton buds and antiseptic wipes. Is that evolution, or a denial of what we truly are?'

Patrick nodded enthusiastically. Julia cocked her head to one side, crossed her legs and was beginning to look at Mark in a fresh light, definitely a fresh light. All she was hearing was 'Blah, blah, blah' but so confident was his 'Blah, blah, blah', she didn't really care.

Mark was in full flow now.

'Without dirt, life is sterile and pointless. It's the same in every area of life. Julia, without pain, how can you know what pleasure is?'

She flashed a sexy smile and uncrossed and crossed her legs the other way, Sharon Stone style. Oh yes, she of all people knew about the pain-pleasure thing. Mark Cohen, who are you? she wondered.

'Without tragedy, how can we truly celebrate happiness, Patrick?' Patrick shrugged and smiled. In his mind, Mark's pitch was certainly more involving than the production of *Madam Butterfly* he'd seen last week. For a start it was in English and didn't last three hours, Patrick thought. At least, he hoped not.

'Without Primo, the uninhibited joy of getting mucky will be lost. Primo reminds us that it's great to be alive and to lose control sometimes.

'Filth is fun.'

By now, Julia was surprised to find herself becoming aroused by Mark's conviction and all his talk of pain, pleasure and, in particular, filth.

'Take our main target audience, for instance. They are human beings, not robotic ABC1s aged twenty-five to forty-four. Just people with families who buy shed loads of Primo or its rival Atomal because they have to, not because they want to.

'I'll bet you that, if we did focus groups with them and got them to talk about their mucky kids, they'd be all enthusiastic. But raise the subject of washing powder and it becomes a chore, and suddenly they'd adopt the facial expressions of an oppressed slave nation.

'We've approached it that way for half a century. Dreaming up pseudo-science and product demonstrations to brainwash the exploited under-classes. Hypnotising the mothers and their mothers before them, and then doing it all again to the children.'

Patrick was now intrigued and, he had to admit, was impressed by this seemingly new, bold Mark standing in front of him, delivering a pitch that would have had Vertec eating out of BC's hand. His mind wandered as he imagined Mark becoming his successor, allowing the balance with God, Andrew, to be maintained. Patrick could float on his yacht, and dabble in the money markets from Monaco. He could see it now, but not twenty minutes earlier.

Mark was still firing on all cylinders.

'What we say is, if you grow up to be a parent, all you can look forward to during daylight hours is a relationship with the Hotpoint washing machine. It should really be called "Hotpointless" by the way.'

Patrick and Julia giggled at this welcome injection of levity.

'Those with careers use housewives as the benchmark for a wasted life. The drudgery and chores that define everything which is unpleasant and demeaning about being a housewife are represented by the very product we're about to pitch for – Primo.

'We should be making them proud of their sacrifice, not undermining them further. Primo should represent Mum taking the kids out to roll in the mud. Dad too, if we can get the fat slob to leave the office early or skip Sky Sports for an hour.' (Mental note: that fat slob is me, thought Mark.)

'We should give away face paint with every packet of the washing powder. Organise paintball contests for families at weekends and huge televised events at which our customers play together and get filthy, in a kind of *Big Brother* meets *The Osbournes* meets *Full Metal Jacket* fashion. Fun in the filth, that's Primo.'

Mark was now moving on to his personal agenda, the reason why he had dragged himself into the office today instead of going to see Gene and unleashing those hooters again, or visiting his kids and acting like a saint.

'I have an idea for a planet-spanning business that will

embody this new theme, and give something back to the children of the world. I have all the contacts needed to create an independent charity, a global organisation to support Primo in their work.

'My wife Grace is working on it tirelessly,' lied Mark. 'She is putting the building blocks in place together with some of the most powerful corporations in the world. Vertec are the missing component to make this dream a reality, and by joining us they can make and take a slice of history.

'This will be my baby if that's okay, Patrick?'

He was drawing his pitch to a close, while simultaneously securing his plan for his Redemption. And he was clearly making progress with the Unfinished Business too. Julia's body language had been speaking volumes for the last twenty-five minutes.

Patrick nodded his blessing. Gotcha, thought Mark.

'I'm blessed to be Deputy Chairman here at the biggest and best agency in Britain. I'm so lucky, and now I want to put something back. Patrick, thank you so much for helping me to help others.'

He had reached the emotional climax of the pitch, and Vertec wasn't even there! But then, it was Patrick's support he needed now, not some crappy advertising account, and his audience were all but lighting their cigarette lighters and raising them over their heads in a collective sway. He wondered if he was the advertising world's answer to Barry Manilow.

This is surreal, Mark thought, like everything else during the past two days. Is this my life from now on? I bloody hope so. He tried to force a tear from the corner of his eye. He had been sobbing uncontrollably for forty-eight hours. Now where was one droplet when he needed it? No matter, he was nearly at the end.

'Primo will become the guardian of fun for children the world over and, in time, maybe their best friend too.' (Careful, he thought, steer the ship away from those sugary rocks before we all throw up and run aground.)

'My new organisation will ensure this. If it's okay, I will brief you both further about this vision and the business plan in the next few days.' (What sodding business plan? he asked himself.)

He drew a deep, theatrical breath before the final sentence. 'This is not an advertising pitch, it is the catalyst for corporate responsibility and for mothers to be celebrated as the liberators of all that's good about being a child in this century.'

Mark sat down exhausted. He deserved an Oscar.

Patrick said simply, 'The pitch date is set for one month today. It is the biggest pitch of the year. Andrew Bond is going away for a sabbatical, to write a book. I am happy to put all this in your hands in his absence, Mark. Make it happen.' Then he swept out of the office with a swagger in his step.

Patrick thought that he could shadow Mark and coach him while God was 'away'. Just to test the younger pretender's mettle before Andrew returned and the real power balance resumed within the BC management.

Julia looked at Mark for a few moments before saying, 'I don't know what vitamins you're taking, Mark Cohen, but I want some.' She added: 'What are you doing later this evening by the way?'

Gotcha, Mark thought.

'Well, Julia, I'm going to work up these ideas at home this afternoon. It's a better use of my time, don't you agree? Would you do the client briefing with Vertec for me at two? Perhaps we could meet later for a drink at the Long Bar at the Sanderson. Say 7.30, if that's okay with you.'

'That's perfect,' said Julia, adding, 'You're the boss,' as she turned and walked to her office with just a touch more swing in her hips than was absolutely needed.

'Gotcha,' said Mark, this time out loud.

CHAPTER NINE

Sleepless Days

Mark was driving home from his day's work and it was only 9.54am. He could get used to this. Last week, Patrick Craze wouldn't have pissed on him if he were on fire, and Julia Hardy-Roberts would have rather stayed in to bleach her upper lip moustache than have gone for a drink with him.

Today, after an hour, his boss believed he was a genius and had fallen hook, line and Lamborghini for his new global venture, attached to a Primo pitch which was vital to BC.

Amazing, considering that the idea had only existed in Mark's head for two days.

Julia was covering for him in the boring, pointless Vertec briefing, coming as it did after he had already dreamed up the brilliant solution. She was acting as his assistant, not a position to which she was accustomed. And he believed she was now interested in him in a carnal way, after his rhetoric-rich performance in the office.

He was talking soap powder at the time – not exactly love poetry was it?

Since fear had packed its bags and joined his integrity on holiday in New Zealand, wonderful things had happened. He just hoped the happy couple were going to settle there permanently.

Life was taking such strange turns. The vast amount of pain he had suffered was finding its match in pure pleasure. He would go home now and take a nap. No more today on his masterplan.

What he must do is prepare a fresh to-do list, as things were moving so quickly now it was hard to keep track of all the spinning plates, or should he say spinnng chainsaws!

He laughed out loud at the conceit, as he swerved into his Woodford driveway at 57mph. He stopped half an inch from the garage door. 'My driving is getting sharper, too.' He was *so* pleased with himself.

Mark walked into his house and all looked perfect. Vicki had scrubbed everything and retrieved the debris from the lawn, disinfecting it before putting it back in its proper place. The photo albums were back in order on the shelves and the loose pictures were all filed.

The empty Jack Daniels bottles and traces of white lines on the glass surfaces had gone. Beds were changed and starched crisp, vomit was mopped up, an immaculate toilet bowl sparkled and the fridge was stocked with basic essentials.

Egg and rice noodles, fresh ginger, bean shoots, coriander, fish sauce, peanuts, soy sauce, tofu. Jar of pre-chopped garlic and real lychees. Curiously, some pork and stilton sausages and a jar of Ragu too. He could only assume that she had picked up those last items in error. Otherwise, there was everything a well-stocked Filipino larder should have.

Four economy bottles of Domestos, twelve kitchen rolls and five Toilet Ducks completed Vicki's eclectic roster of provisions. Mark was grateful for her care and made a mental note to give her a bonus.

It was almost as though Grace had no place any more. It was calm, it was clean, it was quiet and, with the exception of not having Poppy around, Mark was happy in it. To be painfully honest, the absence of his wife's tortured, brooding presence was only really noticeable from the wonderful sense of relief it brought.

For the last year, perhaps eighteen months, Grace had lived almost entirely in her bedroom.

She barely stirred from it except to buy alcohol or run an errand for the children. Her friends had largely been alienated, and Vicki and Denise were her only regular contacts. Mark was a malevolent spirit who pounded on her door at night to demand sex or simply to shout at her through the woodwork.

She had rejected his advances so often and for so long that she'd almost forgotten why she refused him. It became second nature to start her sentences with 'no', before even hearing the question.

On the rare occasions when she did join Mark for an evening out, she was humiliating company. Speaking with a slurred voice, interrupting conversations, laughing at the wrong moments and, memorably, falling over.

Mark would defend himself by belittling her, seeking to present himself as the victim in the relationship, a martyr to her vices. Grace resented it bitterly, as she saw his dark side at three in the morning, in the privacy of South Woodford. The real Mark was a beast that no one but she could know.

He had wished her dead at times. If she simply disappeared, it would avoid all the pain of divorce. He knew she wished the same for him, but this brought him no comfort.

It was bewildering. How could an angel decompose into a vicious zombie in just four years? What had caused it? Was it all Mark's fault? Surely Grace must take some of the blame.

She had had affairs with many men according to Poppy, including that treacherous fat bastard Barry.

Mark stopped torturing himself with these thoughts, concentrating instead on preparing more demonic behaviour. At least that would make him feel better later on.

He set out his next to-do list.

1) See Poppy if they will allow it. Speak by phone otherwise. Text as last resort.

2) Text boys. If not, speak by phone.

3) Speak to Dr Evans and/or Pat re visits and therapy.

4) Visit Grace if possible. (Mention new venture if she's well enough.)

5) Prepare for Julia at 7.30 (At last, some pleasure.)

6) Text Sammy, the later the better. (More pleasure.)

7) If time, speak to Ellie. (Debatable pleasure.)

8) Ignore fat bastard Barry. (Absolute pleasure.)

9) Get some bloody sleep. Set alarm, do not miss 7.00 for 7.30 deadline. (Necessary pleasure.)

10) Gene? (Wickedly indulgent pleasure.)

Fifty per cent pleasure, fifty per cent duty or need. Balance achieved. The only question was, how much of it could he accomplish in a day? Logically he couldn't see Grace or Poppy unless Dr Evans allowed him back into the hospital, so that had to be addressed first.

Mark rang King George's and was immediately put through to Pat. 'Hello, may I help you? Dr Evans' office here, Pat speaking.'

'Hi Pat, it's Mark Cohen. Listen, before you speak, I am

so sorry about the other day. It was a terrible time and I didn't handle it well. Poppy told me something from the leftfield about Grace, and I just lost it. It won't happen again, I promise you. I would love to see my girls, and talk to the doctor about therapy for all of us, including me.'

'The way you drove out of the hospital scared us all out of our wits.'

'I'll take a taxi next time. I will also take you, your sister and George Clooney out to dinner anywhere you choose. Burger King, Kebab City, Subway, wherever. Money is no object.'

Pat was quiet a moment, then he heard a giggle.

'I can't be angry with you for long. I'll talk to the doctor. Can you hold, please?'

It took several minutes, but finally she returned. 'Hello, caller?'

'Yes, caller.'

'The doctor says okay, but just today as a trial run. You can see Poppy and Grace for fifteen minutes each. Can you be here by 11.15? Be a good boy, or I'm going to look an idiot. Dr Evans will speak to you about therapy by phone either this afternoon or tomorrow. '

'That's fine and thank you very much, caller.' (They appeared to have coined a bizarre new term of endearment for each other, but Mark was grateful for the olive branch.) He hung up and decided he would have to postpone a nap.

He called a local mini-cab firm and set off for the hospital in a blue Proton banger that had seen better days, with a driver cursed by severe body odour. Mark opened the rear window and held his breath until he was nearly a matching shade of blue.

Having checked in with 'caller', he headed off to see

Poppy. She was in the toilet when he got there, so he sat quietly by her bed like a faithful old sheep dog, on his best behaviour.

Poppy came back, parted the curtain and was shocked to see him sitting there. She kissed him, but there was no hug.

'Hello. I am so bored. I'm even pleased to see you, dad!'

'Well, that will have to do darling. After my last outburst, I'm only allowed fifteen minutes with you today. Can't blame them. Oh, and thanks for filling in Samuel and Max about my language! Have you seen mum while you've been here?'

'I was so bored yesterday that I went for a walk, and went into Princess Grace Ward. Did you notice the name, dad? So spooky.'

'Yes, I giggled when I saw that too. And?'

'She was sleeping, so I went back after an hour and we chatted but she was a bit confused, but not scary. She's not sure where she is, but she still knows who she is.'

They both smiled genuinely at that.

'She had a visitor turn up with an armful of flowers, so I left. Glad to get out, with all those wrinklies in there dribbling and coughing mucus into their soup.'

Mark gulped at the news of Grace's visitor, but tried not to overreact, for fear of incurring a lifetime ban from the premises.

'So, what kind soul came with the flowers, lovely girl?' he slipped in after some casual chat about the ward, her therapy, and which medication she was taking.

'Dunno. Never seen him before. He was a big bugger in a Boss suit. Mummy recognised him, greeted him like a long-lost friend. I think I was in the way.'

'Ha, ha, ha,' Mark laughed weakly. 'Was he one of the men you dropped into the conversation, in a grenade-chucking sort of way, the last time I came by?'

Poppy looked confused herself now. An eyebrow was raised, her head was tilted and her pupils were large, though Mark thought that might be the medication.

'What are you talking about?' she asked.

Now Mark felt like he was the one going nuts. Was he dreaming it? Was he dreaming everything? Poppy, Gene, Sammy, Barry? No...

He asked the same question about the men, this time though he delivered it very slowly. She twigged, and burst into fits of laughter, chortling and spluttering uncontrollably.

'It's not funny,' said Mark. 'That's what made me blow up. It's okay to have told me, darling, it's for the best.'

Poppy finally brought herself under control and said, 'No, no, daddy. I was kidding. When I said mummy had slept with all those men, you blew up before I could finish my little joke.'

'JOKE?' he began to shout, reining himself back just in time. 'Joke?' now in a huge stage whisper. 'What joke, Poppy?'

She looked down at her slashed arms, avoiding her father's eyes, in some discomfort now.

'Well, when I said you knew them...'

'Yes, yes,' Mark said, aware he had two minutes left of his allotted time, and Pat's back-combed blonde hair was bobbing down the corridor towards them. 'Hurry up, darling.'

'When I said she slept with your best friend, I meant your mate Jack Daniels.'

'Oh,' said Mark, 'and all the other men you kindly hinted at?'

'Johnny Walker, Jim Beam and William Grant. You do know those guys as well as mummy does, don't you daddy?'

Pat said it was time, and Mark slid quietly into shock. He said nothing else but, 'Bye, darling, see you soon.'

He went through the Sammy texts in his head, and recalled all those 'fat bastard' comments he had made about Barry for the past three days. He felt such a fool, but happy that he could speak to the fat bastard again now.

However, he was about to visit Grace, and it seemed that his integrity had come back on a flying visit to taunt him right at the worst possible moment. Sammy filled his head, until she was blotted out by the gargantuan bosoms of Grace's mother. Then he reached Grace's bed and Pat left them alone together.

'Hi' and 'Hi'.

More uncomfortable silence followed, both of them looking down at their laps.

Mark cracked first. 'How is it here? Food any good?'

'It's okay. But why are there so many people in my bedroom?'

'You're in a hospital ward, darling,' he said tenderly, stroking her hand. 'Just until you get stronger, then you can come home to your own bedroom.'

'I see.' But she seemed to have the five-second memory of a goldfish and asked the same question moments later, and every three minutes after that. She was not in distress, and even cracked a joke or two, but she was confused.

Mark felt no anger. The spiteful part of him had been banished as soon as he saw how small and weak his angel had become. He wanted to nourish her, protect her and hold her hand for always. He was spellbound by her face even now.

He brought out the Pentax and took a couple of shots of her. She looked like a child in her first big bed.

He did not bring up the global charity venture he had mentioned to Patrick Craze during the pitch, but hoped it would eventually help rehabilitate Grace, as it was exactly in line with her interests of old. No point worrying her about it now, but it could be an important part of the Redemption entry on his list.

Curiously, Mark found he could separate his immoral actions and dubious behaviour of the past couple of days from his paternal instincts towards Grace. They were separate strands running in parallel.

His time was up with Grace before anything of much substance was said, but it didn't really matter. Enough poison had been drawn from their wounds to allow some respite from their anger towards one another.

Mark said he would be back very soon, and that he missed her, and that he loved her. Grace stared at him with a slightly puzzled expression and offered a cheek for him to peck. She said nothing. Mark was tired emotionally, and physically, but at least he was not crying or screaming.

The smelly Proton was waiting, but Mark had popped into the hospital shop on the way out and bought an in-car air freshener shaped like a traffic light. He hung it from the suit hook in the back as he was driven home. He had been tempted to buy some deodorant and leave it on the back seat for the driver, but decided he would probably never see him again.

On the way home, he texted the boys.

Hi Samuel. Just saw poppy and mum. Both doing well and on the mend slowly. I am busy boy at work. How did rugby go? Love dad. xxx

A reply arrived within seconds, sent from a history lesson.

Hi da. Spoke 2 Poppy . She say u in beter mood. Also she says mum is mad nutter. We lost rugby 52-7. We was bollox. Love ya. S n m. x

The cab arrived in Woodford and Mark was still holding his breath as he shut the front door behind him. The house was thankfully silent – Vicki must have finished for the day.

Bliss, he thought. He went upstairs to nap. Setting the alarm, he realised that it was 1.32pm and he suddenly felt hungry.

He stripped down to his boxers and padded downstairs to find something to eat, as he'd only had a coffee so far that day. Although he enjoyed cooking, he didn't have the energy for it, settling instead for the unusual combination of peanuts, lychees and a glass of rosé.

He stuffed and slurped it down over the kitchen sink, and noticed that the Robinsons next door had thoughtfully returned the dead rat over the garden fence on to his lawn.

He went outside, picked it up by the tail and drop-kicked it over to their side again. He giggled, realising he had invented a new game. Sort of a slow, rodent badminton. He then realised that he had kicked it with bare feet and had rotting rat flesh between his toes.

'Gross,' he muttered, hopping back indoors to wash.

A long, hot power shower, followed by Issey Miyake sprayed all over, and Mark felt relaxed enough to sleep. But, just as he drew the curtains and pulled back the covers, the door knocker banged loudly in the hallway.

'Oh for God's sake. Give me some peace.' But it banged again. He slipped on a bath robe and headed grumbling and muttering to the front door.

He opened it, and there stood Gene. Not in a track suit this time, but some trendy black jeans, a black lace blouse, and black lace bra. She had made herself up and sprayed on Angel scent. Her nails were painted an aubergine colour, like Grace's used to be.

'Well, hello,' she said, 'can I come in? I feel like a scarlet woman standing out here!'

'More like a gorgeous black woman you mean.'

Gene rarely visited, as Grace did not encourage her to. Nor anyone else these days.

She stepped into the hallway, then did something surprising. Instead of heading to the kitchen for a coffee and a chat, she carried on walking up the stairs, discarding clothing as she went.

She had not spoken a word since crossing the threshold. Mark also said nothing, waiting in the hallway for two or three minutes. He heard the toilet flush, then silence from his bedroom.

He padded upstairs into the bedroom, where his mother-in-law was lying naked in his bed. Only the top of her dreadlocked head was visible above the sheets, but her clothes were strewn around the room, so he knew what awaited him.

The lights were off, the curtains still drawn and Gene had lit an aromatherapy candle she had brought with her. She had planned this expedition carefully. Mark slid off his bath robe and slipped into bed with her, taking her in his arms. She was all woman. A Jessica Rabbit cartoon, a diva.

She felt wonderful and different from anyone else he had ever held. It was like passing your driving test in a Ford Fiesta, then jumping into a Ford GT40 (a car from the 1960s that could do more than 200mph even back then).

She was surprisingly self-conscious, presumably because she was older. But she need not have worried, as she was gorgeous and Mark enjoyed her utterly. It was too tender to be called a 'fuck', but too loud and physical to be termed 'making love'. The best description he could come up with was 'affectionate lust'.

She had three orgasms, not because Mark was a super stud, but because she had not had sex for more than ten years. Apparently Harry went off the whole thing when West Ham was relegated one year, and never regained his appetite. They had not talked to each other about their feelings, and had plodded on regardless with a marriage which was comfortable, but little else.

Her daughters did little for Gene either. Mary just pushed and pushed, while Grace was clammed shut. Gene had been feeling old and ugly, Grace was self-destructing, and her affection for her son-in-law changed up a gear when he presented himself in need of a hug.

'I don't expect us to elope, but I do expect us to, well, keep each other company sometimes,' said the enlightened and passionate mother-in-law. 'Oh, and you must continue to lose to me at poker, heavily and often.'

The bed was one big wet patch, tissues everywhere, the KY tube was squeezed flat for its last drops, and items of lingerie still formed a trail up the staircase to his bedroom. They lay panting and sweaty on the duvet, their eyes shut in the darkened room.

Then light glimmered through the doorway, as the door creaked open.

'Hello, sir,' said Vicki, 'I come and check toilet now?'

'No, I'm busy. I thought you'd finished for the day? And what is it with the hourly toilet inspections? Please come back later.'

But it was too late. Vicki was in already, and stood staring at Grace's mother's upturned bum. She knew Gene, but had not seen her naked before, with Mark's hand resting between her large buttocks.

Mark stood up, naked also, found his wallet and gave Vicki an on-the-spot bonus of £300. Vicki was unfazed by the scene, but freaked out by the tip. 'Oh sir, thank you, thank you.'

'A pleasure. To say "thank you" for the last few days. And

to ask you to be quiet about... this,' he said, pointing at Gene's shapely buttocks.

'No problem, sir. Can I clean your toilet now?'

'Go away, Vicki, for a little while, please go away.'

'Okay sir,' she said, shutting the door softy as she went.

Gene left soon after, giving Mark her mobile number for texting.

It was now 5.15pm.

Mark was a dead man walking, his batteries drained after three and a half pounding and athletic hours with his mother-in-law. If he were a stewing steak, he would melt in the mouth after being so comprehensively tenderised.

He had to shower again, but first he called Ellie to catch her before she left the office, as always at 5.31pm precisely. There was no news, but the agency was buzzing with stories of Mark's performance to Patrick Craze.

'You're my hero,' said Ellie.

All hopes of daytime sleep had gone. Mark contented himself with a little private grooming, especially as Julia had made such a big thing of his looking shoddy this morning. Was that just this morning? It felt more like a week ago. He must be living in dog years now.

He trimmed his nasal hair and sanded down the hard skin on his feet. He washed and conditioned his hair, applied moisturiser and toner to his face, exfoliated his back, flossed and brushed his teeth, gargled with mouthwash and sprayed more Issey all over.

Mark fished out some cocaine he had hidden under a floorboard, found the condoms and grabbed a Viagra in case he ran out of steam after the afternoon's session.

This must be what a male escort feels like, he mused.

He got dressed, but avoided black, as Julia had said it was

common. Instead he went for sludgy brown Armani casual, with brown suede Gucci loafers. He wore a black-faced TAG Monaco watch as his only jewellery, and a Kenneth Cole crocodile belt.

If he weren't forty, and getting a bit thick around the middle, he might have looked quite cool. At least he still had hair, after a twenty-three-year reprieve from his dad's dodgy balding gene.

It was 6.28pm and time to head back into town to meet Julia at the Long Bar. He decided to take a mini cab, as he would be requiring a drink or seven. The blue Proton beeped its horn as it drew up outside the house, and Mark regretted not having invested in that gift of deodorant.

He asked the driver to pull up thirty yards short of the hotel entrance, as the cool young doormen with their CIA headsets would be appalled if a Proton arrived at their venue. Aston Martins and Ferraris are the preferred mini cabs for Sanderson patrons, and he was confident that snipers were stationed on the roof to take out anyone who stopped in anything less than a brand new Maserati.

Mark passed through the stylish Ian Schrager reception and entered the Long Bar. It was the best in the area, full of people talking eagerly while glancing over their shoulders to see if anyone more interesting might have entered. It was much like celebrity-spotting at The Ivy, except that the Sanderson staff are all stiff young clones, constantly admiring themselves in the mirrors, whereas The Ivy people are relaxed, larger-than-life characters.

Julia had not yet arrived, so Mark settled on a stool and reserved the one next to it for her. He ordered himself a Manhattan cocktail, based on bourbon, his favourite. He knew she loved a Mint Julep, so he ordered that too (though a couple of Cider Bombs struck him as a better idea).

Patrick was there, but across the bar and locked in discussion with a young blonde account handler called Charlotte. Mark did not interrupt them.

Julia finally arrived at 7.45pm, sweeping in with a mobile glued to her ear. She didn't apologise for her lateness or interrupt her conversation with her girlfriend, Caro St James, about a planned 'shoe safari' to the King's Road. She did mime a kiss in Mark's direction though.

At 7.55pm Julia actually said, 'Hello, sweetness!'

She pecked his cheek and pointed an index finger at her empty glass. She had drained it while chatting to her mate and laughing so loudly that everyone had turned to look. She didn't notice, much less care.

But she was now completely focused on Mark. 'My goodness, darling, I have never seen you like you were this morning. To be honest, only our "God" has been that inspiring in my living memory at Before Christ. What's changed? I love the new you, sweetie.'

He was ready with a bullshit reply.

'Oh, it's just that now I really want to make a difference. The kids thing is so exciting. I also love brands, and I adore working with the top talents in our industry. Andrew, Patrick and you are the best there are.'

He flattered her Achilles heel, her professional vanity.

Julia knew she had the best bum in the business, but resented the suggestion that it did her any favours. She had worked, smoked and sweated to get to where she was, and her bum had very little to say about it.

She smiled and did that head-tilting thing again.

After four or five cocktails they were giggling and sharing stories. They played 'marry one, shag one, throw one over a cliff'. Mark chose three people, and Julia had to say which she'd wed, bed or make dead.

'Patrick Craze, Andrew Bond and Jim Oliver,' ventured Mark.

'Hmmm,' pondered Julia out loud. 'Well, if I knew who this Jim actually was, it would help.'

'Only the office manager for the last million years, that's all,' Mark helpfully replied.

Julia shot back: 'Over the cliff he plummets then – I don't do peasants. I say, this is fun!'

She continued: 'I would marry Andrew as he would be loyal, and he's clever and funny. He is a good person rather than a God person, but with a naughty twist to him. I would shag Patrick, because he would be mustard between the sheets. Anal sex for me, probably him too, toys, the lot. I sound like a perv, don't I?'

'No you don't,' Mark lied, sporting a nice line in erections at the thought of Julia in such wild abandon. Definitely Unfinished Business.

'My turn,' she said, proposing 'Cherry on reception, Penelope Cruz and me.'

'Unfair to include yourself. Against all the rules. Still, I'll answer. I'd marry Cherry. She is fifty-five but gorgeous, and I think women come into their own and are at their most sexy from the age of thirty-five.'

Julia thought she might love this man.

'Cherry is still sexy, feisty and I gather has a trust-fund. She also wouldn't live long, given her age and the strain I would place on her in the bedroom.'

Julia slapped him on the thigh, nearly laughing herself off her bar stool.

'Penelope Cruz is off that cliff. She's a thing of beauty it's true, blessed with a gob like your namesake, Julia Roberts.' (And a mouth like Sammy, he thought to himself.) 'But she's so Spanish and Latin-tempered and has slept with that ventriloquist's dummy Tom Cruise.'

Yet more laughing and teetering on stools.

'As for you, I would love to bang your brains out.'

'Why don't you come back to my flat, Mark? It's getting very noisy here isn't it?'

Gotcha! he shrieked mentally, now in a highly erect state.

'Where do you live? Do you know, I don't have a clue about your private life, even though I've supposedly "known" you for years?'

She replied: 'I live somewhere you'd never dream of in a million years. Go on, three guesses. If you get it right, I'll give you a real treat.' She said it playfully, but with an edge of seriousness too.

'Err, Kensington?'

'Too obvious – wrong!'

'Okay then, Islington?'

Julia smiled. 'Nice try. Close, but too Dido, Paul Whitehouse and Paul Merton, and the media trash.'

What Julia didn't know was that Mark had lied. He knew exactly where she lived, as he had accompanied her home in a black cab two years earlier, and was amazed at her choice of residence. He hadn't been inside, but it wasn't at all what he would have expected for such an upmarket lady.

'My last guess. Hmmm, a wild punt in the dark. Borough?'

'You bastard. How did you know?'

He told the truth about the cab, thinking she might remember anyway, and suspecting she would love his cheeky confession. She did.

'Well, a deal is a deal. One treat coming your way.'

Borough, in south-east London, is bohemian at best, bloody rough at worst. Kebab houses, dustbins and litter dropped by kids and passing van drivers.

She lived above a sex shop on the main road with a metal gate and padlock in front of her front door. The hall was dark, with a bicycle and junk gathering dust. A naked light bulb flickered on a timer switch, illuminating threadbare grey felt carpet tiles.

Julia earned around £250,000 a year. What was she thinking?

Mark was shown into the flat. The lounge was cream, with two low, bright red leather sofas. There was a kitsch mirrored bar in the centre of the room, from which Julia poured two large Jack Daniels with ice. The micro hi-fi was excellent, and she played Mozart while Mark was taken on the tour.

The kitchen was black marble and polished ebony. The bathroom was Philippe Starck, modern and minimal. There was a single black and white photo on the wall of a woman in a tight black leather catsuit and leather mask.

Her bedroom had no windows, and the walls were lined with cream cotton chiffon like a huge flowing curtain. The bed was vast and round, the lighting low and sexy. All of her clothes, TV and other storage were hidden behind the curtain in an area as big as the bedroom. The effect was cool and contemporary without being uninviting.

He was disappointed that they did not linger there, or that she didn't drag him into bed for his treat.

Maybe it's just as well, he thought, flagging from previous wild exertions. Instead, she pulled back the curtain on the other side of that room and beckoned him through. What he saw made his jaw drop.

It was her private dungeon and torture chamber. Chains

with manacles hung from the ceiling. Various whips, dildos, vibrators and electric prods were displayed on the walls like an angler's prize fish. There was a glass table with a hole in the centre, presumably to allow access to the nether regions of whoever sat on it.

Julia turned to him and slipped off her outer clothes to reveal red lingerie. She held up two electric pads, one in each hand, the current crackling between them.

'Get undressed and lie down. Your treat is to experience the joys of true pain.'

Not much sleep for me tonight, Mark thought, what with being plugged into the national grid...

CHAPTER TEN

Faith, Hope and Therapy

It was Saturday morning, and Mark was trying to relax in bed. He was sore in places where he had never hurt before, let alone had electric currents passed through. The phone rang beside the bed.

'Mr Cohen?'

'Yes, speaking.'

'This is Dr Evans. May I speak to you? I'm sorry to disturb you at the weekend, but I need to discuss our recommendations for your wife and daughter.'

Mark sat bolt upright and quickly got a grip of his senses. 'Okay, doctor, fire away.'

'Mr Cohen, Grace is very ill. She has had tests for liver and heart damage, and an MRI scan of her brain. Nothing conclusive was revealed, but long-term alcohol abuse, food deprivation and addiction to various painkillers and drugs will not have left her undamaged. Her mental state is even more troubling, but we at King George's can only deal with the physical aspects of her case.

'We would like to refer her as an in-patient to the Rookery rehab clinic, while continuing her physical treatment through regular appointments and medication. We believe the Richmond branch can take her if we move quickly, as they have a couple of beds available. Will you consent to her admission?'

'Of course, doctor. How long will she be admitted for?'

'A month, to begin with.'

Mark was relieved to know she'd be in good hands. He was also thrilled to be covered by the BC company healthcare scheme.

'And Poppy? What about her?'

'A similar plan for young Poppy, too. She is not in any physical danger, other than from what she may do to herself. Her case is more about depression than addiction, but nothing is that clear-cut. We want her to be admitted to the Rookery too, but separated from Grace obviously.'

After the conversation ended, Mark felt a little numb. He needed to process this information.

It could be a good thing. This could be part of a process that would see Grace returning to planet Earth, and possibly even to Mark. Why not? He could hope, couldn't he? The Rookery would also keep Poppy safe and that was a big plus.

For Grace, it was just plain confusing. Given that she still had not fathomed why there were so many people in her bedroom, being bundled into a car and driven somewhere completely new was disturbing.

To simplify the arrangements, Poppy was taken at the same time. She sat on the front seat and was silent for the whole journey. Both mother and daughter ignored each other.

Poppy was brimming with anger and disgust at Grace; the

hairs on the back of her neck and arms were standing up with utter repulsion at the idea of sharing such a small space with her pathetic mother.

As for Grace, she was lost in her own labyrinth of darkness. Up until recently, she had been suffering hallucinations concerning woolly sheep sporting the distorted faces of old, long-lost school friends. And she was unsure about whether the person on the front seat was actually her daughter Poppy or not. Instead, she chose to let it all wash over her and not to comment or react to anybody in any way. She felt it was safer that way.

The Rookery was set in thirty acres of grounds. In some ways, it resembled Samuel and Max's school, being Gothic, formerly a religious establishment and deeply imposing from the outside.

Grace sat silently in the back of the Ford Sierra, gazing out with no idea where she was going or what was about to happen to her, much like a dog or a cat being taken to the vet.

The huge iron gates opened electronically, revealing a long, winding gravel driveway at least half a mile long. There were woods on either side and cars parked all the way up to the Rookery itself. On each side of the huge white building were annexes, with any remaining overspill caught by Portakabins.

Grace was accompanied by Pat Ballcock from Dr Evans' office, who was the only nurse available for the task. Pat had been happy to come along partly because she was curious about Mark's wife.

They approached the glass doors, which opened automatically. After the impressive build-up, the interior was a disappointment, all threadbare carpets and fire doors and extinguishers, like a cross between an NHS A&E department and *Scrubs*.

In reception, they were registered and asked to sit in the waiting room. Poppy sat a few seats from her mother and picked up a copy of *Cosmopolitan* from 2002. Grace sat staring at the floor, wondering if this place had a bar.

They were shown to their rooms, which were in different wings. Poppy was on the ground floor with the other depressives, or 'shufflers' as they were known to the inmates. Grace could have been assigned a room anywhere, given her various problems, but was placed on the third floor with the alcoholics (or 'shakers') in the West Wing.

Her room was small, with a single bed, and a table on wheels so she could eat in bed, with a jug of water on it. There was also a small TV, a cupboard with secured hangers, and a small en suite with a shower but no bath. Red alarm cords hung in each room. The windows could only be opened a few inches, to prevent suicide attempts.

A kindly junior doctor came by and took her details, or at least those that Grace could remember, which was about fifty per cent.

After that, a mobile drip was attached to her arm to help with the alcohol withdrawal symptoms, and she was shown the communal canteen in the basement.

Grace went back to her room, and was left there to settle in. She lay fully dressed on her bed, feeling sad and lonely. Then there was a tap on her open door.

A short, bright-eyed woman in her early thirties stood in the doorway. She had mousey, shoulder-length hair, bright blue eyes and a creased smile, and was wearing jeans, trainers and an old sweat shirt with 'Relax' on it.

'Hi. My name's Faith. I'm the nutter next door. Who are you?'

'Hi. My name is Grace. What is this place?'

'It's the Rookery,' Faith explained patiently. 'A maximum-security hotel for the terminally hedonistic, optimistic and pessimistic.'

They both giggled and a new friendship was instantly born. Faith went on to explain in more detail, giving Grace a tour, not so much of the place, as the people. She began with herself. 'I'm a journalist. I work on the *Daily Mail*. I'm married to my toy boy, Bill, and have a daughter aged three called Daisy. I'm in here mainly for alcohol, or more accurately to avoid alcohol, but I'm also a sexaholic. I've always craved affection, and my dear sweet bisexual Bill seems to be more interested in chasing trouser than skirt these days, which hasn't been entirely helpful for my raging libido! What about you Grace?'

Grace instantly felt comfortable with Faith, who seemed so at ease with her issues and so full of life. The fact that she was a stranger also encouraged Grace to open up in a way she had not felt able to before. She had been there an hour and the impromptu therapy was already working.

'Well, I'm thirty-eight, I'm a housewife, married to a guy called Mark, and I have three kids. Poppy is seventeen, and the twins Samuel and Max are twelve.' She grew bolder, and some of the pieces that were unhinged in her head started to fall back into place as she spoke things out loud for the first time.

'I've been so unhappy for so long. It's like I don't belong anywhere or with anyone. My daughter hates me, and the other day she overdosed. I couldn't even face going in the ambulance with her because I knew it was my fault – seeing me smashed day in, day out...' She paused and visibly trembled.

'After I called the hospital to make sure she was out of danger, all I can remember is getting back into bed with my whisky and pills – not exactly a change from my usual routine,' she said bitterly. 'I can never forgive myself for what I have done.'

'As for my husband, he rules every aspect of my life. He is a sick, power-crazed thug who is so full of himself and his greed, that I'm just a trophy on his arm. Everyone thinks he is marvellous, but I see him for what he has become.'

The discussion went on and on and they were still talking on their way down to supper. Everyone ate together in the canteen, although all the junkies (or 'stutterers') sat and held hands together like an oppressed minority within the ghetto.

'See that tall handsome Greek guy over there?'

Grace nodded.

'He came in with depression. He's now a sexaholic, and on the way to being alcoholic too. The women all fall in love with him, and the water jug by his bed is full of Smirnoff. The nurses check on every room, each and every hour on their rounds. He's got so many ladies jumping his bones, I don't know how he hasn't been caught!

'I had him two weeks ago. Not bad, but his heart wasn't in it. Nor mine, for me it was just a physical need. Odd thing is, Gabe – that's his name – is married to a vision of beauty. He must be mad.'

'And her?' asked Grace, indicating a young Asian girl in the corner.

'Nisreen. A princess. Very rich family from Bishops Avenue, Hampstead Garden Suburb. Her home looks like the Walthamstow Town Hall. On her seventeenth birthday last year, she was given a red BMW convertible. Gabe has her three times a week at least.'

'Is she nice? Why is she in here?' Grace was getting into the swing now. 'She has a broken nail or something,' offered Faith. There was more giggling, and the paranoid junkies turned to see if they were being laughed at.

'And that family over there, they're the Shelbys. They come here every year instead of a Warners holiday camp. Apparently the daughter likes the salad bar, the mother enjoys the Sunday salsa evenings, and the dad says it's cheaper than a health farm.'

'This is so interesting, Faith. Who's that older guy there? The one with the shaven head?'

Faith turned, and said she wasn't too sure, as he kept himself to himself.

'He's called Andrew. Err... Andrew Bond, that's it. Runs some big advertising agency or other, I think.'

Grace said simply, 'Really?' and smiled mischievously to herself at the thought of finally meeting God after all these years.

CHAPTER ELEVEN

The Eyes of the World

Given the accelerated speed of events in Mark's new world, he felt sure that he could create his global charity before the Primo pitch in just under a month's time.

He would have to leave Grace out of it for the time being, but she couldn't help much from inside the Rookery anyway. However, she would eventually play a pivotal role in the venture, partly because her rehabilitation and his redemption depended on it, and partly because all her best qualities would be harnessed in making the idea a success.

Mark felt sure he could soon tick the Redemption item off his list. He was a genius.

What he needed to do now was refine the vision, and start to form partnerships with the right people and the right corporations. Whom could he discuss it with? Who, ideally, could even part-finance it?

Barry? No way. His mate would be brutally honest, but

sadly had no flair for business.

Julia? Possibly. But, as his colleague on the Primo pitch, she was compromised, and he couldn't trust her enough yet. Not with this. It was too important.

Denise? Not sharp enough. He was talking global conspiracy here, not a local freesheet. Not enough cash either, though her online dating agency was starting to boom.

So who? He rolled the term Make My Mark around in his head. Then it struck him, and he laughed. It was deliciously ironic. And so surreal (that word again). He rang Ellie to buy himself time that Monday to recruit his choice, and absent himself from BC for another day.

'Ellie, how's stuff?'

'Apart from a heavy period and a case of the trots from last night's kebab, not bad.'

'My God, how do men ever resist you? You're so romantic,' laughed Mark.

'I know, it's a gift. How are Grace and Poppy?'

'They're okay, sent to the Rookery for some rehab with the celebrities. £800 a day each for a month! Thank you, BC health scheme.'

'Christ, do NOT get fired.'

'I won't, darling. Moving on from the family (mis)fortunes, I need you to lie, err, cover for me again today.'

He went on to explain that he needed to visit some people in relation to the Primo pitch. He told her how to brief everyone within the agency in order to get things moving, and instructed her to ask Julia to run things, and to call him whenever she thought fit.

He also arranged for a bouquet of flowers in electric blue wrapping to be delivered to Julia's Borough flat that evening, with a card which read, *I was shocked by you. It was lovely! Mark x x x.*

Next, Mark drove to Chingford to visit Derek Peterson.

He pulled up at Wattapenis Palace and announced himself through the gate's entry phone. He had rung ahead and secured an appointment to see Derek, who was still mates with Barry and Sammy and remembered Grace well too.

'Enter please,' said a familiar voice from the gate's loudspeaker.

At the front door stood Fat Dave, the old school chum who had a crush on Grace. He was huge now, 6 ft 5 in, and that was just the width. Wearing a beautiful double-breasted suit, with greased-back hair and impenetrable shades, he looked like a bodyguard to a gun-toting rap star. But he wasn't. He was bodyguard to the king of a dark world. Mark couldn't decide which was worse.

'Hello, Dave, still a big boy I see.'

'Yes, Mark, and a whole lot more too,' he said, with a sarcastic grin.

'Like Grace still, for instance? Thanks for the flowers, big man. I took them home from King George's and they're brightening my days at this difficult time. Nice to know an old friend is there for us. Don't go hiding under any hedges, will you Dave, not in that expensive suit anyway.'

Mark smiled to himself. He felt unstoppable. He took out his camera and flashed a shot straight into Dave's eyes.

Dave hesitated to reply, or to hit him, which he would normally do before attempting a witty riposte. Instead he stepped aside, and Mark strode in to meet Derek.

The lord of the manor was sitting quietly on the huge doughnut-shaped sofa, which had survived all these years, though was now re-covered in snakeskin with mink cushions. He was watching *Countdown* on a projection screen about

100 inches across.

'That Carol V could star in one of my favourite bum epics anytime she likes,' chuckled Derek.

'Yeah,' said Mark. 'Can I have a bowel, please Carol, and an incontinent.'

'So how come you're familiar with the *Back Passage* series I've been known to distribute then?'

'I am a fellow sex-pert,' offered Mark. 'It's the same tragic complaint for all married men.'

'Wouldn't know about that,' said Derek.

Mark changed the subject a little: 'I reckon that the next blockbuster porn feature one of your producer chums films should be shot on location up Fat Dave's rectum. At least there'd be room for the trailer and catering crew too.'

Derek snorted a laugh as Dave went purple, then crimson, and his fists, which resembled whole Parma hams, clenched, ready to pummel Mark's face.

'Relax, Dave, be fair,' Derek interjected. 'Mark here is on cracking form. Get him a JD and the same for me, please. Now, Dave, there's a good boy.'

He winked at Mark. 'Useful chap, Dave. Would do anything for me, like my old Doberman. Eats more than the dog, though. Now what's this about?'

'I have a proposition for you, Mr Peterson.'

An hour later Mark left smiling. Derek was smiling too. Only Fat Dave was pissed off, but his time would come, or so he kept telling himself.

Driving home in the car, Mark played Coolio's 'Gangsta's Paradise' over and over. He had secured more than £1 million of cash funding in just a few minutes, and was now in partnership with Derek. Derek was obviously the silent partner, but he had always been a shy one, reflected Mark. All Del had requested in return for his investment was the right to distribute the products via his packaging and distribution network.

'Easiest million quid I ever raised. All I wanted was his transport network,' Mark said to himself, as if he had ever raised anything like that amount before in his life. Images of the movie *Wall Street* flashed through his mind – 'Greed is good!', to which he added his own 'A friend in greed is a friend indeed.'

Next he rang one of his clients at Max Mobile. Karen Phillips was their marketing director, a lovely, talented woman with a six-year-old son called Martin with learning difficulties. She was about 5 ft 6 in tall, with a shock of wavy jet-black hair down to her waist and one of those creamy complexions sprinkled with freckles.

She had been mentored by Mark years ago and had flown the BC nest to become a top dog at Max Mobile. He sensed that Karen felt that she 'owed' him and that's what counted at the moment – she was also on the board of a global child welfare charity called World Child Care.

Mark called her out of the blue and they chatted for ages about everything. He arranged to meet her that evening for a drink to explain 'this incredible opportunity' for Vertec, Max Mobile and WCC, and for Karen and Mark to make a real difference and leave a fantastic legacy for the world.

Mark had never spoken to her in such an inspirational way before. Karen was intrigued.

'See you at Charlotte Street Hotel bar at 6.15,' she said and cancelled a business meeting just to be there.

Before this appointment, Mark paid a quick visit to BC to prepare more pitch material. Without the Primo business, the whole scheme would fall to pieces, so he needed to take it seriously.

'Hello, Cherry,' he said to the wild grandmother receptionist, 'you still look fabulous.'

'Thank you. Do you mean "still" as in since last you saw me, or "still" as in for my age?'

'Both. One day I'd like to take you for lunch to discuss this whole area closely. All I get to see all day are boring clients and this lot of tossers (pointing at the offices). It would be my pleasure to take you to Mon Plaisir in Monmouth Street, one of my favourite French restaurants. It has great onion soup, coq au vin and steak and chips. What do you say?'

Cherry stared at him and said, 'I would be delighted to join you, Mark, in fact it's about time,' she said, adding with a wry smile, 'but words are cheap!'

A bloody wild panther predator, that woman, he thought, heading for the lift.

As Mark alighted at the eighth floor, he bumped into Julia.

'Evening, Mark, here to review the troops? The research focus groups are arranged, and I've briefed the planners. We'll talk to the creative department tomorrow. Jed and Wolfy, our youngest, spikiest team, are on it. I thought they'd be best to rise to this challenge. You agree?'

'I do, I do.'

Mark was thrilled, as these two were the hottest team at BC, and they were still only fourteen. Actually, they were twenty-three and twenty-two, but looked fourteen.

After two hours, a lot of background reading and an impromptu re-briefing of the planners, he headed for Charlotte Street for his drink with Karen from Max Mobile. He was rehearsing the speech and refining the plan as he walked.

Twenty minutes later they were sitting on two purple tub chairs in the bar, he nursing his beloved Manhattan, she with a Bombay gin and Indian tonic. They had been through the pleasantries and she had just asked him to explain his idea.

Mark introduced a dramatic pause to gather his thoughts, then began sombrely.

'Okay, Karen, the first thing to say is that this is a big idea which is already well advanced and fully funded. At its core is a chance to help children in the most deprived parts of the world, to raise awareness and money for education, to allow them to grow up to be self-sufficient, rounded human beings.'

'Fine so far,' said Karen staring into his eyes. She had always believed in this man, and he was showing a fire that she had not seen in him before. 'Please continue.'

'The first insight is that there is a product out there with an unlimited supply, which is utterly priceless yet completely worthless, and is thrown away every single day. This product is our most precious commodity, because it is the spirit of every person on this earth. It is the naïve expression of a child's impressions of the world around them.

'In time, they'll grow up to be accountants, estate agents or worse, advertising executives...'

'God forbid!' teased Karen.

They giggled and toasted each other, and Mark signalled to the waiter for refills.

'But when they're six or seven, they are fresh, they are funny, they are honest and they have a clean, untarnished view of this world.

'The product I'm talking about is the primitive art of children.'

He paused before asking, 'Karen, your son's name is Martin, isn't it?'

Karen nodded.

'Well, tell me, I know Martin has some difficulties with his speech and behaviour, which we've talked about over the years. Does he paint? Do you keep any of his art?'

'Oh yes, I do,' she replied. 'It's colourful, it's an outlet for him and we love it. It's on the fridge door and blu-tacked all over the lounge. I think he has talent, but then I'm his mum!'

Mark nodded and closed his eyes for a moment like a wise guru. Then he used his best King Cobra stare on her (learned from Patrick Craze). 'My point is that kids all over the world paint and draw in their schools, and only a fraction of this output is ever taken home. The bulk is destroyed, because there's so much of it and who cares?

'Parents think they're the only ones interested in their child's art. And they're right, but it doesn't have to be that way. Like most things on this planet, it's about packaging. You and I, Karen, are experts on packaging. And we can use that cynical skill of ours to the benefit of millions of others.'

'Go on,' she said, as the fresh round of booze arrived.

'If I took this dirty drinks coaster, the cherry from my drink and that napkin with your lipstick smudge on it – nice colour by the way,' he added and she blushed. 'If I then construct a frame in polished black ebony and place these items inside, it becomes art. Not just any art, "impressive" art. And if I then add a story to it, and attach that story to the back, it becomes something mystical and priceless.

'As you know, faraway places seem most exotic to those furthest from them. Croydon is exotic to Mexico and vice versa. It's a global human quality, to wonder at other cultures.

'Now here's the thing, Karen. We are going to source original art from young children in schools all around the world. Beirut, Colombia, Thailand, Lapland, India and the Caribbean.

'Children will paint, sometimes to themes we set, and we will frame their work beautifully and sell it via galleries and the internet, marketed by Vertec and other powerful media partners the world over.

'This new brand will be called "The Eyes of the World".' He paused to let the name sink in.

'The target market is gagging for this product,' he continued. 'When did you last go into a private gallery, Karen? Not the National Portrait, one of those bare white ones in posh side streets?'

Karen thought for a moment. 'Since Martin was born, never, but only a couple of times ever.'

'And you're sophisticated,' offered Mark. 'Now, as you know, I'm Jewish. I know people who live in Edgware with beautiful homes built to impress visitors more than the occupants, and those people are only nervous about one aspect of interior design. Art. It's too highbrow. It's too expensive to get wrong, and they're too lazy to research it and get it right. Prints are cheap and a bit naff, and anyway they're more worried about whether the picture matches the curtains.'

Karen was nodding.

'And these middle-class people who need credible, original art and a story of faith, hope and charity to tell, are in their millions all over the world.

'So where do they go? Where can they find stories that don't require a degree in some pretentious bollocks about a well-known artist that their mates don't care about anyway? Answer, nowhere.'

More drinks were signalled, and Mark continued.

'There will be café galleries in New York, London and Paris, quickly followed by Berlin, St Petersburg, Barcelona, Sydney, Brussels and Rio de Janeiro. Maybe with a coffee-shop chain it could grow faster, but these are early days.

'Our artwork will be beautifully framed, and that's where the money comes from to run this venture. All the paintings will be sold at a basic £150 flat fee, but prices will vary for different sizes and styles of frame. For orders online, it will be bubble-wrapped and despatched by a worldwide distribution group I have in place.'

He continued: 'Every piece is a one-off, no prints. Each will have the story of the child and their part of the world on the back. War zones, floods, disasters, but presented in an uplifting and inspiring way, and far more interesting than some long-dead painter.

'After running costs, the money will be sent back to the schools themselves to fund art equipment, books and computers. Invested in those who create the art and the areas which need it the most.'

'Wow, I like it,' said Karen. 'I have some questions though.'

Mark said she'd have to wait, as he was on a roll, and they laughed. 'As I said, Eyes of the World has the global distribution group in place and they have provided development funds already.

'We have over a million in seed capital to set up offices and infrastructure, and we expect Vertec to take part. Their flagship brand Primo is about the joys of dirt. (Or will be, once we win the pitch, thought Mark.) 'The Eyes of the World charity will give them a source of worldwide publicity outside the traditional advertising channels, at a fraction of the cost.

'I can see huge posters on the sides of skyscrapers in New York with kids' paintings on them, and the Eyes of the World logo, sponsored by Primo. It will touch mothers the world over.'

Karen slapped his knee playfully and said, 'I love it, Mark. Love it. But how can I help you? It sounds like it's all set to run without any contribution from me.'

Mark smiled, pausing again for dramatic effect.

'That's where you're wrong. We need you totally. This has to have complete credibility. We want the WCC to monitor and run the collection of art and the distribution of funds in each local market. It becomes their – or rather, as you're a director – your money to use to improve the lot of the children.

'I propose that a panel of the great and the good are recruited to ensure the quality of the work and maintain the non-profit-making aspects of the charter. We're talking to Geldof, Tracey Emin. And you remember my wife Grace? She'll be working full time on that and the sourcing.'

'Ah yes, I remember Grace,' said Karen. 'She's lovely, and really into kids and art as I recall. A perfect choice!'

Mark continued: 'Marketing will be down to me. Vertec will put it on all of their packaging worldwide, and will be able to use the artwork exclusively to sell Primo. They will also sit on the board of the Eyes of the World. I hope that you too will be available to sit on the executive committee with that great team and, of course, humble me.

'As you know, our media people at BC are the largest spenders of advertising in the UK. Our clients include newspapers, TV stations and most of the powerful media owners, so I see no problems with PR. Christ, we couldn't be better placed.

'That's the pitch, Karen. What do you think? Are you in?'

Karen sat there for a moment saying nothing. Then: 'It's fate. I was sold the moment you mentioned Martin's artwork on our fridge door. I promise that I'll talk to the WCC board this week, and maybe Max Mobile as well. May I do that?'

'Oh yes, you may.' (Gotcha, he thought for the umpteenth time that week.)

It was now 8.30pm and Mark was very happy. He had no

plans for the evening and thought he should have an early night but, when he was in this mood, there was little chance of that.

So he made that call to Barry.

'Baz, it's Skid.'

'It's about time. Where have you been? No calls, no e-mails, no texts. What's up?'

'Sorry, Baz, but you won't believe my last few days.'

He went on to describe everything except the Sammy texting episode. When he got to the Gene story, Barry interrupted him.

'I-AM-SORRY. You did what to your mother-in-law? This is gold dust. This is amazing! I always fancied Sammy's mum but, Skid, this is unbleeding believable. R-E-S-P-E-C-T.'

Needless to say, Baz demanded every detail, and Mark didn't disappoint. They agreed to meet up in the following few days for a drink. Mark felt better to be back in contact with Barry, as he had missed him.

Back at home, Mark bypassed Vicki's fresh selection of healthy food and enjoyed a meal of ancient fish fingers instead, dredged from the back of the freezer and served on toast with ketchup. Once full, he texted Sammy.

Mark: *Hi Sammy. How you been? Any more thoughts since we last texted?*

Sammy: *No. Must be why I keep walking into walls and closed doors. I haven't had a single thought about anything.*

Mark: *Ha ha. Sarcasm, my favourite. It's after midnight. What you up to?*

Sammy: *I'm in Tescos. Actually I'm just squeezing the watermelons. That's not a joke either.*

Mark: *The thought of those firm orbs in your hands is a turn on.*

Sammy: *I'll pass on your compliment to the fruit and veg*

section. The cucumbers and marrows look very flattered by it.

The banter continued for some while, until Sammy returned home, unpacked her late-night shopping and went into the bathroom for a relaxing soak. By this time it was 2.11am.

Then the texting turned blue. She described all the things Mark could do for her sexually, and took some pictures of herself using her mobile. Mark was thrilled that someone else was taking the shots for a change.

Then he asked the key question: *When are we going to meet? I have in mind a suite at Sloane House Hotel. It has a huge four poster and is the sexiest place on earth. All piled cushions, low lights and faded glory. Would love to meet you there. 20 years is a long time to maintain a hard-on.*

Sammy replied after fifteen-minutes: *Name the date and time, and I'll be your date with wine and no dress.*

Mark resisted the urge even to think 'Gotcha'. Instead, he went off to sleep with a smile on his face, feeling absolutely no guilt over Grace or Barry.

CHAPTER TWELVE

The Boys are Back in Town

Samuel jumped out of bed in the room he shared with his brother at St Edmund's and woke Max with a shake. This morning was special, as it was the end of term. They had to pack and be out of the dorms by 10.30am.

Max went for a shower while Samuel packed for both of them. They had a military-style respect for packing, folding clothes neatly and placing them in an orderly fashion, so as to fit everything in their kit bags; qualities that are unusual even in a twenty-year-old man, let alone two twelve-year-old boys.

Samuel set about the task briskly, if a little bleary-eyed, as the previous night there had been a party. St Edmund's was a mixed school, and some of the girls had sneaked out of their dorms and joined the boys for dope smoking and Cider Bombs.

Kids grow up quickly these days, as Mark often reflected nervously. Neither of the twins had even got close to a sexual encounter so far, but booze and dope? No problem.

They went down to a breakfast of bacon and pork sausages, perfect for the 'Jew boys', as the twins were affectionately known by the Korean, Asian and Arab crowd. As full boarders, they had fellow inmates drawn from the four corners of the world and, although a Catholic school, all religions were represented. To be called Cohen was no big deal.

Mark had told the boys to book a cab through the school to bring them home, as he was busy at work that day. He would be at home later that afternoon, but not until around 3.30pm.

The boys said they would be staying overnight with a friend, Jason from Potters Bar, and would be gone by the time Mark got back. They would definitely see him the next day.

Though their dad was at work, Vicki was waiting to cook them a meal when they arrived home. For the second time that day it was sausages, but they wolfed them down. Then, after she had gone, they attacked the larder like a swarm of locusts, consuming the contents without rhyme, reason or mercy. Max had tinned spaghetti and raspberry jelly cubes. Samuel combined a jar of peanut butter with a packet of Minstrels, topped off with salt and vinegar crisps.

Samuel's mobile phone beeped as a text arrived.

Hi. Bad news. Mum said I have to visit my nan, so you can't come over after all. Soz. Jason.

'Bollocks, Jason just blew us out, the git. So we'll have just the pleasure of dad and a DVD in our room tonight. Bor-ing.'

As boredom is perhaps the greatest curse of being twelve years old, they immediately tried to think of a new scam.

'Samuel Ponsenby-Smythe, if you could stop eating like a nuclear waste disposal unit for just a second, old bean, I've had a simply spiffing idea.'

'Now what might that be, Lord Maxwell of Pooshire?'

For some reason best known to themselves, they began

speaking like a couple of toffs. The twins clicked into such 'themes' together at will, each feeding off the other. One minute they were astronauts, the next Eminem or a pair of old women from Scotland.

They decided to play private detective. Poppy had sent them a text that got Max thinking.

Hi there boys. I think dads up 2 stuff. Don't ask y but I just do. He's acting kinda strange don't u think? Do me a favour in ur half term hols have a snoop. Report back. Luv ya. Poppy. x

'When is father, the Duke of Puke, due home, Maximillion?'

'About fifty minutes, Prince Albert.' They giggled at this, as they were aware of a penis piercing by this name.

'Right then,' said Max, 'this is the plan. We'll sort out enough food and drink for a few hours, and take an iPod each too. Then we'll camp out in dad's wardrobe and maintain a surveillance operation, see what he's up to. We can take one of dad's cameras and a Sony movie camera. And go through his drawers and stuff too, while we wait for him to get back. Okay, bum face?'

'Cool.'

Mark's key rattled in the lock at around 3.30pm, as he had told them. He called out to see if anyone was around. You can never totally trust a twelve-year-old, let alone two twelve-year-olds.

'Hello?'

Nothing. He went into the kitchen and opened the larder door. Nothing except mustard, garlic and a couple of stray bean shoots left on the shelf. Bloody boys. Impossible to fill them up. He shut the door and spotted a note from Samuel:

Hi dad. We've gone to Jason's in Potters Bar. We took £15

from the emergency fund in the wallet in the drawer. See you tomorrow. We're not home tonight, def. S+M. x

'Brilliant!' Mark said out loud.

Meanwhile the boys were already in base camp, inside Mark's bedroom wardrobe. It had louvered doors, which meant that they could look out without being seen themselves.

Sam and Max were thorough. They had brought torches, soft rolls (crisps being too noisy), cheese, cake and marsh-mallows (the quietest sweet of all). Also, two beers and a bottle of Evian. When the water was drunk, they planned to use the bottle as a portable loo. Dad's spare Pentax digital camera was fully charged, as were their phones and camcorder so that they could keep Poppy up to speed.

They were playing cards among the shoes at the bottom of the wardrobe. To avoid giving themselves away by speaking, they were texting each other, despite being only a foot apart.

Do you think Dad will turn up and do anything? His shoes are stinky.

Sod off Max, and stop cheating at whist.

Downstairs, Mark was restless. A house to himself and no plan? It was unheard of. So he sent his first-ever text to Gene, the minx mum-in-law.

Hi. Mark here. I'm home, boys back from school but out for the night. I'm in a naughty mood. You?

See you in 20 minutes! replied Gene.

Partly out of respect for Gene, and partly because he found it exciting, Mark decided to set the scene a little.

He went up to his room, drew the curtains, and placed the KY Jelly under his pillow. He found some vanilla candles and lit them, then went to the boot of the BMW and retrieved the vibrator and ropes he had bought on impulse from a sex shop on the way home. He showered, sprayed thoroughly with the

Issey and selected the music. A bit of Michael Bublé.

Having put everything in place for a great afternoon of passion, he sent another text to Gene.

All set. Will leave the front door on the latch. Just come straight up. Will be waiting for you in bed. M x

OK lovely boy. On way. Be there in 5. G x

Mark got undressed, stepping towards the wardrobe door to hang up his trousers.

The boys held their breaths, shut their eyes and waited for the biggest telling-off since they had faked their own kidnappings at age eleven. The ransom note had only demanded £50 which, while a fortune for a kid, was implausibly little for a hardened criminal. This lack of fiscal ambition was the only thing that gave the boys away, as their planning had been impeccable. Mark was secretly proud that they had inherited his eye for detail.

Mark did not open the wardrobe, as he was distracted by a candle going out. Instead, he dropped his trousers on a chair and re-lit the wick. Then he dropped his pants, scratched his groin and admired his hair and teeth in the mirror.

Max texted his brother: *Oh my God. Dad's dick is horrid. If he bends over I will be sick.*

Samuel was trying not to laugh.

Wonder wot babe is coming. Hope she is buff. Get camera ready, I will use the Sony.

Mark went downstairs and put the front door on the latch as he had promised, then returned to his room and slipped into bed. Everything was hushed, apart from Michael Bublé crooning softly on the CD player-alarm beside the bed. Mark lay with just his hair visible above the sheets, as Gene had done the last time they met. The tension was electric, both in the bed and in the wardrobe.

After several unbearable minutes, they heard the sound of the front door closing. Then footsteps padding up the stairs.

The bedroom door opened then closed, and the boys could just make out the dark silhouette of a woman as she crossed the room, pulled back the sheet, and climbed into bed next to their dad.

The twins were delighted. This was great. They clicked their cameras but it was not possible to use the flash.

Can you see her tits? They look massive. Lucky old dog.

Max replied: *She's a bit fat and old. But dad no oil painting. Pass me a marshmallow.*

No words were exchanged in the darkness between Mark and Gene, but panting, moaning and shouting were in abundant supply. The ropes came out, and Gene was bound to the bed posts and given a thorough workout with the dildo.

Samuel and Max were confused. What the hell was going on?

Max, wot r they doin? This not wot I was told birds n bees do by mum. Is dad Michael Jackson?

It's getting well odd. Did you get a foto of what he did with that long thing?

Hope so. Bit dark 4 camera. Still must tell popy.

Mark and Gene carried on. And on. And on. The boys grew so bored that they went back to playing cards.

Eventually the adults gathered their stuff and went downstairs. They were whispering, which was strange given that, as far as they knew, there was no one in the house. It was just so naughty an afternoon that whispering seemed appropriate.

Samuel and Max stayed in the wardrobe for a while, until the muffled discussion downstairs became a constant drone. Then they gathered their surveillance kit, including empty sweet wrappers, various items of technology, and an Evian bottle filled with their urine.

Well pleased with their afternoon's work, they retreated quietly to their bedroom to text their sister with the juicy gossip.

Max wrote: *You r rite sis. We just sat in dads wardrobe n c him bang a big titted old bird. He was well rude. Later. M+S x*

Downstairs, Gene got dressed, used the mirror in the loo to reapply her makeup, and kissed Mark bye-bye for now.

He had enjoyed the lust, and was very fond of Gene, but he was not satisfied. This had been a repeat performance, and some of the spark had gone, along with the intoxicating risk of the unknown. It was beginning to feel more like 'Finished' than 'Unfinished' Business.

I hope life is not about to become dull, he mused.

Meanwhile, the boys were discussing their stakeout.

'Samuel, did you get a good look at her? I didn't really. Saw her bum more than her face and that was BIG!'

'Me too, and the pictures and film are too dark to see much,' replied Samuel. 'I did manage to zoom in on that big wobbly arse so close that I think I could make out what she ate for breakfast this morning. We could take it to the lab in the photography club at school and print off some of the clearest bits.'

'Cool. When we get back after the hols then.'

Mark was blissfully unaware that the fuse of a time bomb had just been lit in his underpants. So much for life becoming dull.

CHAPTER THIRTEEN

Wow, wow, wow, wow, wow, wow...

Mark pottered about in Woodford for a while, then went to the office. It was after hours so he had to sign in with the security guard in reception before heading up to his eighth-floor office.

He spent a few minutes catching up with correspondence on the Primo project, which had accumulated while he was busy with 'other engagements'. Then he began drafting a proposed new pitch flow.

Mark had an idea for how to inject some theatre into the presentation which he knew would need the team's approval. More importantly, it would also require Patrick Craze to agree.

'Still, he did put me in charge. I guess it's my call,' he announced to the empty room. But an answer came right back at him, and he nearly jumped out of his skin.

'Talking to yourself is confirmation of what we already know, that we at BC are fully-paid-up members of the straitjacket club.'

'Patrick! Blimey, you scared me! Working late? Thought

you were off home by seven o'clock normally.'

'Normally, yes, but I had some calls to make to the States. Actually, I was pleased to hear your voice. How's the pitch going? Not long to go and we really need it, as you know from the figures at the last board meeting. Any progress?'

'Yes. The research groups are going well, and have confirmed the principles. We've filmed them, but I want to do something different with the whole presentation. It's radical, so there's risk attached, but I don't think we should play safe on this one.'

'Well,' said Patrick, 'as you said, you're in charge, it's your neck. Muck this up, and you'll face the guillotine treatment, I can promise you. Now tell me the idea.'

Mark outlined the various elements. Patrick's jaw dropped open, but no words emerged. He turned quite ashen.

Then he burst out laughing. 'Wow, Mark! Balls of steel,' he said. 'You've surprised me – I love the new edge you seem to have found. But you'll need some luck now, too. That'll decide whether I have to fire you or give you my job.'

Patrick looked Mark in the eye with that Cobra stare, full on, leaning six inches too close to Mark's face for added impact. It wasn't needed.

'Are you up to my job, Mark?'

Uncharacteristically, Mark stared right back at him without flinching or blinking. Two King Cobras locked in a staring contest. He waited a beat before replying.

'I am the next and best Chairman of this agency. I was born to do it. I always knew it, and now you know it, too.'

'Okay then. Time will tell. Three weeks, to be accurate. Make it happen.'

Patrick turned and headed towards his corner suite, trailing a smile. 'Be lucky, Mark.'

Mark took out the Pentax and flashed off a shot of Patrick

disappearing down the corridor into his office. Who knew where all this was heading? Maybe this was an important moment, to be captured forever. It felt that way.

In the past, if Mark had been asked whether he was up to the Chairman's job (which, of course, he never would have been), his initial response would have been very different. He would probably have begun by defending the incumbent Chairman by trumpeting Patrick's abilities for fear of being deemed a disloyal BC citizen. Safeguarding his own tenure in a job for which he was well paid, but in which he felt trapped.

He would have followed this cautious opener by saying that he hoped to be considered for the role one day. In this context, 'one day' would mean that at age forty he was not ready, and probably never would be. It would shriek, 'I am too comfortable and too nervous.'

He would have sealed his fate with a quiet assertion that he would like the position and accept it as an honour, if he were deemed to be the right man – an open invitation to be treated as a happy little doormat forever, in other words. Dead in the water before he had barely begun speaking. No manager wants a weak piece of shite in the role of Chairman, particularly when co-founder Patrick Craze had been so extraordinary in the role.

Craze was powerful, wise and charismatic but, lately, he had become a little bored. He had only £11.35 million in the bank and wanted much, much more. He was only interested in people who could replace him and safeguard his BC shareholding. He would then be liberated from his principled partner Bond so he could take on the city alone with his own independent ventures.

Mark's clear and confident strike, sinking his fangs unhesitatingly into his jugular showed Patrick that he had found his fellow Cobra in the serpent's pit of BC. Only luck or, in other words, the Primo pitch, stood in the way.

Minutes later, Patrick strode across the car park to his Lamborghini and drove home to Sussex a contented man. That evening, he banged his wife with gusto for the first time in a year, happy that his search might finally be over.

Mark remained at his desk for a time, equally content. He had won the necessary approval for his pitch presentation, and now could simply tell Julia and the rest how things were going to be done.

Phew, he thought, life just got its momentum back.

He moved on to the next item on his agenda, something to follow the Unfinished Business represented by his mother-in-law. Of course, that was Sammy.

He reached for his mobile and texted her: *Hi you. Not to put too fine a point on it, I want you. I want you now. I don't care if you need to wash your hair, or if you fancied watching* EastEnders. *I have already booked the most erotic sexy space in the world and am waiting for you.*

He was not telling the truth here, but…

Can you meet me in an hour and a half? Isn't this Barry's night out at Secrets? Life is for the living and I'm burning up for you. Be spontaneous, impulsive and dangerous. Will you answer the call? Sloane House Hotel. In the bar downstairs at 8.30pm. I dare you. I double dare you. M. xxx

He then rang Sloane House to find out if any rooms were available. He could only get a suite, but he thought that was perfect, and money was no object when fulfilling a fantasy.

Rooms 'Pearl', 'Jet' and 'Red' were available. One was huge and Venetian-styled, virtually a flat with its own kitchen. Another was all cream-faded glory with a ceiling up in the heavens. The third projected a more masculine ambience in a dark, brooding, red and purple scheme.

He chose the brooding one. So much more demonic.

Mark had no idea if Sammy would, could or wanted to travel across London that evening at such short notice. But he was quite happy simply feeding his impulses and trusting to spontaneity. What the hell, anticipation is always so wonderful.

The suite came to £700 before VAT, but at least if Sammy didn't show up he would have a good night's sleep, and the boys were well used to fending for themselves. He took his pack of emergency overnight things from his office drawer: shaver, Issey Myake aftershave, deodorant, hair brush, toothbrush and paste, spare boxers and socks.

He took a cab, stopping off at Oddbins to get a bottle of Jack Daniels and at his dealer for some high-octane cocaine. It was 7.45pm as his cab pulled up at the entrance to what had been four of the grandest houses in London, now combined to become Sloane House Hotel, one of the sexiest spots in the world. More powerful than a thousand Cider Bombs on the most stubborn of knicker elastic.

Mark checked in and his bags were taken to the room.

The 'Red' suite had a unique, ornate walnut door and vast surrounding architrave, with no room number on it. Beneath the high ceiling, its sultry red and black interior was filled with gorgeous silk sofas, cushions piled one on top of another, thick baroque drapes and magnificent oversized antique furniture, scattered over polished wooden floors and thick rugs. The lighting was elegantly dim throughout, and no technology was on show but the Bang and Olufsen was only a fingertip away.

The bathroom was all marble and faded gold, with ancient framed mirrors. But the centre piece was a black granite sculpture of a giant ram set in front of the king-size four-poster bed with shot-silk and dark red velvet curtains The lights were set low inside the canopy itself, and tissues were piled neatly in stacks beside the bed, with ribbons to bind them.

It was a fantasy bubble, safe from life's realities. A passport to a forgotten time and place. A fitting location for the seduction of Mark's life.

After a bath and a brush-up, he dressed and headed down to the Asia Room in the basement, reclining on a sofa amid bamboo, terracotta walls and hundreds of coffee-table books about interior design and travels to exotic parts of the globe. It was 8.15pm and he treated himself to a Manhattan and a Davidoff cigar.

Time dragged for a while, but in an agreeable, reflective way. But he did not reflect on Grace or on Barry. Sloane House was so magical that it had the ability to dissolve feelings of guilt, like Domestos eliminating germs. That was, if Mark had felt any guilt to start with. And he didn't.

He was absorbed in the perfection of the moment, far away from family, work or any of the mundane aspects of life. Not that he had suffered from many of those lately either, but he remembered them well enough.

Instead, he reflected on the here and now, and the prospect of pleasures to come. Would Sammy turn up? Would she have to make excuses and leave after a few minutes? Was this going to be a massive anti-climax?

Suddenly, he became aware of movement out of the corner of his eye. Someone was coming down the stairs. Mark tingled like a sherbet fountain. It was Sammy. She was dressed in a floor-length fur coat buttoned up to the neck.

She said nothing and drifted toward him as though gliding. He sat there mesmerised, legs apart, with the cigar dangling slackly between his lips. Sammy stopped right in front of him, standing between his parted feet. She unbuttoned her coat and let it fall loosely open. Underneath the fur, she was totally naked except for a pair of black silk, skimpy knickers.

Mark gulped and thought, she probably hasn't ordered a mini cab for ten minutes' time, then.

The night that followed was so charged and passionate, providing a sexual zenith of such giddy altitude that it made every other night in Mark's life seem tame.

In some ways it ruined him. For once, reality exceeded fantasy by such a margin that Mark knew he would spend the rest of his life trying to recapture that feeling. An impossible dream had been replaced by an impossible reality.

This did not feel like the progress he had hoped for, and it was a surprise to Mark. Sammy felt it too, but less acutely, as her motives for being there were more of the moment than bound up in a lifelong dream.

She went home around 3am in a limo Mark ordered on his company account. A last, deep kiss at the door as they parted matched the chemistry of their first kiss as they had entered 'Red' some six hours earlier.

Sammy received a text on her journey home past Harrods, Piccadilly and on eastwards.

That was the most incredible night of my life. I will never receive such pleasure again in my lifetime. I know it. You are my sex goddess, my fantasy and my friend. You hold a unique place in my heart. Always. M. x

Sammy replied: *Ditto wanker. x*

He laughed. Sammy could always make him laugh. He returned to bed and spread out like a starfish in the luxurious, if now somewhat damp, space. The 'Red' suite was so drenched in their DNA that it would have provided enough material for analysis to keep an entire police forensic department busy.

Mark didn't care. He drifted into the deep, dreamless sleep reserved solely for the sexually satisfied, completely unaware of what Grace was up to at the very same moment.

CHAPTER FOURTEEN

State of Grace

The Rookery had been good for Grace already. She was sober, laughing and more open after a couple of days than she had been in her whole life. She made new friends who seemed to like her without the benefit, or drawback, of knowing her before she had entered the gates.

So much so that Grace had avoided visiting Poppy, despite being in a different wing of the same clinic. Grace was still too embarrassed to face her own daughter, and was too wrapped up with the heady joy of being happy and safe.

Here she had a clean sheet, and a clearing mind. She could focus and was becoming less confused about where she was, and what she was doing.

Faith, her new journalist mate, was very caring, and they would wander off around the grounds for cigarettes between therapy sessions.

'I'm a good journalist, you know, Grace. I've won awards.

My colleagues praise me and rival newspapers regularly offer me better-paid positions. My husband Bill loves me, and I have a lovely daughter. It's pretty good really. Nothing much to complain about, is there?

'So why do I drink and smoke and screw around without the strength to control what I do? I think I'm an intelligent person, or at least I'm not stupid. But I do things which are ungrateful and selfish and will cut my life short. And all the therapy in the world hasn't yet been able to tell me why.'

Grace thought about it.

'Who am I to tell you? I'm in the same boat, minus the career stuff, of course.'

'That's why I'm asking, in a way,' said Faith. 'You have more excuse to be here, because you have less than I do.'

Grace dug deeper to answer her new friend. She wanted to help, and to find the answer for herself too.

'I think it's an ache,' Faith replied for her. 'A gap. A vacuum. Here.' She pointed at her own heart and at her friend's chest too.

Faith held Grace's hand and cupped it around her breast so Grace could feel her heart beating. This took her aback, and somehow transported her back to that time at Derek Peterson's mansion, in the study with Del and her best friend Sammy. The night of her lost virginity and the out-of-body experience on drugs.

Grace drew her hand back sharply, as the resentment at her friend's betrayal that night long ago pierced the present like an arrow through her breast bone.

'I'm so sorry,' said Faith, 'there I go again. Can't let the situation go, or keep my hands to myself. I need affection – either that or to be locked up!'

'It's okay,' said Grace, 'it's just, you conjured up something I'd forgotten a long time ago. I hadn't thought of it in years, and it came out of nowhere. It's probably nothing.'

The friends turned and headed back towards the main building for the first group session of the day.

The room was large, with a dirty, orange carpet. Bits of discarded equipment were scattered around the mainly empty space. A circle of plastic chairs was arranged in the centre of the room, and a whiteboard and range of coloured marker pens stood at the ready for any note-taking.

Some of the group were already seated.

Bob Shelby, patriarch of the family who attended the Rookery every year in place of a holiday, was there. So was Gabe the Greek stud, flanked by female admirers, among them the doting young Asian princess Nisreen. There was a man called Russell, to whom Faith had not yet introduced Grace too, and sitting beside him quietly in a world of his own was God. That is, Andrew Bond of BC.

The group therapist came in. Liz was a pretty lady in her early thirties and, like so many of the Rookery staff, an ex-patient and ex-cocaine addict. She sat down and said nothing at all. The group sat in total silence too.

Grace had discovered that the group therapist did not run these meetings. Her role was not to chair the proceedings, or to ask all the questions. The patients themselves were expected to do that. This was self-help, not a nanny state.

Consequently, they typically got off to a slow start, which could be very uncomfortable for new recruits. Grace had been to several of these groups already, and had hardened to the silences.

Someone stood up first and took the inevitable plunge. Group discussion followed and Grace eventually said her piece. Her own views, though not the most vocal, were given respectful attention. All so very different from any home life she had known, both before and after her marriage to Mark. No one had ever really listened before.

Her input was particularly heeded by one Andrew Bond, who similarly was not the most vocal, but who was easily the most eloquent and considered of contributors in the group.

Grace thought it was like being granted an audience with a wise guru. He was attractive in a father-figure way despite being only forty-nine years old, possibly because he was Mark's hero and boss. This worked on so many levels for Grace.

After several of the group had revealed their psyches, like onions peeling their skins in public, Liz thanked everyone and declared the session over. They dispersed, heading off to the canteen or for a walk and a fag.

Andrew sought out Grace as they left.

'Hi. I enjoyed your contribution to the session very much. Would you do me the honour of meeting me for a chat over coffee tonight, in the kitchen on the first floor at, say, 10.30pm?'

'The honour would be all mine, Andrew,' said Grace, without a moment's hesitation.

At dinner she received a message that she had a visitor. Grace wasn't keen to see anyone, but she turned round just in time to see her old friend Denise walking towards her.

Denise was still sporting the same short and spiky hairstyle she had always worn, though it was now tinted a purple colour. Only 5 ft tall, she was dressed in jeans, with a sweat top layered with lace, velvet and safety pins. She looked good and was a bundle of energy.

'Darling, how are you? I brought you some grapes. That's what you're supposed to do, isn't it? Are there any celebs in here? Any gossip? You must tell me everything.'

Grace bundled Denise off to her room in order to contain any collateral damage caused by this mini whirlwind. Only Faith joined them, and soon the three were giggling together.

Faith entertained them with stories about Hillary Clinton, the Queen and Boy George (individually, not together), taken from the mental vaults of her journalistic experience.

In return, Denise recounted tales from her online dating service, concentrating on some of the juicier and more disastrous encounters between her customers. Soon they were crying with laughter, tears pouring down their faces. Then Grace asked about Mark.

Denise said she had heard things through Barry, and that Mark seemed to be doing okay. He was spending time with Poppy and was even talking about taking some therapy with her.

Grace's eyebrows hit the ceiling. That doesn't sound like my husband, she thought. Maybe he is changing for the better...

Next she told Denise and Faith about her rendezvous with Andrew Bond later that evening.

'You're meeting God?!' exclaimed Denise.

'God?' queried Faith, and the girls went on to explain Andrew's relationship to Mark, and how brilliant he was reputed to be.

They giggled some more, and Grace was warned that all men are the same and she should be on her guard.

'That is, unless you feel randy. In which case, go for it, girl! Oops, there I go again. Ignore my nymphomania, darling,' said Faith.

Actually, being sober had reawakened Grace's libido. She was excited, as it was only an hour until her meeting with the man.

The girls said goodnight and Grace went to her room and showered. She looked eye-catching in an underweight, waif-like way. For a woman approaching forty who had abused her body grievously, her exterior was unnervingly unspoilt.

'There must be a portrait of me all aged and haggard in a loft somewhere,' she said into the mirror, in an uncharacter-istically confident mood. She was definitely getting stronger.

Grace went up to the first-floor kitchen and found Andrew already sitting there. He had made two coffees.

'Do you take milk and sugar?'

'Please.'

She sat down next to him and looked into his face properly for the first time. It was lean and lightly tanned. He had a shaven, perfectly formed cranium and a large, beak-like nose. Deep lines and crow's feet around the eyes made the face more interesting. She suspected that, like Clint Eastwood, he looked better as an older man than he had when he was young. His small rectangular TAG Heuer glasses provided much-needed horizontal balance to his face, and he sported a slightly incongruous diamond stud in his left ear.

Andrew wore a black linen suit, with a loose white cotton shirt and immaculate trainers. On his wrist and just visible on his hairless chest were tiny orange love beads. This was a man comfortable in his own skin, without being arrogant or conceited in any way.

He proved to be a wonderful listener, too, and spoke about one word for every ten of hers.

Grace told him everything about her drinking, the kids, her family upbringing and her husband. He was shocked that he knew Mark and yet had no recollection of meeting Grace before at some industry event or other.

'I'm so sorry. I must have been blind.'

'No sweat, Andrew. I was probably blind drunk.'

They laughed, and the years fell away from the gorgeous man. Then she asked why he was in the Rookery. She had noticed he had offered wise advice to others, but had not opened up about his own problems.

'Well, you know a little of my background, so I won't bore you with BC and all that nonsense. But did you know they call me God?'

'Really?' said Grace, feigning polite surprise.

'Yes, they do. After thirty years, it's a tall order carrying that sort of pressure. Everyone you meet expects to see flashes of genius in you, every single time. It's been relentless, every minute of every day, every week, month and year. I feel like a performing monkey – I should wear a fez and carry a pair of cymbals.'

They smiled at this image of the great Andrew Bond.

'It builds and builds. You see less of the kids you never knew. Less of the partner you once loved. You're sucked into a vortex of ego until there's no escape. Unless, that is, you break down, or lose yourself in addictive distractions until you do.'

Grace had a tear running down her face. She stared into the deep, still waters of his pained blue eyes.

'Don't cry, Grace.'

'I'm not crying just for you, Andrew. Everything you said is an echo of what my husband Mark must have been going through. He never put it like that, though. He's so angry, but you're so much more balanced about it.'

'No,' he replied softly, 'it's just that I'm here in this calm place, talking to a delicious stranger.'

She smiled and blushed. Her libido was definitely back.

'I was angry with Joan, my ex-wife, too. Then a few years ago, she passed away. I threw myself into the business and shut out everything else.'

He went on, enjoying talking about himself for once.

'Then a few weeks back I had a heart flutter. I'm okay, but it made me stop for breath. And suddenly it all collapsed in an avalanche. I'm finally grieving, and I'm depressed for the first time in my life. I miss her, and all the lost years.'

There was a silence for a few seconds.

'That's the story, Grace. That's why I'm here.'

It was now 2.30am and they were alone. The Rookery was not a prison or a school, and patients were treated as adults. They were protected from themselves and others, checked for illegal substances, illicit sexual activity or signs of self-harming, but the hours were their own. Even the therapy wasn't compulsory. If someone did not want to get well, they were sent away.

Nurses patrolled every hour, checking all the rooms. A nurse had just looked into the kitchen and moved on.

Grace and Andrew walked back to his little room, holding hands. They sat on the bed. Without a word he moved his face toward hers, and then stopped. She hesitated, and then met him half way in a soft, full kiss.

They lingered for several minutes in the slow magic of a first embrace, then he cupped her chest in the palms of his large hands.

'You have beautiful breasts,' he whispered in her ear.

At this, something was unlocked inside her, and she jumped on him like a hungry bird of prey.

It was 3.07am and, in the 'Red' suite of Sloane House Hotel, Mark was just nodding off in the sticky, damp bed.

At the same time, Poppy was wandering the corridors of the Rookery, unable to sleep. She was carrying her mobile phone, hoping that someone out there in the free world might be up and feel like chatting by text. But nobody was.

Poppy was still angry with her mother, but even more enraged by the absence of her mother during her stay in the clinic. There had been no visits from her at all. Poppy had wanted to shout 'Just die, you bitch' to Grace's stunned face and to throw her out of her room. Instead, Grace was ignoring her.

So, desperately, Poppy had decided to take a casual-looking stroll round the floor her mum was on, in the hope that she might be 'accidentally' seen by Grace. Then Poppy could deliver the well-rehearsed 'Just die...' speech.

As she passed the kitchen on the first floor, she heard a familiar low moan coming from a nearby room. The door was invitingly ajar. She peeked through the gap and saw Grace. Eyes shut, mouth wide open, riding a strange man in a state of naked abandon.

Poppy jumped back in surprise. Then she stuck her hand round the door, pointed her Nokia in the general direction of the scene and pressed the camera button. It flashed and clicked like a camera shutter.

'What the hell...?' exclaimed Andrew.

Poppy ran as fast as she could to the safety of her own room. She was seventeen and had a head start, they were naked and had to pull on some clothes, so Poppy was long gone before they emerged to give chase to the 'paparazzi'.

Back in her room, Poppy sent a text to Samuel and Max.

You'll never guess. Mum is banging some guy 2. Can't believe anyone could find that drunken skinny bitch attractive! Love ya... P xx.

CHAPTER FIFTEEN

Pitch Black

The big day was looming.

The preparation by the agency had been intensive. While he had seen Grace a few times at the Rookery and had noticed that she was becoming stronger, Mark had decided not to mention the Eyes of the World art venture to her until after he knew the result of the Primo pitch. It might set back her recovery if he were to raise her hopes, only to dash them again. And he didn't relish being cast as the villain again if he could avoid it.

Worse, she might actually say no, presenting him with a pitch problem that he'd rather not know about.

In the meantime, Mark had been practically living with two families, doing some in-depth focus group work and learning how 'normal' family units work and play together. This was very time-consuming, but really helped him hone his arguments with first-hand experience.

Julia Hardy-Roberts was brilliant. She ordered people about, attended all the research groups, steered the strategy meetings and flattered the young creative teams into going the extra mile.

Building contractors had been arriving at BC's Soho Square address for days now, their purpose a closely guarded secret. The boardroom and car park had been declared out of bounds, and even Patrick had to park his Lamborghini in the local NCP.

'You'd better win, Mark. You'd better win...' he remarked ominously every time he saw him.

Cherry in reception grew increasingly fed up with the intrusion of workmen and their mess in her domain. As Mark arrived early one morning, she piped up, 'I've got a bone to pick with you, Mr Cohen. First, what about my lunch date? Second, why are you mucking up this lovely building? I spent an hour scrubbing this limestone floor yesterday. I'm not a washer woman, you know. It's a disgrace.'

'Cherry, I'm sorry. It's absolutely necessary, I'll make it up to you. I'll upgrade our lunch to dinner, and make it the Michelin-starred Hakkasan instead of Mon Plaisir. Sound okay?'

'Hmmmm. Words are cheap. You got your red card, Marky boy.' She smiled at him with a raised eyebrow. 'You can forget it. Now run along, little boy.'

No time for this now, thought Mark, filing it mentally back under Unfinished Business. However, this first refusal in a very long time threw him a little, and he hoped it wouldn't prove to be an ill omen.

That was a few days before, and it had been quickly forgotten in the flurry of last-minute preparations. All too quickly, the big day itself had arrived.

It was time to pitch for Primo and give birth to the Eyes of the World project.

To redeem himself, this was far more important.

The Vertec people were due at 2pm.

The reception was now pristine and sparkling. Stylish flower arrangements were placed everywhere. Coffee was percolating, not for consumption, but to spread delicious aromas through the building. Cherry was wearing her best sexy grandma gear and people were running about with an excited spring in their step.

The atmosphere crackled with pure electricity. And it was only 8.30am. Mark had been in for an hour. Julia had not gone home at all. The team had worked through the night on charts for the handout document, and on dressing the rooms and the sets. There had been tantrums and tears and pizza and beers for two dozen panicking people at one in the morning.

The drugs had flowed by 2am, provided as a pick-me-up for the crew by the young creative team, at BC's expense.

Throughout, Julia remained an oasis of calm, though her stomach felt as though if it were playing host to a dozen dizzy eels.

The technology had broken down completely at 5am. Reinforcements of sleepy, stoned IT experts had been bussed in to fix it by 7am. All in all, it was a fairly typical pitch day for any advertising agency, anywhere in the world. It just happened to be a particularly big and important pitch for BC.

Andrew Bond was back at work, though his role that day was simply to meet and greet the clients. This was a welcome break from the pressure of being 'God' and carrying the entire pitch himself. He was a little unsettled at the thought of looking Mark Cohen in the eye, but he was professional enough to pull it off.

By 1.50pm everything was set. Andrew was chatting casually to Cherry with one eye on the large chrome doors.

Two people arrived wearing business suits and a 'go-ahead-and-impress-me' manner. They were obviously hardened to the marketing merry-go-round and the usual agency bullshit. Seen it, done it, got the washing powder for the T-shirt to prove it.

Andrew held out a hand to Jim Smith, Head of European

Group Marketing. Then to Helen Chapman, UK Marketing Director, Soap Powders. They were friendly and courteous, and not about to give their emotions away.

'Did you have a good morning?' asked Andrew, knowing they had already been to AFT, the incumbent agency on the Primo business.

'It was satisfactory,' said Jim without emotion, adding, 'Where do you want us?'

'Well,' said Andrew, 'I'd like to introduce you to the only member of the team you haven't met. This is our Deputy Chairman and pitch leader, Mark Cohen.'

Jim and Helen looked at him with disapproval. Why would the main man not think it important to meet the clients himself before the presentation? Didn't Craze know how influential they were to this decision?

A definite black mark against Mark.

Andrew continued, oozing charm: 'Mark will take you through the whole process today. He's the architect of all you are about to see, and he's been practically living here, and with your customers, for weeks.

'I'll see you afterwards to answer any questions about the agency, and to give you a tour of anything you may wish to see. I know you only have two hours here, so that part is optional. Good luck, and I hope you enjoy your time with us at BC. Mark? It's all yours...'

Mark took a step forward, but his tongue was stuck to the roof of his mouth. No recognisable noise came from his throat and everyone looked around at each other nervously.

Suddenly doubt had entered Mark's mind as he realised this was his moment – Redemption and making his mark, with God and the Devil passing it all over to him. It felt serious and he had a sudden attack of stage fright. Luckily the cavalry arrived – in the form of Ellie.

In the background, and only just in his line of sight, Ellie opened her wide lips and using hand and cheek movements mimed a blowjob. She mouthed 'Later' and winked.

He spluttered as if jump-started into life.

'Hi,' said Mark. 'This isn't going to be a normal presentation, so don't expect to be assaulted by graphs, charts or death-by- PowerPoint. Now, I know we have never met, but I do know quite a lot about you both nonetheless. Don't be alarmed, I haven't hired a private detective or become a stalker. You're quite safe I assure you!'

The two clients looked at each other through nervous, fixed smiles, not sure what version of office etiquette this guy was operating from.

'Now, I believe you're both good sports, and I don't want you to ruin those beautiful outfits. Kenzo, Jim? That one is only available in Tokyo, I think. Cost about $875? And Helen, I believe that one is from Barneys in New York? Nice buy at $760.'

'Now wait a minute,' said Jim, growing agitated. 'What's this about? We're here to see a pitch for the UK advertising budget for Primo. I suggest you back off or...'

'Okay, okay, please bear with me. There's a purpose in my rude behaviour. Would you please go along with it? Trust me, I'm in advertising!'

That lightened the mood, just a little, and just enough.

Despite his initial stage fright, Mark was now becoming confident to the point of utter fearlessness. If Patrick was there, he would have fired him already. Yet he was able to get these two people to undress in a private room and change into purpose-made white combat outfits bearing the Primo insignia, with combat boots to match.

Mark met them outside the room, dressed in an identical

fashion – all spotless, perfect and brilliant white.

'Please follow me into the first room.'

They did as he asked, sitting down in the empty white room feeling very warm towards AFT at that moment.

Mark said: 'We have constructed a simple six-point plan for the Primo brand, represented by the letters A_B_C_D_E_F.'

They nodded, feeling patronised now. More points lost. This was an embarrassing farce, they thought.

'This is point A. A is for Atomal.'

He delivered the 'dynamic tension' speech, describing the opposites as he had to Patrick and Julia a month earlier. He cited Coca-Cola, Tango and Pepsi once again, using bottles as props, smashing the Pepsi-labelled one for dramatic effect.

When he got to the part describing how this principle affected their own market, Helen and Jim straightened a little in their chairs. They were with the argument so far, and wanted to see where it was leading.

'Atomal is all about product performance and product demonstration. But don't take my word for that. Please help me out, Benny...'

The door opened and TV presenter Benny Walker entered, dressed in the same white overalls, but with an Atomal insignia on his chest.

'Hello there. Yes, I'm the jolly wally they pay to stand on the windswept doorsteps of the industrial north, flogging boring boxes of soap powder to shackled housewives in Bolton, Burnley and Birmingham.'

The clients were quite enjoying themselves now. Helen had defrosted and even Jim was tepid towards Mark, whose enthusiasm and confidence were infectious. Significant progress from such a poor start.

Benny went on to explain the largely impersonal brand

characteristics of Primo's main competitor, Atomal, and how they used celebs like him to make some connection with the public. But, at best, people felt neutral about Atomal. Usually, they thought of it as dull and all about chores. Benny assured them that personally he was much more exciting.

'Ha, ha, ha. Ta very much, Benny. See you later on,' said Mark. 'So, A was for Atomal. Now on to B.'

'B is for "Before time began".'

The door opened and the revered wildlife filmmaker Sir Albert Longthorne walked in.

'Oh my God!' squeaked Helen uncontrollably, displaying more emotion than she could help. 'I loved *When Reptiles Attack* and *Our Dying Planet*. My kids worship you!'

'Bugger me...' was all Jim could think of to say.

'Why, thank you, Helen. Good to meet you too, Jim, but I think a handshake will do until I know you a little better.'

Laughter erupted.

'I'm here to talk about where man came from. We originated in the primeval swamps. This was where our DNA evolved...'

He went on to develop the thesis that we are born to live in dirt. How micro-organisms in our bodies help us digest food and fight disease. How we need to get dirty, in order to fulfil primitive instincts to hunt and play.

'It is what we are, and we cannot deny our roots.'

Jim loved this and questioned Sir Albert for ten minutes. Mark had to cut it short, but promised they would see him again at the end of the six-point presentation: 'We're only on point B so far!'

Sir Albert left the room and Mark continued.

'The next section is C. C stands for "Celebrate housewives". As you know, I've not met you before today. That's because for the past two weeks I've been pretty much living with two families. Bright young families who meet the definition of the Primo target audience, as specified in your brief. Actually, they're a little more upmarket, but not where it really matters. The breadwinners of these families have been absent from the research, because they've been so busy with their careers. Let me introduce our research stars.

'Family One, the Smiths, and Family Two, the Chapmans.'

Jim's wife and six-year-old twin boys entered the room, together with Helen's house husband, his fourteen-year-old daughter from a previous marriage, and their seven-year-old son.

'I only commented on your suits because I knew exactly what you paid for them, and where you got them. Jim, you bought yours in Tokyo, and yours, Helen, came from New York. You've both recently been away on business trips, as your other halves told me. And you've sacrificed so much while you were away...

'I wanted to prove to you that I understand the pressures of the work-life balance, and how hard you both work to build lives for your families. This is not an attack on you.

'Christ, I do it too! I gave up my kids to live with yours! I hope you can forgive me.'

Jim and Helen were speechless. They felt bruised and battered emotionally, and hovered somewhere between mortally offended and deeply touched. This was like no agency presentation they had ever seen before, and they thought they had seen them all.

They nodded their forgiveness feebly.

Gotcha, Mark thought.

Their partners went on to describe what they had done with the kids while Jim and Helen were at work, or abroad, or playing golf, or too exhausted to join in.

Mark showed some film he had shot of the kids during his weeks there, in the park, at the school sports day, around the family home. He was definitely still his dad's little boy at heart.

The Smith and Chapman kids were laughing on the film, as well as now laughing at it, while it was hard to tell if Jim and Helen were crying or laughing. Mark took out his Pentax and shot a few discreet pictures of them.

'Sweet,' he said softly. Yes, Sid's kid alright.

Mark moved it on from C to D on the plan.

'D stands for "Dirt is for living".'

'Primo is about the greatness of getting dirty. About liberating who we really are, and nurturing the same in our kids. Helping them realise their full potential by developing their physical and communication skills.'

At this point he introduced the young creative team who went on to show a whole wall-full of work. TV ads, posters, in-store promotions, new packaging and radio scripts, all on the theme 'Fun in the filth'.

The TV ads showed adults in serious grown-up mode, at the office, reading the Sunday papers and so on, then suddenly standing up and throwing themselves into the nearest puddle or pool of mud to the slogan, 'Release the child in you'. Then the rest of their families joined in, the spots ending simply, 'Primo, fun in the filth'.

The MTV ad involved two log-like turds talking to each other in a toilet bowl. (The clients' children howled their approval at this one.)

At the end of this presentation, Mark ushered the families out of the room so they could get their breath back. They had a cup of tea with American Mud Pies from Patisserie Valerie, courtesy of Ellie. Then Mark resumed:

'Okay, on to point five, or E.'

'E is for the "Eyes of the World".'

The door opened again and Jim and Helen held their

breath. Who would come in next? President Bush? Madonna?

They were slightly disappointed that it was 'only' the Marketing Director of Max Mobile, Karen Phillips, who as Mark explained was also a director of World Child Care.

Karen outlined the idea of using art from deprived kids worldwide for charity, promoting free expression and sending money back to the places which needed it most. She told them that Max Mobile had pledged £1 million (news to Mark, at which he smiled) and that the WCC would police the project, helping to distribute the art and channel the money. She said that they would be honoured to change the world in partnership with Primo, which would be the lead sponsor.

Mark added that Vertec would have exclusive rights to use this unlimited supply of children's creativity worldwide, on any of their brands including Primo.

They were impressed. Then the door opened, and they were way beyond impressed as rock superstar Bruno walked in.

He was on the board of the WCC, and worked alongside Karen. And he happened to be both Jim and Helen's favourite artist, as Mark had discovered while doing his homework, browsing the CD collections in their respective houses.

He took out his Pentax again and snapped Jim and Helen standing either side of Bruno with beaming smiles tears.

Bruno agreed to be on the 'great and the good' board of the Eyes of the World, as a WCC representative with Karen. He remarked spontaneously that he hoped to see Jim and Helen there as the Vertec representatives. God bless him.

Mark hoisted his voice over the excitement.

'Okay everyone. Please come out to the car park now, for point number six.

'In case you're wondering, F is for "Fun in the filth".

'You too, Bruno, and put on a Primo combat suit please.

By now, Jim and Helen thought Mark was the best ad guy in the world. So did Mark.

The car park had been transformed into a giant, muddy outward-bound assault course. Around the perimeter was a kind of toboggan track, while in the centre was various equipment to jump over, scramble through or crawl under.

The idea was to get round in the fastest time. The toboggan track allowed the competitors to become human projectiles and hurtle round at speed, while spectators could try to slow them down with mud balls shot from mini rifles.

All the kids came out, with Jim and Helen's other halves, Benny Walker, Sir Albert, Bruno, Mark, Julia and the main pitch team including Ellie. They were all caked in mud from top to toe within seconds.

Patrick watched the mayhem from his office with a smug smile on his face. He called out excitedly for Andrew Bond to join him at the window.

'What do you think, Andrew? Our next Chairman?'

Andrew felt compromised, as he knew far too much about Mark Cohen to be objective.

'If you are hell-bent on invading the city then you know the deal,' he stated. 'All I ask is for you find out if he is trustworthy enough.'

Given he and Grace were sleeping together, this line of discussion was uncomfortable for Andrew, as he was breaking his own impeccable code of trustworthy behaviour.

Patrick replied: 'You're not going anywhere are you? As long as we have Good God Almighty working here, that's enough trust for any advertising agency!'

Andrew grimaced and left the building without waiting to see if the Vertec people wanted the tour or not. They didn't.

Jim and Helen stayed for three-and-a-half hours, not the

two hours specified in the brief, but they had the best time of their careers that day. Their families had bonded again too. When they left after showering in Patrick's corner bathroom, they were each handed a huge package as they climbed into the two family-sized stretch limos provided by BC.

These included signed copies of the creative work and media plan, an Eyes of the World DVD narrated by Bruno, photos of them with the celebrities, T-shirts saying 'Fun in the filth' and a digital film of the mud competition. This had been won by Helen Chapman, who also received the 'Mud Cup'.

Two days later, BC was awarded the Primo business across Europe and not just the UK, and on very generous terms. There was the promise of more to come, too, if they delivered all that they had promised.

BC celebrated with the biggest party in the agency's history. The cocaine was piled up in the meeting rooms like snow drifts on the slopes of the Alps. Mark was made Chairman that same day, and delivered a drunken speech at the party that made him cry, then kissed Patrick Craze (now the non-Executive Chairman) full on the mouth to the applause of the entire agency.

Mavis cried too, when her boy phoned with the news. He couldn't get hold of Barry, despite making calls all night. He gave up ringing him after a while as his presence was required by everyone all over the agency building.

Mark adored the mass adulation but, as if on automatic pilot, he would still regularly check his mobile for news of Barry and any interesting new texts. Sure enough, among a batch of bland congratulatory messages, was one from Ellie. This was interesting as she was standing only five yards from him at the time.

It read: *Dear hamster knob, remember the Xmas party 2002? See you on that fire escape in 5 mins.*

He made for the fire escape on the roof of the office block, pushing the metal door open to emerge into a cold evening.

Ellie ambushed him before he could say anything, clamping her lips to his and pushing her long tongue deeply inside his surprised mouth. She tasted vaguely of doner kebab, but that was no bad thing for Mark.

She dropped to her knees, unzipped his trousers and clasped his cock and balls in both hands before saying, 'I won that pitch for you by showing you what I was going to do to you when those "clunts" first walked into reception.'

'It is rude to talk with your mouth full,' he replied, but was then struck dumb by the fellatio skill that Ellie applied to his penis.

Fifteen minutes and one exquisite ejaculation later, they went back downstairs into the celebratory crowd of well-wishers, all still gathered in the reception area. Mark was a hero – except to Cherry, who made a point of ignoring him – and was being hailed as the new God, at least in the office at Soho Square.

'Personally I'd prefer to be the Devil,' he said to Patrick.

'That's still my job for now, so "f" off,' Patrick replied. Relenting, he added: 'Devil-in-waiting, if you like.'

The party began to break up, and Mark told Julia how incredible he thought she was. She was the most amazing woman he had ever met and he couldn't begin to express his thanks to her. Well, he was very, very drunk.

Happily, Julia could think of several ways for him to say thank you. They retired to her place in Borough around 3.30am.

'About time I mentioned the Eyes of the World to my wife, I think,' Mark mused out loud, while using a leather whip on Julia's fine rear quarters. This after binding her to the bed.

'Never mind the world's eyes. Just keep yours fixed on my arse for now, there's a good boy,' said Julia.

And what an arse, thought Mark as he flicked the whip, and what an incredible day.

CHAPTER SIXTEEN

Barry is White

The phone rang at 6.30am.

Mark had crawled gratefully into bed at 5.30am after leaving Julia and taking a black cab home, just as an eerily beautiful dawn was rising over sleepy suburban London. He was tired and ready to sleep deeply.

It felt as though he had only just closed his eyes and sunk his head into the squashy feather pillow, when the phone rang loudly and woke him. As he fumbled for the receiver, he was reminded of the Michael Caine movie *The Ipcress File*, where sleep deprivation was used as a form of mental torture.

'Hello,' he answered in a semi-comatose state, 'who is it?'

There was a long pause and then a voice said:

'Hello... It's Sammy... Barry – is – DEAD.'

Time stopped. His heart stopped. Mark could not take this in. He could not respond.

'Are you still there?' Sammy asked.

'No, not really,' he replied. 'How, when, where?'

Slowly she told Mark all she knew, which was not much. That was a mercy, as the full story was more painful than they could have coped with at that point.

That story began two days earlier, when Barry arrived at work as usual in Doris, the 1973 E-type Jag he had been given on his seventeenth birthday, which was growing old and temperamental like its owner. As he pulled into the parking lot, he was cursing the start of another boring day serving the 'bastard' public in a draughty furniture warehouse. Work was crap and home was crap, and Doris was playing up this morning, so she was crap too.

Sadly, it was a long time since his relationship with Sammy had been able to cheer him out of such a malaise.

She was less attentive to his needs, less 'there' for him generally, and more critical and unwilling to share the blame for any problems. For someone who had been rejected by his parents and who thought he had found his soul mate for life, this was a devastating development. He was not equipped to deal with it, nor to confide in anyone about it, even his best friend Mark.

Instead, Barry resorted to the childish arsenal of responses epitomised by his habit of spitting in his mother's tea, and most often deployed against customers at work. Sammy had been spared this in the past, but recently she had felt the full force of his 'toys out of the pram' tantrums.

This may have been Barry's way of reacting to her distant behaviour, but it had the effect of pushing her further away, making her feel like a total stranger, or at best just another abused customer at the warehouse. Sammy was too smart and self-willed to live with these antics, and too incapable of taking responsibility to meet him half way.

Consequently, their life together was locked in an alarming downward spiral of denial and broken communication. So it was that Barry arrived at the furniture warehouse that morning in a dark and brooding state of mind – and that would prove fatal.

Doris wheezed into the car park and Barry got out, glancing sourly at the weather-beaten 'Regal Furniture' sign and graffiti-scarred walls as he unlocked the shutters. A cup of sweet tea and a chocolate biscuit lifted his spirits just enough for some smutty banter with the cheeky-chappie drivers as they turned up for work. Then the morning settled into its familiar, slow, incident-starved routine, to the soundtrack of melodic tunes on the radio.

Barry organised deliveries, ordered stock and dealt with tiny trade issues with characteristic foul humour. By lunchtime he had used the words 'piss', 'fuck' and 'bollocks' so often that if there had been a company swear box, Doris could have been replaced by a Bentley Continental GT from that morning's take alone.

Then a couple entered the showroom, or 'slowroom' as Barry had coined it years ago. They pottered around, bouncing on the beds, checking the badly scrawled sticker prices, and picking up brochures as they went. Barry wafted over after fifteen minutes with a half-hearted offer of help.

The man was in his late thirties and obese, with a shaved St Paul's Cathedral dome of a head. His ears were pierced with diamond studs, and he had a closely cropped greying beard that was still ginger at the chin. A thick roll of blubber around his neck gave the impression he was wearing a polo-neck sweater, even though he wasn't. He had the look of a muscular man who had gone to flab some time ago, with his brown leather coat only partially concealing the fact that his Farah slack-style trousers sat too low, tightly belted under his overhanging gut.

Fat men do this to kid themselves and others that their waist is 38 inches not 46, reflected Barry with an unconscious sneer.

'Hi there, can I help you?' he asked with forced interest.

He was facing the guy as he spoke, but his eyes were instantly super-glued to the girlfriend's pendulous, surgery-enhanced breasts.

Barry raised his head with some effort, and saw her face for the first time. She was about twenty-eight, blonde and pretty, with round doe-like grey-blue eyes. She had a strangely familiar vacant expression on her face.

The fat man was irritated by Barry's unsubtle inspection of his girlfriend's assets, but managed to remain calm. 'Yeah, we're looking for a deal on a new bed. I'm big and heavy, she's little and light.'

The girlfriend giggled and covered her mouth and nose, so just her eyes were visible. And then the penny dropped. This was the girl who had given Barry a blowjob in the cubicle next to Mark at Secret's lap-dancing club, a few weeks ago.

As usual, Barry's immediate reaction was not diplomatic.

'I know you! Secrets! Lap dancing...' He stopped short, realising his mistake.

The girl looked horrified, the fat man confused, then angry. Then very angry and sweaty.

A plump Cumberland pork sausage index finger pointed accusingly at her face. 'What's this about, Stacey? You promised...'

He then prodded Barry's cheek. 'As for you, pal, back off or else.'

'Or else what? You might get even fatter and even more ginger with your tits getting even bigger than they already are?'

At that the boyfriend lost it. He slapped his great white hands round Barry's face, gripped his cheeks and bit deep into Baz's right ear.

'Ahhhhhhhhhhhhhhhhhh' he screamed in agony. 'Boys, get over here. AHHHHHHHHHHHHHHHHHH...'

Barry's drivers rushed over en masse, unceremoniously escorting the by now near-hysterical brute off the premises with a final kicking into his ribs and balls for good measure. Feeling well protected, Barry shouted after him, holding on to a torn ear lobe: 'That's the closest you'll ever get to whispering sweet nothings, you bastard. And by the way she gives a good blowjob, mate. Now fuck off, you fat ginger wanker.'

For Barry to insult the guy's girth was undoubtedly a case of the pot calling the kettle black, but that was him all over. He would not have been quite so provocative had he not been particularly frustrated with life in general that day, but he felt better for having let off some steam on this hapless stranger and he busied himself tending to his ear using the company bottle of TCP, Regal Furniture's only health cover.

The day dragged on, a plaster now taped attractively against his weeping wound. At 6.30pm Barry headed with weary relief to Doris the Jag, braced for the slow commute back to an uncertain atmosphere at home. 'Maybe I'll get a kebab with salad and fries on the way back,' he consoled himself, smiling at the prospect of adding another layer of grease to Doris' steering wheel.

The smile was still on his face as he snapped the padlock shut on the rusty metal shutter and turned to find himself staring into the huge, leering face of the bloated customer he had insulted earlier that day. It twisted into a grimace as he felt the sharpened carving knife slam into his gut and rip up his stomach like a butcher slicing a lamb's tender underbelly.

The man said nothing by way of explanation, and Barry could only gasp feebly before the slash across his throat killed him stone dead.

His blood-drenched body was packed unceremoniously in an industrial black plastic bag, then bundled into the back of the old Ford Granada estate from which the fat man and his two equally rotund henchmen had been patiently watching the furniture warehouse. They filled buckets with water from an outside tap and sluiced down the sodden, red concrete. No one was around to witness anything, as most of the other lock-ups were vacant, and the housing estates were more than half a mile away.

The body was dumped in a trench deep within Epping Forest, and lightly covered with leaves and earth. Ironically, Barry's second-to-final resting place was near a local lovers' spot called High Beech, where he had sometimes taken Sammy before they were married.

The thugs left laughing and congratulating the murderer on his latest exemplary revenge attack. They also approved of his ridding the world of one of the worst customer service personnel of all time. Barry lay undetected and unreported for more than a day in the forest ditch.

Sammy didn't worry that he had not returned home, as he was always staying out late these days. Mark had called him repeatedly, but again was not unduly concerned. Indeed, Barry would have remained nestled in the flora and fauna for much longer, if a frisky young couple had not pulled up nearby in their 1987 white Escort van, eager for an al fresco physical workout.

The back of the van was littered with empty KFC boxes and used Castrol oil cans, and Essex girl Sharon insisted that it was no longer a romantic enough environment for her to perform sexually. Trisha had hosted a programme about women's sexual self-esteem on daytime TV that morning, and Sharon had taken the sentiments very much to heart. She wasn't that cheap or easy any more.

'Fussy cow, you used to do it for a Cider Bomb a year ago,' her boyfriend muttered, as they walked hand-in-hand towards the spot where Barry's corpse was hidden.

'Get 'em out then, girl, those tits needs an airing,' said Kevin. 'I'm feeling in the mood to pork you rigid.'

Sharon lay down on the mulch and opened her legs obligingly. She spread her arms wide over the ground, feeling classy and liberated.

Her hand brushed Barry's frozen fingers, protruding stiffly through the carpet of leaves. She turned, stared, and screamed, leaping to her feet in an instant fit of hysterics. Kevin's erection wilted, then drooped completely as he scooped away some leaves to reveal the bleached white face of the very cold and dead Barry.

Kevin called the police. They found Barry's wallet and his identity was confirmed. Investigations began, but the well-oiled funeral machine kicked in immediately the coroner had finished with Barry's remains. In the Jewish religion, a burial is a very quick process. Indeed, if funerals were an Olympic event, the Jews would win the gold medal every single time.

Sammy, who was in a crushed state of shock, had very little to organise personally. Many people lent a hand – through love of them both, or because they were busybodies who thrived on playing a part in a human tragedy.

The ceremony was held at the Waltham Cross Jewish cemetery, near junction 26 on the M25, on the following Friday at 11am, in the kind of drizzly, windy weather invariably reserved for such occasions. Despite this, Barry was a very popular chap and well over three hundred people made the effort to attend at virtually no notice.

Everyone was crammed into the small, concrete chapel, men on one side, women on the other, as tradition dictated. Those men who were not close to Barry treated it as a business networking opportunity, or a chance to catch up with old friends. The girls looked critically at each other's outfits and figures, with a keen eye for anyone who had recently piled on the pounds.

Those closest to the deceased were a species apart. Ashen-faced, somehow shrunken, numbed into stricken silence or sobbing uncontrollably with no regard for their neighbours' ear drums.

Maurice and Shirley, Barry's parents, were quiet and dignified in their loss. Sammy cried softly, subdued by a diet of strong painkillers which made her feel like a shadow or a detached phantom hovering at the fringes of this terrible event.

Gene and Harry Christmas were there too, shaken by the untimely end of this young man whom they had known personally, if not well.

Denise cried loudly and her eyes were puffy and swollen. Fat Dave looked stoical, but in truth he didn't really care very much, and was only there because his boss Derek Peterson had insisted that they both attend. Derek was dressed in an appropriately sombre black suit, though he couldn't resist a rather flashy, frilly lace shirt.

He was focused on the widow Sammy throughout the ceremony, in an overly-concerned, vaguely vampiric sort of way.

As for Mark, he sobbed and sobbed and sobbed. He had filled the wad of tissues that he had brought with him long before the rabbi had spoken a word in serious prayer.

The coffin was eventually wheeled slowly out to the

graveside on an ancient, rickety cart, followed by Sammy, only held upright by her slightly-built mother. Close behind shuffled Shirley, Maurice, Mark and Grace, who gripped hands tightly together, weeping as one in their shared anguish and pain. Poppy and the twins followed. They were upset, but still held their mobiles in their hands just in case they missed a vital text.

The mourning party went back to Barry's house to drink tea, eat bridge rolls with smoked salmon or pickled herring, and to console the bereaved widow and parents. Yet, in a way, it was Mark who was most fundamentally affected by Barry's death.

He had lost his only confidante, the one lifelong friend who could know everything he did and give him stick for it, but without passing judgement on him.

When it had been Mark's turn to take the shovel at the graveside, scoop up some of the wet heavy clay, and tip it on to the coffin, he thought the sound of the dirt hitting the lid was the worst one he had ever heard in his life. It was so final. It was the sound of nothing ever feeling complete or balanced again.

CHAPTER SEVENTEEN

Sex, Lies and Videotape

It seemed that the list written on Armageddon evening was in a state of flux now. Priorities were shifting as a direct result of this traumatic catalyst, the untimely and violent death of Mark's best friend. The more parochial and personal goals on his agenda had either been quenched already, or were now somehow relegated to a far lower priority.

Most of his Unfinished Business was done and dusted by now anyway. Sammy no longer wanted him. She withdrew into herself, becoming a recluse, isolated from her old life. Only Derek Peterson, who was forging a determined path into her head, managed to reach her through her pain. He was an odd choice of comforter for her, but this was a case of a man in the right place, at the right time, with a plan.

Similarly, Gene, Mark's mother-in-law, ended their illicit sessions together after the trauma of Barry's death. It was not a bitter or brutal rejection, but was simply as though she had suddenly come to her senses. She felt at peace with her age now, and no longer excited by the danger of their liaisons. Mark knew that Cherry on reception was still outstanding, but she was hardly in the same league as Gene or Sammy.

No, this was a time for getting serious about the tougher objectives. This was the stuff which would stretch him, which might create a lasting legacy. These remaining aims duly moved to the top of the previously equally weighted agenda.

Mark was now focused on two things. Achieving Redemption for himself through being a true father and rebuilding Grace. And acquiring a previously undreamed of degree of influence, via his bold plan for Make My Mark.

The Eyes of the World project was a major vehicle for both of these objectives, though only a long-term investment of time and energy into committed parenting would restore his status as a father. His stamina levels when it came to emotional commitment were notoriously poor, so this undertaking concerned him somewhat.

On the other hand, everything was going amazingly well where the art venture was concerned. Numerous highly motivated people were involved in the charity from day one, which helped create an unstoppable momentum behind the company, and established a brand with its own distinctive personality.

The WCC handled the educational remit, sourcing suitable establishments to provide the supply of art and identifying the most worthy recipients of the revenues. Some of these locations were proposed by Mark himself, following suggestions from his silent partner, Derek Peterson.

Every box of Primo carried a promotion for the Eyes of the World, and an advertising campaign was launched on building-sized posters, on TV, in women's magazines and on branded postcards distributed in cool bars, galleries and clubs. All paid for by their generous sponsor, Vertec.

God bless Jim and Helen. But then, sales of Primo quickly rose by eight per cent, so everyone was happy.

The PR campaign saw ambassador Bruno featured prominently in *Hello* and *OK!* magazines, as well as on MTV and many digital platforms.

Mark had arranged prominent launch articles in the quality daily newspapers. It was also featured in the regional TV news, and on numerous radio shows, including a prime slot on Radio 4's *Today* programme. The ad guru and art fanatic Michael Greta (of Greta & Wendla) bought ten pieces, which was reported in all the papers. Entrepreneur Dick Branston bought a hundred, which made the national TV news.

Britain was seen as a test market to measure consumer demand for the Eyes of the World artworks, ahead of a possible global roll-out. They need not have worried about the consumer.

Some of the better-known pieces of art, those featured in ads or editorial articles, were reselling at healthy premiums almost instantly at online auction. A market in collectables was quickly established, despite the huge supply of original art pouring from Colombia (Mark's suggestion after he was prompted by Derek), Thailand and Iraq.

One piece in particular, called 'Good Morning Mummy' was painted in Iraq by a six-year-old, gap-toothed little boy called Ahmed. It was a typical child's picture, a jolly breakfast table scene with flowers, flat bread and a jug of milk, and mother smiling sweetly in the background.

Unfortunately, Ahmed had been killed in a car bomb incident the day after he completed his otherwise unremarkable work. 'Good Morning Mummy' hit the newspaper front pages and sold on eBay for £12,000 to a Japanese businessman who had read an article about the Eyes of the World in the *FT*, and thought it would be a shrewd fiscal move to get in early.

Bargain hunters moved in looking for the best investments, those pictures with the most heart-rending tales of woe attached. So began a popular stampede to the Eyes of the World website.

This online gallery had been devised by BC's in-house web design agency, and allowed people to browse the artworks, read the kids' background stories, select their own picture frames, make their payment and arrange for delivery. A typical picture cost £170 including delivery and took less than a month to be framed and shipped.

The entire operation was hailed as a triumph, a commercially driven charity which recognised a genuine consumer demand, offering a value-for-money solution which benefited the needy. Unlike other charities, it managed to avoid being depressing, as it celebrated the creativity and joy of children. It was a model for corporate responsibility, and reinforced Britain's world role as a leader of grass-roots cultural expression.

Given these credentials, it was no surprise that it attracted the interest of politicians. The Conservative Party contacted Mark, making noises about meeting up soon for an informal introductory 'chat'. Wow! Mark thought after taking the call. Even the big boys want me these days. Clearly it takes one to know one, after all.

The Eyes of the World was his ticket to such elevated circles, but its significance to Grace was far more profound. She had been allowed home on the condition she attended therapy sessions at the Rookery, and on the second evening of her return to the family nest Mark finally plucked up the courage to pitch the Eyes of the World to her.

He needn't have worried about her reaction to the project

– while she had done her level best to appear nonchalant as he told her about it, by the end of the pitch, all she could muster was an incredulous 'Oh my God!' She was dumbstruck when Mark informed her that Andrew Bond was also set to work on the charity.

Once the pitch was over, the couple had done something which would have seemed unimaginable twenty-four hours earlier – they went on a date. After dinner and a trip to the cinema, they had spent the night in the Covent Garden hotel and had made love for the first time in years.

The only potential fly in the ointment had been the fact she was using the very same hotel to have an illicit affair with Andrew Bond. She had been somewhat relieved that no one on reception had enquired, 'Your usual room, Grace?' when she and Mark had arrived.

Her work on the Eyes of the World began in earnest and, for the first time in a long time, she felt alive. It swiftly became a consuming passion for her, all the more so as it was such an unexpected guest in her previously bleak and narrow existence.

Whisky was absent, and not missed. Her feelings of guilt and failure towards her own children were being washed away by her efforts on behalf of thousands of strangers' offspring, rather than by the anaesthetic effects of alcohol.

This was of little consolation to Poppy or the twins, and surprisingly it was Mark who proved to be there for them through all the texting, phone calls, joint therapy sessions and occasional shared meals at the home in South Woodford, which Vicki kept reassuringly clean and sparkling.

Grace had simply slipped too far to attempt any comeback with the children, at least in her own eyes. So she didn't try. She was almost never at home, instead touring the world's poorest spots to meet the children, visit their schools and understand their needs. She saw little of Mark or her lover, Andrew Bond. Andrew did arrange to go on the occasional 'fact-finding mission' with her, and their sex continued to blaze in this exotic and highly charged atmosphere.

She had also changed beyond all recognition.

Physically she was no longer a skeletal figure, but curvaceous, slim and beautiful. Her newly discovered power appeared to radiate from within her. She was a beacon with a magnetic field, irresistible to all the needy losers that now swarmed around her.

Grace was not complaining, though. She loved being listened to after so many years of being ignored by everyone, especially her husband. This greatest of her wounds had been unwittingly inflicted by her husband. A good person who was not confident enough to blossom on her own, she had chosen Mark to protect, encourage and nurture her. He had failed her utterly, lavishing all his attention on his own passions and needs, pushing hers aside with barely a thought for her welfare.

Grace had supported him, and waited patiently for her turn in the sun. It never came, and she gradually turned into a quietly bitter dissenter. She hated the person she had become and, perhaps unfairly, blamed Mark for it entirely.

Today, though, she had morphed into someone totally different, independent and robust. She felt capable of almost anything, except perhaps of being the front person for the art brand. Showing off would never feel right to her. Mark was better suited to that, and he was welcome to it. She also did not feel the need to be grateful to him.

As for Mark himself, he was simply revelling in being Mark. He was thrilled to be asked to be a guest on the Charlton show that Saturday, to talk about the Eyes of the World phenomenon. It was TV's biggest chat show in its last series, and the invitation was ample evidence that Mark was achieving his most ambitious objective. Even Patrick Craze was impressed and urged Mark to slip in a mention of BC's role in the project, or preferably to shout it at full volume in the middle of the live, peak-time broadcast.

Grace was away, and Andrew was travelling with her. At least the kids would see his public triumph, though, thought Mark. They were appropriately excited, but more because Johnny Depp and Wayne Rooney were their dad's fellow guests, and they hoped to meet them as they were going to be in the audience with backstage passes.

It had been some time since the twins had carried out their surveillance mission in their father's wardrobe. Barry's funeral and the family fall-out following his demise had postponed any plans to explore the mischievous possibilities of the pictures and video.

Poppy had kept the incriminating shot of her mother riding a strange man in the Rookery stored on her Nokia for a while. It was no award-winner, but was clear and sharp enough to be family dynamite. This made her nervous, as she knew anyone could find it, should she misplace her phone. It could also be deleted accidentally, and she had a feeling it might prove useful at some later date, for blackmail or revenge.

She approached the twins, who printed it off along with the shots they had taken from the wardrobe. Some painstaking after-school work in the photography club had significantly enhanced the original quality.

All three were shocked to realise that it was their grandmother bouncing around in bed on top of their father.

'Isn't that illegal or unhygienic or something? Couldn't they go to prison?' asked Samuel earnestly.

'I'm never eating her fairy cakes again, not now I know

where her hands have been,' Max said to Poppy in disgust.

They all made a pact not to speak of it or tell anyone, until they could decide the best way to benefit from their parents' filthy fun.

On the night of the Charlton interview, the photographic evidence was hidden in Poppy's bedroom in South Woodford, in a locked red money box in her wardrobe. Appropriately, she had labelled it 'Future Gold Mine'.

Mark was the first guest on air, but he was not even remotely nervous. He was relaxed, even elated, as though he had waited his whole life for this moment. 'Bring it on...' echoed through his mind as he descended the studio's stairway, his hand outstretched to grasp the nation's favourite chat show host, Terence Charlton, a grandfather figure to the nation who sported a fine mop of grey hair and a silver tongue.

'Hello, Mark. Before we talk about the Eyes of the World project, how are you coping, given all the media attention you've received recently?' asked Charlton.

'I'm nervous to be honest. Being in advertising, I'm trained to sell, sell, sell, and this is all about do, do, do. There can be no more inspirational thing than the joy of life as seen through the untarnished eyes of a child. It's a celebration, it's nourishment for the human spirit, and it's a chance for the most disadvantaged kids to express themselves to the wider world. And all this noble ambition is in the hands of a jaded old ad man. How sad is that?'

The host laughed, along with the studio audience, appreciating a bit of self-deprecating humour.

'Terence, have you ever felt so strongly about something that you would sacrifice everything for it? Not because it's a personal mission, or an ego trip, but because it is just plain right?'

Charlton was surprised by this direct line of questioning

from a broadcasting virgin. It took him off guard, and as a result he answered from the heart.

'Actually, there are many things I believe in and would defend to the end. But I can't think of anything that really meets the spirit of your question.'

'Well, I'm a lucky man, Terence. The Eyes of the World has captured the imagination of enlightened commerce, whetted the public's appetite for creativity, and harnessed the human desire to be true to our consciences. I've found my cause, and hope I might be able to expand the goodwill to many more enlightened people.'

Mark had the feeling that his nose was growing right there and then in front of an audience of millions.

Charlton then asked, 'Do you think you might be persuaded to enter politics? I wonder if you are just the sort of chap that this country needs in government to shake things up.'

With a wry smile, Skid took his time to answer his host. 'Well, as we all know, politicians are hypocritical egotists who only care about themselves.

'Hello?' he said, pointing to his own chest. 'Clearly I'm perfect for the job.'

The studio audience laughed loudly.

'At least everybody can see it coming this time – "I does what I says but with sin" – to paraphrase a famous advertisement, Terence.

'But seriously,' he said with a cheesy wink, 'I am in very early discussions with a certain party about my possibly taking up a publicly spirited challenge in the near future.'

'Well, good luck,' offered Charlton. 'I'm sure many people watching will hope you do decide to follow that path.'

Gotcha, Mark thought.

CHAPTER EIGHTEEN

The Business of White Powder

Derek Peterson was a man who was rarely satisfied. On the issue of whether a glass should be considered half empty or half full, Derek was firmly in the former camp.

He was an only child, born in the austere 1940s in Catford. Today, the sheer density of Southern Fried Chicken fast-food outlets in this neighbourhood is an indication that it is spiritually very far from leafy St John's Wood or chic Mayfair, despite the fact that all three are regarded as slices of the same London cake. It was no better in the post-war years.

Derek's father was Greek and his mother was from Peckham, which proved to be a volatile mix. As far back as he could remember, the two of them were always rowing in front of him. Plates of food would fly across rooms, and he would be shouted at and sent to his bedroom for no offence that was ever adequately explained to him.

He grew into a quiet, withdrawn chap who was largely

ignored, except when used as a weapon by one parent or the other in the heat of battle.

It wasn't that he was not loved, but they never told him so. They were too wrapped up in their selfish adult needs. Derek was a factor in their unhappiness, a reason (or an excuse) for them to stop trying to become whatever they wanted to be.

He was never a cause for celebration, or a person who existed solely in his own right. It was no wonder then that he always sought approval and recognition, but was never in any danger of finding any, no matter how successful he became in later life. No, Del was a short, round, insecure little boy who grew up to become a short, round, insecure man.

The local school was rough, South London rough, and rugby was the preferred contact sport. Given Derek's disposition and distinctive build, the natural role for him on the field of play was to be the ball. His peers did not fail to deliver on this potential.

Kicked at home, and then kicked at school was not a good start for a small, lonely child.

Derek was good at art and came top of his class, but had no one to tell or be praised by. He learned to survive by being good at business, dealing in trading cards and later in stolen exam papers. This kid would never be a sports star, but would always have money in his pocket. And he knew the value of paid-for protection by the age of ten.

He was never popular with girls. Instead, he bought his way into their bras and beds, after the initial painful rejections had finished shredding any of the little self-confidence he had left after such a debilitating childhood.

So, to Derek, women were paradoxically both a commodity and set on a pedestal.

In the early 1970s, he founded a company which filled a

gap for the blossoming pornography sector. He fulfilled huge demand by providing a way of avoiding the embarrassment of going into a shop. To enter a newsagent to buy *Hot Hooters* and to be served by an Indian lady with her young child at her side was a humiliating experience.

Derek worked that out, not least of all because he had to ask twice, as he could not even reach the top shelf. So he decided to build a business based on removing that indignity.

Through a combination of direct mail, leaflets in pubs, phone boxes, toilet posters at football grounds and word of mouth, he offered a means by which men could reliably receive porn at specified times, at home or by hand in any location. He pioneered the idea of the 'late-night, brown-paper-bag home delivery service', locally, then regionally, and then nationally. They traded under the name of Blue 2 U.

At the beginning, anonymous white Escort vans would drop off dirty mags from 9.00pm until 1.00am, fulfilling telephone orders. He employed only male drivers to do the courier work, and they had discreet identity badges bearing 'Blue 2 U' in very small letters on the underside. Men would pay double the cover price to avoid humiliation.

Derek's potential market widened vastly when he extended his operations through supplying out-of-hours booze, the rental of washed sex toys and then full escort companionship 24/7. He was one of the first to compile data about his customers, and used this information to sell more and more specialist items to a sex-starved audience of mostly, but not exclusively, men.

Eventually the country's every whim or excess were funnelled in some way or another through his underground organisation. He sourced and distributed an ever wider array of items for his punters. Gradually that included more and more drugs, such as heroin, MDMA, GHB, cocaine and pills, but all via more discreet personal deliveries than white vans – by young runners on foot or riding mopeds.

He kept his competition sweet in all of these markets by cutting them in on his monopoly – for a healthy slice of their revenues naturally.

He made millions, and the pickings were easy.

He acquired respect through his conspicuous wealth.

He could buy adoring friends by the dozen.

He had also had the ultimate satisfaction of having buried both of his despised parents.

Or, at least, he had attended their funeral service. Their bodies were never found, but some unusual sausages were on sale in the speciality delis of East and South London that month, thanks to an errand carried out by his one trusted mate, Fat Dave.

'Greek pork mixed with the best of British beef and hot chilli, to make a spicy seasonal sausage treat.' Derek had laughed out loud when Fat Dave informed him he had sold a batch of the sausages to the local school. What poetic justice, that such bad parents should ultimately be eaten by innocent children.

But he was still not satisfied. The glass of life had grown to the size of a bucket, but it was still half empty in Derek's eyes. He wanted love.

Of course, there was still not enough money stashed away either, there never was, but he wanted love more. Money brought him little satisfaction now, but he was addicted to the habit, and it amused him that everyone else seemed to find making it so difficult, when to him it was as natural as breathing.

Ironically, he really wanted what everyone else seemed to find so easy to acquire. He ached to be cherished by someone who was not a paid employee or a fawning lap-dog. Derek had only once had a fleeting glimpse of what love might be, in the eyes of a young girl who crossed his path many years before. The lovely teenage Sammy.

Sammy had popped in sometimes on the way back from school or from work for tea and a chat. She had been free and wild, had laughed and had fun with him, and had not been judgemental about his height or his modest genital cluster. She'd liked him because he was a nice guy, and it seemed that was enough for her.

So why couldn't he have Sammy?

He was not a rough man. He was polite, gave to charity and was generous with all the pandering, blood-sucking people around him. Who had ever said 'Well done' or 'Thank you' or in any way nurtured Derek Peterson? Sammy was the only one. And he had believed her interest in him was genuine, so he allowed himself the secret romantic dream of having her one day.

Then, in the wink of an eye, that loudmouth oaf Barry had come along and Derek had lost her. But he had unfinished business there, and he was not going to let her go without a struggle. He could be patient, and play a long game. A very long game.

Because of the newlywed couple's lifestyle, they were in his orbit most of the time anyway and thus fell under his stealthy surveillance. Their social life was played out in his clubs and at his parties, fuelled by the drugs which were becoming a bigger and bigger part of the Peterson distribution empire.

In later years, the porn industry had moved into DVDs and the internet.

He had been a pioneer in these and other emerging areas of the UK 'blue' market, but the competition was more fragmented and widespread, and his capacity to control the distribution was much reduced.

So he had sought to expand his drug importing and distribution business, focusing particularly on increasing the volumes of his bread-and-butter product, cocaine. When the price was right, he would 'come on down'.

Derek had established links with Escobar, the notorious Colombian narcotics baron, many years earlier. They had liked each other, sensing similar hang-ups perhaps, and had become friends and associates, until Escobar's untimely and messy death. Del dealt in large quantities of product, paid promptly and was businesslike at all times, so it proved to be a fruitful long-term relationship even with those who succeeded the baron.

As always, the transportation and smuggling part of the operation represented the greatest challenge and ongoing risk. Typically, containers of medical products, tractor parts or tinned fruit arrived at the docks, and were whisked from there by trucks to remote packing and processing units in the more isolated parts of Essex, for final delivery to the familiar list of usual suspects supplying the smaller drug dealers nationwide.

But, with the quantities Derek was moving, something new and bold was required, and it was not at all clear where this big idea was going to come from.

So when Mark Cohen, an acquaintance made through Sammy long ago, came to his gates in Chingford, Derek was in a receptive frame of mind. Mark required a supply of custom packing racks designed specifically for the safe transportation of delicate Eyes of the World artwork. And he needed some 'seed money'.

It struck Derek that the transportation of these containers, backed by the cast iron credibility of global charity WCC and triple-A sponsor Vertec, was likely to attract far less scrutiny than his regular trafficking channels. It could also very quickly become a daily shuttle service. He 'got it' instantly and jumped in with both feet.

Eureka! he screamed mentally.

Aside from the practical advantages, it tickled him that one business based on white powder, the washing detergent Primo, and a second, the narcotic cocaine, could cohabit in some small way, like one brother brand sponsoring another.

After Mark left, Del talked it over with Fat Dave.

'How elegant this is. It's like the respectable parents covering up for the black sheep of the family,' he said, glowing with self-satisfaction. 'You see, my friend, "fun in the filth".'

Mark and Derek had toasted the seemingly innocent venture with Jack Daniels, and shaken hands to seal the deal. Derek had also signed off £1 million to have a special packing rack designed, and business operations quickly set up in the UK.

Unknown to Mark, art initially sourced from Colombia, and then from other trafficking hotspots, would provide the opportunity to transport cocaine to practically anywhere in the world. For now, the UK would be the test market, where the art (and its illicit excess baggage) could be unpacked by Derek's people, in Derek's warehouses.

Having pointed out the brilliance of his plan to the loyal Dave, Derek stepped to the phone and called in a favour from a fellow Essex businessman.

Colin Black was an ex-poker pro who had suffered a run of bad luck. He had turned to Del for a life-line, before his knees were blown off by an Irish family with a short fuse (at least where credit control was concerned).

He now ran a flourishing packaging business called British Bulldog Packaging, located in the Lea Valley industrial estate in the flattest, ugliest part of Essex.

Derek had backed Colin as a start-up, writing off the gambling debts first, and owned a fifty per cent share in the business. It was by now a massive group, after years of profitable trading – it would be British Bulldog's track record in packaging which would reassure the WCC and Vertec, when Mark presented the business plan.

Derek quickly explained the design brief to Colin, who was familiar with all current customs laws and inspection techniques, as well as the detection tools used to sniff out drugs at entry and exit points.

He also knew what quantity could be shipped in each consignment, and therefore how many containers in any one batch needed to be specially modified. The fewer custom racks per shipment, the lower the risk, but it was crucial that all the racks (modified or not) were exactly the same in appearance and weight.

Derek was a valued client, so work began that same night, and a prototype was ready inside a week. The World Children's Charity logo was prominent on its side, as was that of the Eyes of the World. Ironically, making them stand out would help ensure the containers were ignored.

Each appeared to be made of a single piece of blue moulding, with thick strengthening ridges along the bottom and a removable sealable lid. In fact, there were fine seams across the bottom section, but these did not follow the line of the ribbing, instead cutting across at an unexpected angle. The panels slid out at this angle if they were pushed hard and the fine glue seal broken. The ridges were solid plastic, but in the modified versions the cavities were filled with cocaine.

The racking method and moisture-absorbent interior linings gave credence to the use of these particular containers for this unique task. The lining also allowed for the impregnation of a subtle but effective masking aroma, designed to defeat the nasal powers of even the best-trained customs dogs.

A standard version was sent for clearance by the authorities, and passed with flying colours after just two weeks. Production commenced, and the Eyes of the World art (and cocaine) business was effectively up and running, at least from a logistical viewpoint. This dovetailed perfectly with the commissioning of a framing facility (again courtesy of Colin Black's packaging empire), the first supply of art from the schools, the marketing campaign, and the establishment of admin offices and a call centre.

It was a masterpiece of organisation, to the tightest of deadlines. Initial strong demand went ballistic following Mark's Charlton appearance and the eBay stories. The kids of Colombia and Thailand were virtually put on full-time painting shifts, while more territories were hurriedly signed up by Grace and the WCC teams.

The revenues from the art sales made their way back reasonably quickly to the originating schools, and were put to good use buying art equipment, books and computers.

The first illegal drugs shipment sailed through as part of a consignment of Colombian art in week three, after two dummy runs using Primo as a cocaine substitute.

'White powder is white powder,' Derek had joked to Fat Dave, repeating the jest to Colin later the same day.

Mark was blithely oblivious to this underworld activity, but to be truthful he wasn't really looking for trouble. He had enough chainsaws spinning of his own.

The cocaine shipping and distribution process thus established, it was further refined through trial and absolutely no errors ('Or else') into a slick drug-running machine.

Mark was thrilled to receive the first cash 'bonus' payment

for his part in the supply chain, personally delivered by an equally satisfied Derek. Fat Dave felt like an outsider, mute and motionless as a rock, not at all delighted at the turn of events. He was reduced to playing the role of servile chauffeur, waiting obediently in the car, while his boss greeted Skid like the long-lost son that Dave was supposed to be.

He had earned that role the hard way, with blood, guts and unswerving obedience.

If he hated Mark before for his intimacy with Grace, he loathed him all the more now for inadvertently usurping his rightful place Derek's side.

Del handed Mark a six-figure sum in neat bundles of £50 notes, intimating that there were going to be many more of these massive backhanders to come. And long may it last, Mark sincerely hoped.

Derek wanted to make it clear why he was so grateful to Mark: 'This deal is a right result for me. I am usually mixing with the low-lifes and on the filthy fringes of crime. This is my chance to do something good, and for it to be all above board and proper. You done that for me, you did. And my Sammy.

'Me and her are getting closer and closer every day, and you helped do that an' all. As long as this gig lasts, I will show you my gratitude by sharing the wealth. Just make sure no one else can muscle in on our lovely work, if you know what I mean.'

He winked as he returned to his new green Maybach limousine. 'This is the only one in Essex,' he called back to Mark as Fat Dave opened the door for him. 'And you could afford one soon. You lucky, lucky boy,' Derek said before sliding inside.

Not if I can help it, Skid, thought Fat Dave, slamming the the door shut a little too hard before opening the driver's door. Your luck just ran out, big time. Take my advice and buy a hearse instead.

And he meant it too, big time.

As the Maybach pulled away, Derek waved a cheerful goodbye through the rear window while whispering 'Bloody mug' through his tiger's smile. Mark smiled and waved back, feeling the warm glow of satisfied if temporary sainthood in his heart. It was surely part of his Redemption.

In honour of his late best friend Barry, he was putting things right for Sammy. He was setting Derek Peterson on the path to honesty and happiness. And, besides, this money could fund his final ambition – Make My Mark – just as he had vowed he would do on 21st February, 2004.

With money like this, never mind making my mark, I can blow a bloody great crater in the side of the planet, thought Mark. He sat on the carpet surrounded by a moat of £50 notes, like George Best but without a Miss World. He counted it all, set his camera on timer, and photographed the scene of excess and success for his albums, followed by a bottle of Jack and a gram of the finest Colombian fairy dust. 'What can possibly go wrong?' cried the naïve fool gleefully.

One should never ask that question out loud. It is unlucky.

CHAPTER NINETEEN

The Lies of the World

Mark lay in bed next to Julia Hardy-Roberts in her Borough flat, wondering what to do with his ill-gotten gains. By now he had £1 million tucked away in odd places, and in the care of a few trusted people like Mavis. Derek had helped 'invest' some of it out of sight of prying eyes before returning it, considerably bloated by yet more illegal interest.

Cash under the mattress seemed a primitive and risky investment strategy in this day and age, but Mark could hardly bank it in the current account he shared with Grace at Lloyds TSB. A bung was a bung, after all, even if he had no idea where it came from really.

Although he and his wife still co-habited, and even enjoyed a sexual relationship on an occasional basis, he had grown used to sleeping alone in Woodford. He was not the victim, and she was not the enemy. It was a lifestyle choice they both gratefully made. Sex was very good, if irregular, their mutual anger still a big element of the energy vented during it, but the loss of individual space was not a price that either wished to pay for such pleasures.

With Julia it was different. He wanted to hold her all night.

To be there at her side was to be at peace with the world. To study her every detail and every movement was a joy. Her removal from the list of Unfinished Business and their ongoing sexual adventures had elevated her to a more meaningful place in the Cohen world order.

Ironically, Grace shared much the same feelings for Andrew. She no longer needed to tame the dominant male, and had begun to respond to Andrew's vulnerabilities rather than competing with his strengths. Grace knew he was a father figure to her, which was hardly surprising given the weak casting of Harry Christmas in that role, but their relationship had become much more than that.

The odd thing was that both Mark and Grace were coming to respect each other again. He had impressed her lately, it was true, but Grace knew that she would be in the driving seat of their relationship in the future. She felt she needed to inflict some retribution and punishment for his previous neglect, if she were ever to move their relationship forward again. Still, it was not out of the question, and the possibility did intrigue her.

They had shared much of their lives for better or worse and had three children – it was hard to admit failure after that huge mutual investment, to shrug lightly and just walk away.

But they both had things to go to now, not just things to run away from. Whatever they chose to do would mean sacrificing something as well as gaining something.

If things had remained as they were at that moment, the smart money would have been on a compromise and a reconciliation, followed by a try at another probably doomed attempt.

After achieving most of his list, such a route back offered a certain symmetry to Mark, but it was deeply unappealing in its timidity. His new life was an addictive cocktail of sexy thrills and heady spills, while this other, safer life looked about as addictive as a long queue at the checkout in the local supermarket.

He was not there yet emotionally. There was still a healthy glow in his embers. Indeed, he had recently stretched himself still further, spending 'quality time' with the Conservative Party and managing, at least in part, to synchronise their political goals with his own ambitions.

The fund-raising part of their organisation had spotted his commercial prowess, his money, and his reputation for reaching out to the population of 'Middle England'. They did not seem to mind that he had fibbed on the Charlton show about how he was already being courted to join them. It was taken as a prompt for them to act and not as an indiscretion by him.

Through the post, he had received an invitation to join a small gathering of influential party people, mixed with current media movers and shakers, at a private dining club discreetly located close to Berkeley Square.

This group included a Shadow Minister, who in a previous life had been the chief executive of a major electrical retailing chain. Apparently a commissioning editor at Sky TV was also going to be there, and Mark could not resist the lure of more access to publicity, let alone the thrill of being noticed by such an A-list elite.

It was a cold, dark evening and he felt that Jack might be taking the blame later, so he took a taxi. Avoiding the prospect of another embarrassing arrival in a smelly old blue Proton, he ordered a chauffeur-driven Mercedes from a new limo service in the area.

An efficient text announced that his carriage had arrived and he adjusted his cuffs and collar as he approached the gleaming long-wheelbase version of 5-litre German S-class engineering.

As he shut the heavy Aga-weighted door with a satisfying clunk and admired its leather and walnut facings, a familiar pungent odour greeted his nostrils. The one-time mini-cab driver turned to him and proclaimed proudly, 'Hello, sir. Nice to see you again. As you can tell, I've upgraded since we last met. Life is much sweeter in a Mercedes, don't you think?'

Unable to hold himself back, Mark replied, 'Clearly not in the underarm department...'

The journey proceeded in utter silence, with the windows lowered, until they reached St Matthew's Club. The back door was icily opened for him to get out. There was no eye contact between the men, and Mark hoped this was not an omen for the evening ahead.

To hell with him, Mark thought, he needed to know. Be brave, Mark Cohen, hold your nerve. Bring it on...

The doorman, in a top hat and green uniform, nodded as he admitted Mark into a different, altogether more classy world than he had experienced before.

He was shown into a private dining room which, despite its scale, held only a single round table. The 1970s TV series *Upstairs Downstairs* immediately sprang to mind and he surveyed the area for Gordon Jackson, the butler. He smiled at the care with which the napkins had been folded into their silver napkin rings. Just then, a large freckled hand was extended towards him. It belonged to a huge ginger-haired man in a double-breasted blazer.

'Hello,' boomed the voice, blowing Mark a centre parting. 'You must be Mark Cohen.' It was Leon Philpot, a senior Tory and fund-raiser who was co-host of this little soirée with Roger

Fulton, a Shadow Minister.

'Delighted to meet you,' said a younger man of around Mark's age, dressed formally, though more Boss than Savile Row. 'I watched you on the Charlton show and thought you might enjoy this sort of thing. Natural communicators are so rare, and you came across as having the common touch.'

'Praise indeed,' said Mark. 'I have the advantage of having the common touch because I am not so much rare as, actually, deeply common.'

'So am I,' whispered Roger, 'but don't tell anyone.'

A bond was forged between these grammar school boys, and the night rolled on with Mark telling stories of his life and his hopes for the Eyes of the World and the world in general.

'Sorry I said that I had already been approached to enter politics,' he said to Roger to one side. 'I got a bit carried away with myself.'

'No problem, dear chap,' said Roger, 'we all thought it was a great idea. And you seem full of them.'

When the dessert was finally served, Mark excused himself and went in search of the loos. He made for stall number two which clearly displayed the word 'vacant' in the rectangular brass-framed lock.

He pushed the door and entered the cubicle, which disappointingly was not entirely enclosed, being open above head height and below ankle level. As an experienced coke snorter, this did not faze him but was an annoyance, as it required him to be more discreet, and to flush the loo to cover the noisier parts of the ritual.

As he took a packet of Colombian fairy dust from his trouser pocket and began to chop it up with a small, silver blade, he noticed that someone else had entered the toilet immediately to his left.

The same chopping noises could be heard from within and, so the pair's ritual became synchronised. Mark peered under the separating partition and saw Roger on his knees hunched over the lavatory seat. The brandy got the better of common sense and he impulsively spoke up.

'Need a decent chopper?'

'Piss off,' came the reply, then a giggle that turned into uncontrollable rib-aching laughter from them both. Mark passed the solid silver blade under the partition.

They walked back to the table together like naughty school-boys returning from the headmaster's office.

The discussion about more lofty matters brought them back to maturity and, with Mark and Roger behaving like a pair of hunting lions, everyone was coaxed into having opinions about everything. Mark honed in on Garry Barnett, the Sky TV executive, exchanging business cards over coffee. They were relishing an intimate debate about corruption in politics and football's influence over the sex drive of the British male.

'We must do lunch,' stated Garry.

The evening was a success. Leon said it was the best they had held in years.

So impressed with Mark were Roger and Leon in particular, that his name was spread throughout the organisation in record time. The guilty cocaine moment had somehow made Roger all the more determined to nurture a friend to share and trust in such a hostile environment. Christ, he needed to laugh more.

To the Conservative Party, Mark had huge potential, miraculously raised from nowhere in particular to help them to escape from a millennium of uninterrupted Labour rule. To them, he was the logical offspring of an unlikely liaison between Dame Margaret Thatcher and Sir Bob Geldof. Terence Charlton and Bruno both approved of him, and he was in his early forties with a full head of hair. This boy could go far.

So Mark was duly called by Roger personally to explain the process of becoming a candidate, should he feel that was something he would be interested in. Oh, he was so very interested.

He was flattered to be approached so directly and privately, and took heart that he was favoured so quickly. Never one to queue for anything these days, this was preferential treatment at too lofty an altitude to ignore.

Mark wondered if a failure to return to the bosom of his family might scupper his new political challenge. The process of becoming an MP seemed laborious and to try and be faithful to one woman again felt beyond him. The two tasks combined might be too much to bear.

According to Roger it would require auditions, attending church halls filled with other hopefuls, while being observed by the local and central office representatives who would assess his suitability to the task.

Debating issues such as capital punishment and forming playground groups in the style of some low-rent reality show frankly filled Mark with dread. Queuing and hard work no longer interested him as a route to improvement since his transformation that long-ago evening on the carpet with that rat.

Reluctantly therefore he decided to trust to luck that he would be catapulted to power by some other means, but to prudently keep his options open as well. He rang Roger and said that he was flattered, and motivated, but was going to be cheeky and ask a favour.

'Is there a way I might jump the usual protocol and be fast-tracked with your private support? Then I would give it my all. Trust me, I want this but I am a man on a mission.'

'Keep in touch, Mark. Who knows where fate may take us?'

World domination was not a bad demonic dream, given he had hardly even attempted Make My Mark on his list yet, and he felt something would happen because, lately, it always did. Until that day came, he would back off and let matters take their course...

He pumped some personal wealth into Conservative campaign funds to show his intent. Where the money had come from nobody knew, or asked, as it was donated anonymously via his new best friend Roger and through the fund-raiser, Leon. The favour he gained straight away was to be put on to the advertising pitch list for the account. Once given a shot at presenting their vision for the Tories, they won the business fair and square from Greta & Wendla which had held the party for more than a decade.

This was much to the pride and pleasure of Patrick Craze, who had assumed this was an impossibly prestigious piece of business to wrestle from Greta's, at least in his lifetime.

'That's my boy,' he had said to Julia and Andrew over *Campaign* magazine's headline, 'BC in amazing Tory triumph'.

Andrew quietly blushed at the means by which Mark had won the account. Patrick could not help but boast to him how 'Mark pulled that business in by knowing that even the powerful are susceptible to human weaknesses, like a bribe'. Julia secretly glowed at the unlikely achievement, alongside Patrick's open euphoria. Results, not methods, were all that mattered to them.

In the press, there was now official talk of Mark standing as a Conservative candidate in the next general election and the Make My Mark entry on his list began to swell. Given the dwindling list of objectives which remained to be completed, and the outbreak of peace (or at least a ceasefire) on the domestic front, Mark was certainly fired up to take on the globe.

When it came to personal family relationships, Denise became a more regular confidante for the Cohen couple, particularly Grace, who had lost touch with Sammy over the years and did not have the time or energy now to repair the damage.

However, Grace did feel the need to share the secret of her relationship double-life with someone after bottling it up for so long, and that someone could only be Faith or Denise.

One evening when Mark was out, she invited Denise over for a drink. (Coffee for her, wine for Denise.) They talked about their exciting businesses, people they had lost touch with or recently met, and other superficial chatter. Then at around 10.30pm Denise asked what was on her friend's mind, as she had noticed a tension in her expressive eyebrows all evening.

'Is there something you want to tell me?' she probed.

Grace drew breath. 'Well, I've met someone special, and I care for him a lot. But I also have feelings for Mark which I'd forgotten I ever had. I don't know what to do, Den. I think I'll go mad, off my head and out of my depth all over again...'

She went on to spill all her feelings, going into detail about the hot sex and the thrill of the foreign trips, and telling her friend that her secret lover was 'the' Andrew Bond himself.

'Oh my God,' said Denise, 'or should I say, oh Mark's God!' and they both laughed.

By coincidence, Denise was due to meet Sammy the next day. They went for a curry and talked about Barry, Sammy's guilt, and Derek's surprising support and friendship for her in her time of need. Sammy was falling for him. Ever the gossip queen, she repaid Sammy's trust by telling her all about Grace's ongoing affair with Andrew Bond. All in the strictest confidence, of course.

The next day, Sammy repeated every detail to her trustworthy new partner, Derek Peterson. Unbeknown to her, this took place within earshot of Fat Dave, who was hovering silently outside the study door in Wattapenis Palace, like a monstrous humming bird. Dave had many years' experience of concealing his vast bulk from those he was spying on. Indeed, it was skulking under the hedge outside Grace's bungalow in Hillsdale Gardens, in the hope of seeing her vest removed, that had first honed his undercover skills.

Given his proximity to Derek at all times, it was easy for Dave to find out when Grace was away overseas, when Mark was away at work, and when the kids were boarding or staying at a friend's house overnight. He also knew when Vicki was working, as he asked her outright when he called one Thursday morning claiming to be delivering a package from work to Mr Cohen.

The various elements coincided to leave the Woodford house empty on Thursday afternoon quite soon after he had eavesdropped on Sammy's revelations. He asked Derek if he could take that afternoon off to run a domestic errand. His brother, Fat Kevin, could step in for him if needed, Dave ventured helpfully.

'That fat ginger wanker?' responded Del, employing a description which had haunted his brother since childhood.

Dave said nothing in reply. Some weeks before, his brother had come over late one afternoon, after visiting Barry in the Regal Furniture warehouse to buy a bed with his big-titted fiancée, Stacey. Evidently Kevin had been insulted, humiliated, beaten and then thrown out. Well qualified in thuggery, Kevin was gagging to get even in the most severe and vicious of ways.

Years earlier, Kevin had enjoyed the Peterson parental sausage mission, albeit as a young and green apprentice, and like a rabid dog had discovered the lust for blood.

After a brief description of the incident in the furniture warehouse, Fat Dave confirmed to his brother that the culprit was indeed Barry, and reminded him of the unfinished business Kevin had with him, the man who (as a teenage boy) had first coined the epithet 'fat ginger wanker' at Mark's Bar Mitzvah. Dave could have defused the situation now, but chose instead to pour petrol on the flames, then to blow on them just for good measure. Kevin was so thick and so open to his influence that it was a pleasure to wind him up.

Fat Kev went back to Regal Furniture that very evening to deal with Barry. Perhaps if he had slept on it without his brother's council, Barry might have survived with just a beating.

But to Dave, Barry's demise served a practical purpose, too. He was performing an unasked-for favour for his mentor, Derek, by removing Sammy's husband. He was leaving the coast clear for his boss to be happy and this was his duty as Del's surrogate son. Inflicting pain on Mark was a nice bonus for him, too.

Barry had been no more than meat to him. Butcher's meat.

After such a display of loyalty and Derek's new-found and insulting affection for Mark, Dave felt wholly justified in going on another mission without authority, and for mostly his own ends. But he thought he could present it as good for business too, as the pious Grace might persuade her husband to follow the straight and narrow path with the charity, if they were reunited as a true couple. Dave concluded he was acting like a saint by looking for filth.

He pulled up near the Cohens' home in Woodford one afternoon, parking out of view of any nosy neighbours. He rang the house to make sure it was empty, and there was no answer. He let himself in using a duplicate key cut from the original, borrowed from Mark's jacket pocket while it hung in the mansion's hallway a few weeks before.

Once inside, he crept about like a bloated ninja, looking in drawers and sideboards, and skimming the photo albums in the lounge. Upstairs, he went to the master bedroom, and rifled through drawers, wardrobes, pockets and linings, bags, purses and shoes. He took a couple of pairs of Grace's dirty knickers from the laundry basket, sniffed them deeply and stuffed them in his coat pocket for later.

Next he repeated the procedure in the spare bedroom, again with no joy. He did not know what he was looking for, but he was sure he would know it when he saw it. A diary, a love letter, a photograph, or... who knew what else?

Growing frustrated, he went to the twins' room, then to Poppy's room. In the wardrobe he found a red locked money box labelled 'Future Gold Mine'.

I wonder, he thought, and took it under his arm.

He left after searching the garage, loft and under-stairs cupboard, all to no avail. For all his efforts, he'd netted two pairs of knickers and a red money box that was probably full of bubble gum or, at best, some soft porn. Still, this was his last, faint hope of finding any evidence of the Grace affair.

'Why would that kind of dirt be in the kid's room?' he chided himself as he drove home, depressed and defeated.

It wouldn't be there he knew, but some hunch had made him take the box anyway. He took a screwdriver from the kitchen drawer and levered the lid of the money box off its thin metal hinges. He peered inside and chortled, 'Yo, ho, ho.'

Among some remnants of grass in a little plastic envelope, a couple of girlie diaries and a bit of loose cash, lay a few fuzzy amateur photographs and stills taken from video footage.

He stared at them with wonder and dawning realisation.

A grin as wide as a banana crept across Fat Dave's face,

exposing his irregular, ochre-coloured teeth. He felt like a lottery winner.

'Gotcha!' he shouted. 'You are a dead man walking, Skid, my old friend. Prepare for pain.'

He sat and considered how to use this photographic dynamite to inflict maximum damage on Mark and ruin Grace's fun, but without harming Derek at the same time. It took him nearly all night to work it out, but he finally got there at around 4.15am. Mark was going to get such a huge surprise. Not the Christmas present kind, but more like Pearl Harbor.

Dave giggled, shut his eyes and slept contentedly, like the well-fed butcher's dog he was at heart.

CHAPTER TWENTY

War and Pieces

Poppy had been allowed home and was now a day patient attending therapy sessions four times a week. The regular counselling was working for her, especially since Mark had accompanied her once a week in order to confront any family or personal issues that they were harbouring. They had grown closer – to her, Mark was now a man as well as a flawed father, while, to Mark, Poppy was now a young woman as well as a pain in the arse.

The twins were less wilfully independent, now that home had become a more harmonious place in which their mum and dad were able to peacefully co-exist. The couple had even kissed romantically in front of their three offspring, and were given to occasional displays of spontaneous affection. Max would always make fake gagging and retching noises whenever this happened, pushing his fingers down his throat and muttering 'Gross' or 'Get a room'.

Such general good humour was a major miracle, given the troubled history of this family.

One morning, Pat Ballcock rang Mark on his mobile.

'Hello, caller.'

'Hello, caller. That's the lovely Pat, isn't it?'

'It is,' she confirmed. 'Dr Evans was speaking to all the therapists at the Rookery, and he said to tell you that you had done a wonderful job. Grace's physical damage is not as bad as we first feared, and she is still dry and clean. A strong woman that.'

'Thanks, Pat. I did very little, but I appreciate the call. Yes, Grace is amazing in every way. I'm very proud of her.' (He meant it, too.)

Pat concluded: 'Well, it looks like you'll have to pay full price on British Airways from now on, as you won't be getting any more air miles from us! Good luck to you all. My sister says hi as well. Maybe we could meet for that lunch with George Clooney you promised me sometime. Bye, caller.'

Could life be any less troubled? Mark was warming to the notion of slowing down all the recent madness. What else did he have to prove, after all?

Forgiveness was in the air. It seemed that Grace's rehabilitation, and their reconciliation, could mark the end of his search for Redemption. Together they could return to the light, after an extended shared journey through the darkest of the dark side.

Redemption might be to grab a life for the whole Cohen household, now so tightly bonded together, after being torn apart and close to death for so long. But just when these tender shoots of reconciliation were rooting in their minds, the shit chose to really hit the fan.

From nowhere and with no warning, two vast lumps of pungent personal poo were lobbed at them with devastating accuracy by Fat Dave.

First, the picture of Grace writhing naked on top of Andrew Bond was posted to Mark at his BC office. He opened the green envelope and sprayed the mouthful of coffee all over his ordered desk. He sat there stunned for a while, wondering if it was a hoax perpetrated by those rascals in the creative department. It wasn't April 1st, was it? No, it wasn't.

After a closer inspection of the shot, he realised it was real, and broke down, weeping uncontrollably in his office in utter despair. All his worst fears and insecurities suddenly rose up to torture him, summoned by the arrival of a single picture, sent anonymously, by some unknown malevolent 'well-wisher'.

It seemed that Grace did not want him back after all. Or worse, she had wanted Andrew more than him all the time, and was laughing at him behind his back.

He wanted to die, then he wanted to introduce Bond's skull to a baseball bat, then he ached to rant and roar at Grace. He did none of these things, instead sobbing into a sodden tissue.

'Spineless twat,' he called himself and went 'home' to Julia's place early without telling anyone, even Ellie.

Meanwhile, back at the South Woodford family home, a copy of the latest *Readers' Wives* porn magazine was hand-delivered through the Cohen letterbox, addressed to Grace and bearing the scrawled legend, 'Private and Confidential'. A bookmark was helpfully placed between pages 22 and 23.

Grace opened the envelope, saw its pornographic contents and went to throw it in the bin without a second glance. However, the bookmark stopped her in her tracks, and she opened the magazine at the sign-posted pages.

'Oh, my God, I do not believe it... no. No. NO. The bastard... the bitch...' She screamed out loud, and the sound was gradually replaced by an interior cry of anguish.

The magazine featured a three-page spread of her bastard

husband, unmistakably screwing her bitch mother, and to add insult to considerable injury the photos were obviously taken in their own spare bedroom. The headline read 'Mother in Whore'.

When Mark eventually crawled home to Woodford, he shoved a copy of the Grace/Andrew picture under her bedroom door without comment and tiptoed past silently. He entered the spare room to discover that she had left the *Readers' Wives* magazine open at pages 22 and 23 on his pillow.

What followed was not so much a showdown between any of the named and shamed, but a mental meltdown of the individual parties involved. Muffled sobbing and a grinding of teeth were a constant background noise all through that night, but there were no explosions. It was the calm before the storm.

Needless to say, any hopes of a fresh start or a new partnership between them died utterly and forever in an instant that day. Fat Dave had achieved his version of Pearl Harbor. This was war and he was the Japanese. By the next morning, the papers had got hold of the story. The *Sun* headline read 'Lies of the World'.

It went on to reveal how Mark had been having an affair with his mother-in-law, while serving on the board of the Eyes of the World with his wife Grace. They called him a 'love rat', a 'revel devil' and, more simply, a 'cad'. The article also claimed, 'You can never trust an ad man', and went on to talk about BC (wittily glossed as 'B*stard Creeps') and included a picture of Patrick Craze with the caption, 'This man hired the love rat, will he fire him?' This was yet more damaging for Mark, like a last kick in the nuts after being beaten up and left for dead.

The game is definitely up, thought Mark. I'm screwed.

Meanwhile the children's reaction to the exposé, after a general chorus of 'What the...', was to discuss if their undercover roles in the operations codenamed 'Hi-Gene' and 'WrinklyGate' were blown. They met in the 'emergency war-room' (Poppy's bedroom) that morning.

Max opened the court case. 'Poppy, you twat,' he stated for the prosecution. 'I think I can speak for both myself and the right honourable Sam-wise Cohen QC when I say, what the bleedin' hell happened?'

Sam interrupted. 'May I add at this point in the proceedings, and with our total respect for you as our older and more mature sibling, you cunt.'

Poppy replied: 'Listen, the security box was nicked.'

'Oh really! How convenient!' said Max.

'Along with your emerald-encrusted crown and sceptre I suppose,' added Sam.

'Look, I am in the do-do as deeply as you two and have nothing to gain by going to the papers. So, are we up to our ankles, necks or drowning in it?'

Eventually the general consensus was that they were 'not in the poo' and they should play it 'by ear'.

'Case dismissed, M'Lud,' proclaimed Max, 'due to lack of evidence.'

Back in his Chingford mansion, Derek Peterson was not in such a relieved mood. 'What the bloody hell is going on?' he shouted. 'How did *Readers' Wives* and the *Sun* get hold of this stuff?'

Fat Dave stood quietly, suppressing a smirk of satisfaction and restraining himself from claiming this as a triumph of his planning, initiative and loyalty. First, he sensibly grunted one question, just to test the temperature of the water with his boss.

'Dunno. Is it important?'

'Is it important? IS IT IMPORTANT? You thick sack of shite. Without Mark there, we can kiss goodbye to our little money-spinner tout de suite.

'This is a disaster. He was the reason we had the contract. I'd bunged him so that, if there were problems, he'd be willing and able to dig us out. My insurance policy was that I could put the squeeze on the little runt any time. With this sort of attention, the authorities will be all over the books like rabid lice on a dirty scalp. We have to shut it all down, right now.

'I can promise you, someone is going to lose a hand, a head or their bollocks, or all of the above, over this cock-up. Sharpen your hacksaw, Dave, we're going back into the butchery business one more time.'

Dave no longer had to struggle to stop himself smirking. Instead, a deep, fearful frown was etched into his brow. He had to think quickly, which was not easy for him.

Meanwhile, in the bungalow at 53 Hillsdale Gardens, the daily copy of the *Sun* dropped on to the doormat and Harry Christmas carried it to the breakfast table. He sat reading the sports section, while Gene sat opposite him staring at the front page in horror. It showed her bare arse, blown up large and printed in colour for the delectation of its millions of readers. Gene's jaw dropped open. This was a nightmare. She would wake up in a minute.

Harry glanced up and saw his wife's expression so turned the paper round to see the main picture and lurid headline ('Lies of the World'), then swallowed hard. He looked once into his wife's eyes before calmly returning to the sports section.

God bless that emotionally constipated man, thought Gene.

Grace was less reserved. She rang her mother and, before Gene could say more than 'Hello….', her daughter began a rant which lasted without pause for a full twenty minutes. It felt to Gene like twenty hours stretched on the rack, with thumbscrews attached as a bonus.

The tirade went something along the lines of:

'How could you?

'How could you screw my husband? He's your son-in-law,

for Christ's sake!

'You've never loved me, and this is proof of your lack of respect for me, too.

'You've betrayed me, my father, and killed any love I ever had for you.

'I don't want to see you, and I don't want you to see my children.

'I have no mother, I'm an orphan, but then that is clearly what you have always wanted.

'I was a mistake and, if you'd had your way, I would never have been born at all.

'I hope you're happy now. You got your wish, you bitch.

'I won't be coming to your funeral, but I hope that I'll miss it some time very soon.

'Give your favourite child Mary my regards, and tell her to drop dead too.

'That would make two burials that I don't have to go to.

'My hate, loathing and contempt for you are so great that they cannot be measured.

'So I won't bother to try. You're not worth it.

'Goodbye forever, bitch.'

The phone was hung up with a slam and Gene was left in floods of tears, overcome with grief, guilt and remorse for what she'd done. She turned to the sink to wash up the dirty breakfast bowls, and Harry stood up, stepped behind her and quietly whispered in her ear, 'I still love you, baby.'

Gene looked at him with watery red eyes, smiled through her sobs, and suddenly knew just how lucky she was to have Harry Christmas. That night, she made love to him like it was the first time, and he was the only man she had ever wanted.

West Ham won that Saturday, 3-0 against Aston Villa at home, and it was like a very happy Christmas for Harry

Christmas, even though it was still only October.

Grace was in a less forgiving mood than her dad, instead becoming a ruthless predator with no room for mercy. Vengeance would not be enough; she would have to destroy Mark. If nothing was left standing after the blast, then so be it.

She telephoned her Rookery buddy Faith, who was now back at work as a journalist at the *Daily Mail*.

'My word, Grace! That husband of yours really is a pig. Don't just be angry any more, you have my full permission to hate him now!' Adding, 'Do you want to rub salt into his wounds and make him squirm?'

'With your help, Faith, I can do more than that.'

The next day, an article detailing everything that was reprehensible about the celebrity monster Mark Cohen appeared exclusively in the *Mail*, based on Faith's interview with the wronged wife, Grace Cohen. (Grace was paid £20,000 for it, but she was not concerned about the money.) It ran as a series in the paper for a week, with television commercials to promote the saga of the rise and fall of a two-faced bastard.

Mark was, among other things, described as a drug-taking womaniser and inadequate lover. A power-crazed beast with no talent for anything except feathering his own nest, he had driven Grace to drink and was a poor father, too.

The article also made it clear that the 'wronged wife, Grace Cohen, would now become the Chief Executive of 'the Eyes of the World', and that the *Mail* would be contributing double its editorial fee directly towards 'her' cause. She was a saint and, unlike the evil pervert that she married, she was not in it for the money. 'She has been insistent that she makes no personal gain from this incident and that her work continues solely for the benefit of the world's children.'

The scoop, which mostly centred on Mark and his disgrace,

ran a full four pages, and included quotes from ex-colleagues, ex-lovers (including Kerry Goldstein, the thwarted swimmer) and even his neighbours. They spoke of him rearing giant rats and flinging them into their garden 'as some kind of perverted sport'.

Mark was ground to dust. He was no longer the confident, swaggering winner of just a few weeks earlier.

He sat in Julia's flat with the curtains drawn, huddled on the lounge floor with his head in his hands, eerily echoing that memorable evening in Woodford back in February. The maggots were missing, as was the rat, but the darkness was as deep and depressing as it had ever been then. He wasn't even motivated to take any photos of the scene. Mark preferred to feel these days, rather than filter out his emotions.

As a momentary distraction from his agony, he wondered how the pictures of him having sex with Gene could have been taken. A hidden micro camera placed by a journalist or private detective? This seemed too far-fetched and probably illegal.

Could it have been MI5 or MI6? Perhaps he represented a risk too far for the politicians and they wanted to get rid of a security threat. But that too seemed implausible.

And then, quite suddenly in a flash of clarity he knew exactly who had done it and how this disaster had been so skilfully accomplished. Which two characters were smarter than journalists, detectives and the entire British Secret Service put together?

'Samuel and Max.'

He smiled just a little, pinched the bridge of his nose hard and shouted in a Homer Simpson voice, 'DOH!'

It broke his rage, and then he immediately remembered the image of Grace on top of Andrew again, and the twins' crime paled into insignificance. He would speak to them another day when he could be more rational about it. For now, self-pity had made its Sinatra-style comeback and filled his brain with pain once more.

Is that it, then? Am I back in hell once again, he wondered. What else can happen to me?

He shouldn't have asked that question. His mobile rang and Patrick Craze was on the line. 'Listen Mark, it's hard to say this, so I'll come straight out with it. You're fired. Those are the breaks, I'm afraid. Your luck ran out, that's all. We'll send your stuff over in the next few days. Good luck.'

The WCC had also called to say that his involvement in the Eyes of the World project was no longer welcome, and that they would seize his shares under the clause in his contract covering gross misconduct.

Clearly he was certain that any aspirations towards a political career were as dead as his marriage and his reputation. If a man ever needed the reassuring hug of a sympathetic friend and lover, this was that moment.

The front door rattled with the sound of a key being urgently inserted into a worn old lock. Julia Hardy-Roberts walked into the lounge in a highly excited state.

Mark looked at her, and smiled with gratitude. Before he could utter the words he was bursting to say ('Thank God you are here...'), she began one of her trademark one-way broadcasts and pre-empted him.

'Listen, I have some news,' she said. 'Patrick called me up and I was promoted today. They made me Chairman! Yes, your old job my love, and your old office in the Tower of Power too. Darling. At last! And it wasn't my bum that got me over the last chauvinistic hurdle, it was your inspiration and confidence in me. Thank you, my lovely boy.'

Mark, unsurprised by her lack of sensitivity, just stood and beamed blankly from ear to ear and ran to squeeze her tightly, as though genuinely pleased.

In his ears all he really heard was 'Blah, blah, blah.'

He was still unable to get a word in about his predicament, despite his urgent looks and increasingly desperate hand signals. She went on, oblivious. 'Listen, I've been thinking for a while now. I'm the breadwinner round here...'

Julia mimed pulling a pair of braces out with her thumbs while rocking back on her heels, like a plutocratic big-shot.

'And I think it's about time we broke up,' she said with very little emotion.

'Oh...' he whispered. His final hope had just kicked him full on in his exposed bollocks. The pit of his stomach was knotted, his bowels were loose, and he felt dizzy.

Pure rage grew in him rapidly, but he stood there outwardly emotionless. He then moved almost in slow motion, gathering up his personal items before calmly walking right up to within an inch of Julia's face. He stared into her eyes unblinking and delivered four icy words, spraying his breath into them so that it made her flinch away from the toxic mixture of bile and saliva.

'Bring it on, bitch.'

It was the final straw. Unfinished Business no longer represented past frustrations but had been reframed and refuelled in the present. Head-on confrontation and payback were the items on the new agenda.

Skid drove off at maximum wheel-spinning speed towards Soho Square, heading for a showdown with Andrew Bond. On the way he felt weirdly calm, listening to Classic FM and thinking beautiful thoughts about clubbing Bond's cranium to a fine paste.

He screeched to a halt in the car park, defiantly blocking in Patrick's Lamborghini, slammed the car door and stomped purposefully into the hushed reception of his former employer.

Cherry said cheerfully, 'Hi there, Mark.'

'Fuck off, grandma,' was his curt reply.

'Charming,' she said, glad now that she hadn't gone on a date with the rude pig. Still, she was concerned that Mark had lost it this time and might actually be dangerous. What should she do, she wondered?

The high-speed lift whisked Mark to the top floor. He was now talking to himself like a homeless derelict with too much booze in him. He stormed out of the lift and along the corridor, still muttering, and barged into Andrew 'God' Bond's offfice.

Andrew sat alone and serene behind his enormous walnut desk. He had the look of a man who had found peace through born-again religion, or perhaps a hippy high on some very strong skunk. He was too relaxed, given the loud bang with which his door bounced back against the wall as Mark stormed in, a murderous expression on his tortured face and hatred shining from his eyes.

'You bloody bastard. I worshipped and served you for twenty years, Bond. You were my hero. But you're just scum after all, just like all the other weak losers out there,' Mark shouted.

He pulled out the photo of Grace and Andrew screwing and, tears welling up in his eyes, pushed it into Bond's curiously impassive face.

Bond said nothing. Instead, he went ashen and blue-lipped, then clutched his chest, collapsing in slow motion to the floor beside his desk, whispering hoarsely, 'Help me...' just as Grace had done that terrible February evening.

'Oh no, not again, not again, not bloody again. Oh bollocks...' said Mark. He picked up the phone, fully intending to call for an ambulance, as he was sure Bond was having a heart attack. Then he did something quite alien to him. He put the receiver down, sat next to Andrew Bond and stared into his eyes.

A shark has black, fathomless discs for eyes, as did the dead rat that lay under the sofa in Mark's lounge that same February evening. Now Mark had them too, and they were looking straight and unblinkingly into the face of his erstwhile God.

'Just die, Bond. Make it quick,' he whispered, but didn't touch him. Bond smiled at that, despite the fear and pain he was suffering, recognising that he was paying the price for his own unprincipled behaviour. Somehow, the feud between them had vanished like a puff of smoke. Life, and death, can be odd that way. He was about to meet his maker, and apologise in person for being mistaken for him all these years. Andrew knew God had a sense of humour.

'I love you, you bastard, now slip away, there's a good chap,' muttered Mark. Bond smiled again at this intimacy and obediently slipped into unconsciousness, sighing his last breath. Mark smiled and felt elated at the sudden surge of power that swept through his veins.

Cherry had been standing at the office doorway and had seen Andrew die, and noted Mark's whispers and smiles, hunched over the corpse like a vampire. She ran downstairs in terror and rang for an ambulance. She did not say anything about what she had seen, too scared to tangle with the owner of that demonic face.

Mark had taken the back stairs to the car park and was nowhere to be seen.

For someone who prided herself on taking no shit, Cherry was spooning the stuff down her gullet by the shovel load, but she would not remain happy keeping that indigestible secret for long.

For now though, back in the safe haven of her Putney flat, Cherry did her best to drown out that horrible event she'd witnessed with a bottle of gin.

CHAPTER TWENTY-ONE

Politically Incorrect

Derek and Sammy were now together.

Sammy felt safe with this kind, older man, and was drawn to the sensitivity, love and tenderness he showed her. Money was never a concern for her – she did not understand it, covet it, or want any part of it. Derek simply made the nightmares go away, making her feel safely cocooned in bubble wrap.

For his part, Del was happier than he had ever been in his life. He was disappointed to have to let the Eyes of the World scam go but, as he had already made mega money from it, he was pragmatic about the situation.

After all, he had not been caught, and his plan had proved a winner. That still made him The Daddy. He could hold his head up high among the fake terracotta-tanned faces in the Blue Mondays bar in Buckhurst Hill, and that was the main thing.

However, he did feel the need to start a witch hunt to discover who had leaked the incriminating pictures. The application of harsh justice to the culprit was necessary to reassure Derek that he had not been 'turned over' by anyone. This had never happened before, and he had standards to maintain.

A killing was on the menu, and it didn't really matter who it was, or what body part happened to be on the chopping block. Ego and reputation both demanded satisfaction, but Sammy need not know about that unsavoury side of his character. This was purely business.

Helpfully, Fat Dave provided his beloved mentor with the identity of the traitor. Unsurprisingly though, he did not own up to committing the crime himself. He was not that stupid.

Shockingly to anyone who did not know Dave well, he chose the safest scapegoat he could think of and he did so without breaking into a sweat.

'Derek, it pains me to tell you but it was my own brother, Fat Kevin, who stole those photos and sold them on. I can prove it,' he lied, 'but all you need to know is that my loyalty to you is so strong I'm prepared to wipe out my own flesh and blood, if you say the word. Your wish is my command.'

Derek's eyes welled up. He gripped Dave's shoulder with affection and said: 'Kill the fat ginger wanker.'

So Fat Dave obediently killed his own brother, in an unnecessarily gruesome and messy manner. He used rusty blades and jagged saws just for the fun of it, while wearing an apron emblazoned with a picture of a smiling Delia Smith. The bloody deed was done in an old lock-up in Dagenham, the tightly bound Kevin crying, pleading and screaming even before the first cut was made into his plump, white limbs.

He did not realise that years of raw, loveless survival had transformed his brother into a cold killer who cared nothing for anyone, even his closest kin.

The speciality sausages which went on sale that month in the delicatessens of East and South London were a little fatty and not quite up to the quality of the Greek pork and British beef of years before.

Later that week, Fat Dave raised the subject of his brother's death with Derek.

'He was a fat ginger wanker, and bloody useless. He couldn't even make a decent banger when he was dead! To be honest, I never liked him much anyway. Turns out Barry was right all along, the poor dead oaf.'

'Good riddance to both of them,' Derek said with a contented smile, thinking about taking Sammy to the Bel-Sit Italian pizza restaurant in Woodford Green later that evening. She was easily pleased, and asked for very little, which charmed him.

Unaware of all this, a few miles away, Mark was sitting on the lounge floor of the Cohen residence, leaning back against the base of the sofa. His once mighty list was strewn out in front of him. Things had changed since Andrew's funeral (held in a Surrey crematorium, with more than five hundred people there to pay their last respects).

Grace had relapsed into drinking, and Mark had become super-attentive and indispensable in the role of covering for her with the children. It gave Mark a purpose, and at least he could delude himself that he was choosing to turn his efforts toward the Redemption element of his list. It represented a faint hope signifying that all might not be lost, although, in his heart of hearts, he believed it was over on every front.

Grace was not very proud of herself but, on the other hand, she had bloody earned this position of power over Mark. She knew that the right thing to do would have been to kick him out, divorce the bastard, and strip him of everything (with considerable help from the legal system).

Instead, she sheltered herself with the comforting platitude, 'I'm doing it all for the good of the children'.

Grace knew that she had failed Poppy, Sam and Max in recent years, and she could not deal with that failure. She preferred to focus on her husband's faults rather than confront her own issues. To her it was mostly about torturing Mark, and gaining some payback for her years of suffering.

She relished the idea of his servitude. She also knew that she was barely holding down the CEO role at the Eyes of the World, as her booze habit, or 'pick-me-up' as she called it, was getting beyond the stage where she had any choice in the matter.

Grace barely spoke to her husband unless it was to bark orders at him as she left for the office each morning. The preferred communication route was yellow Post-it notes stuck everywhere, patronisingly setting out his menial tasks for the day.

'Take the rubbish out.'

'Buy milk, bread and whisky.'

'Get me some Lil-lets.'

There was never a 'thank you' or 'please' or any kind of warm greeting offered, but Mark never complained. He saw it as fair punishment and came back for more like a dog that has been kicked too often. Yes, she had cheated on him with Bond but Mark knew that he'd helped push her down that route because of his past neglectful behaviour and anyway, compared to his crimes against holy matrimony, she was still just a beginner. The word 'hypocrite' would hover in the periphery of Mark's mind whenever he felt a flash of anger about her affair with Bond now.

Poppy and the twins were happy with the family setup as

long as their father was close. They were used to the drunken mother scenario, but a dad as the buffer zone represented a great improvement.

The twins were faring less well at school, though. Many of their friends, who represented the inner circle of coolest kids, were suddenly not including them in their web of information. Max remarked to his brother: 'Is it me or are you getting less texts than usual?'

'Thought it was bust until I got some dodgy sextext.'

They walked into the common room and the lively discussions among eight of their so-called bros suddenly stopped. The twins turned tail and walked out, hearing giggles, no doubt aimed at them, just as they cleared the door and entered the echoing corridor.

'Christ, Sam, I think we just turned into tragic dorks coz of our grandma's norks.'

They were not happy.

And nor was Mark.

He was growing restless at being a house husband and invisible dogsbody on the edge of things. He had started to wonder what he might do with his time now, other than be there for everyone else's needs, like one of the bored housewives he had interviewed for the Primo pitch a lifetime ago. The days ticked by, the school runs and washing-up were ever present, and his only company for long periods of the day was Vicki.

One day, as he was polishing the floor tiles alongside her to a chorus of 'Oh what a beautiful morning', he stopped in his tracks.

'I've got it!' he shouted.

Vicki turned to him and enquired, 'What, sir?'. She did not know if he was announcing that he had cancer, had won the

Lottery or had found the missing floor cloth that she had hunted for that very morning.

Mark knew the idea was ambitious. It was outrageous in fact. His heart stepped up a couple of gears, as suddenly he knew where destiny was taking him next. It required him not to aim low, but to carry on where he had left off.

He got on the phone to his old contacts in politics, the media and PR. He talked animatedly for hours, in his best pitch-winning voice, with a compelling and logical argument which was crystallising even as he spoke the words for the first time.

Then the following afternoon, Grace was uncharacteristically working from home. While Mark was hoovering, she was collating a new batch of artwork just delivered from Iraq in readiness for the art board to evaluate. She was in a good mood and, as he placed a cup of tea on the coffee table, she unthinkingly said, 'Ta.'

Seizing the moment, he summoned up some courage and asked a direct question. 'Darling?' Grace looked up and bristled at this term of endearment. 'Would you mind if I applied to become an MP and fought the next election as an independent candidate?'

'Knock yourself out,' she casually replied, unable to suppress a smirk of enjoyment at his next, no doubt self-inflicted bout of public humiliation. He said no more and returned to the hall floor tiles, and she went back to her work, not giving it a second thought.

A month later, in the period leading up to the general election, a new independent candidate for Islington South appeared on the freshly printed ballot cards: 'Mark Cohen, Independent, Conservative Ideals'. But there was much, much more than this summary of his principles to expose to an unsuspecting public.

Mark's masterstroke was to realise that his celebrity was still highly potent. This, despite the unfortunate slurs and accusations which had seen his popularity plunge after the heady days of Eyes of the World launch parties and Charlton show appearances.

His skill was in being a brilliant judge of the public mood and its willingness to back plucky losers as well as winners, if they demonstrated a refreshing honesty. And he had lost all fear of consequences now. Mark was back hovering far above everyone else, all helplessly held back by their fear of failure or rejection. Next in his crusade for an unlikely maiden election victory, he unleashed his nuclear PR weapon.

CHAPTER TWENTY-TWO

Don't Let the Sun Go Down on Me

One Saturday morning Julia awoke in her Borough den, aware of the empty space next to her. The young blond, graduate boy who had enthusiastically tried to impress her last night had all the character of a mannequin. It was just too easy; like a Chinese meal, it left her quickly feeling hungry again.

After he was kicked out (with a wave of her foot protruding from the satin sheet and with the curt instruction 'Dismissed, thanks for coming...'), she recognised this early hours routine as an annoying itch that demanded to be scratched.

It was not going to be enough for her, ever.

She pulled on a comfy pink towelling dressing gown and picked up the papers that had been delivered. Sitting at her kitsch bar having a light breakfast of fresh sliced pear and instant coffee, she tried to wake up fully.

Julia unfolded the *Sun* and, after reading the headlines, turned through the pages listlessly – until she reached a double-page spread which demanded her full attention. Half-chewed pear pulp dribbled from her mouth, pooling into her lap as she read on.

It featured a picture of a devilishly smiling Mark Cohen and brutally listed his life's sins. Drugs, sexual acts, tax avoidance, mistreating his wife, affairs, and even the incident where Vicki cleaned up his vomit as he slumped in front of her.

The end line said, 'Britain is alone against the world. Wouldn't you rather the Devil was fighting on your side?', adding, 'Mark Cohen, nothing to hide, everything to prove. Trust me, I'm the Devil.'

Julia held her hand over her mouth before erupting into laughter. Her mind floated back to when Mark had taken on Patrick Craze at BC for the first time. Back to the pitch triumph that he had outrageously orchestrated with such conviction and verve. Back to his dominance, even when faced with the high-voltage sex toys she had displayed in order to intimidate her prey in the private dungeon. No one had ever been a better pupil, or graduated to become the dungeon master before.

Now, just when he was vanquished and discarded by everybody, trust him to take on the entire population of Great Britain, she thought. 'That man never fails to surprise me,' she whispered, reaching for her mobile phone.

She'd really had enough of a diet made up solely of those mannequins. She texted Mark and suggested they meet up very, very soon.

Elsewhere, the impact of Mark's ad campaign was huge too. He had taken out double-page spreads in all the national and local newspapers, paid for from his considerable fortune of amassed bungs. He booked them all for the same day, so that it would be too late to pull them if the authorities thought his message too political or unduly heavyweight.

He appeared on *Newsnight* on BBC2 and the national news on BBC1 and Channel 4, and featured on Radio 4, on the cover of *Esquire* and in numerous other consumer magazines, plus all the national newspapers. The debate raged as to whether or not he was suitable even to stand as a candidate.

He went down a storm hosting *Have I Got News for You*, too. Practically everyone in Britain now knew who he was. He was charming, funny, honest and clever, and no longer a mere perverted, womanising crook. Mark became a complete media tart, an omnipresent rent-a-gob. 'Have mouth, will travel' was his motto, and it worked. But now he needed some weight behind his campaign. It was time for stage two of the operation. He called his Tory contact, Roger Fulton.

'Hi, it's Mark Cohen. Can you speak?'

A long pause followed but after a time Roger confidently replied: 'Hi, how are you doing? Talk about playing with fire! Being in politics you come to expect scandal, but usually exposure happens after being elected and not before you even reach the starting gate! If I had any sense, I would just cut you off right now but... bedding your mother in law? I don't mind admitting I am in awe of your chutzpah – but never quote me on that. Anyway, sorry about the rambling lecture but you caught me by surprise. I suppose I'm asking – how can I help, dear chap?'

'Well, as you know by now, I have decided to fight this general election as an independent, but I do want to test the water with you about my long-term plans and how they may benefit the Tory Party, which I'd like to serve one day.'

Roger was left speechless – something unheard of in ten years of his political career.

'I actually think I can pull it off, Roger,' Mark said.

Still reeling, Roger managed finally to rustle up a reply. 'If you honestly think that all this PR and revelations about your private life might cut it – and you are the media expert, I suppose – then I guess I should talk to some people back at HQ. But I can tell you right now, I see a blot on the landscape, Mark – the state of play between you and your good lady.'

Mark inadvertently let rip a cacophony of wind from his pants. Even his body instinctively understood the accuracy of Roger's statement – and the impossibility of addressing it.

Roger continued: 'You know Middle England is still quite conservative with a small c, and, in order for them to even consider forgiving you, they might need to witness a full and convincing reconciliation. You know, happy again, love conquers all, a changed man but better for the experience. Understood?'

'Roger, Roger, over and out,' said Mark.

It will take a lot more than Jack Daniels and Valium to put this back together, Mark thought.

Roger in the meantime returned to base and consulted the statistics boffins for ammunition before braving the party powerful. The independent research company, which collected data from a large panel of the electorate, continuously polled public opinion on various topical issues.

These last weeks' results were showing some unique tracking trends. It was becoming clear that a significant slice of the affluent, young and wavering Labour voters were excited and broadly supportive of this searingly honest approach by a politician.

However, as Roger had predicted, the lack of a wife, or Grace in particular, was beginning to have a negative impact on Mark's progress.

Roger had told Mark the news in an optimistic tone, but

tinged the delivery with firmness: 'Read my lips. Bloody do what it takes to win this and get Grace to co-operate. And do it now...'

Mark took this order on board. He had arranged to take Grace out to dinner to celebrate her success at opening yet another gallery café in a new territory, Dubai. He opted for his new favourite restaurant, St Alban, where Mac, the ex-maître d' of The Ivy, had recently moved. Mark took care to brief Mac to make a huge fuss of her and largely ignore him.

'No problem. Who are you anyway?' he had replied. 'Quite frankly, she is the celebrity these days.'

You wait, he thought, just you sodding well wait...

He and Grace took their seats in the favoured corner, opposite the entrance, where one could get a panoramic view of the diners. Tom Toumazis of Disney was having a close family dinner and nodded at Grace warmly before turning back to his wife Helen with a kiss. David Emin from the Mirror Group, a short man resembling Morocco Mole from the 60s *Secret Squirrel* cartoon, mouthed a greeting to Mark and gave the Barry-like wanker sign.

'Charming,' said Grace.

Vanessa Redgrave, Ricky Gervais and Lenny Henry raised the level of celebrity star value though, even if they did only say hi to Grace and ignore Mark completely.

After a few pleasantries, and an excellent pork belly which appealed to Mark's Kosher upbringing, Grace asked: 'What is the fish of the day?'

The waiter replied: 'It's Brill.'

Mark couldn't resist interjecting with, 'I'm sure it is, but what is the fish of the day?'

Grace, not amused, just glared at him.

The conversation then became more serious as Mark

needed to raise the subject of his imminent ambitions.

'Grace, I know I do not deserve to ask anything of you, ever.'

'True,' she retorted, 'so don't bother then.'

He persevered. 'The Eyes of the World was originally my creation, and you now do a wonderful job. I absolutely admire and respect what you are doing. You know that don't you? It would not exist without you.'

'And?'

'You know I'm doing this election thing?'

'I cannot believe you are, but yes?'

He swallowed a glass of Chablis. 'I need you.'

Grace smiled, and sat there staring at him like a cat playing with a mouse. 'Well?'

'Well, the bottom line is that I can't win this, even fight it, without you by my side. I don't expect you to mean it or anything...'

'I should hope not,' she whispered harshly, out of Dame Judi Dench's earshot, who had acknowledged her at just that moment. 'Why should I, Mark? Why, in all that's right and fair, should I support you in any way?'

'Because it will take your Eyes of the World organisation to a completely new level if I do win, and provide lots of free promotion for it even if I don't. It will help the underprivileged kids out there.'

Grace just sat there and listened.

Mark continued. 'Life is about helping others, and not being selfish. I know I need to put something back, as I am a self-centred tosser, and, for once, I am happy to be in the shadows to champion your superior skills. Show me the way to being a better person and worthy of your respect.'

He paused, trying to judge if any of this was making an impact. Her face was giving nothing away.

He went in for the kill. 'Most importantly, this will make our own poor bloody children proud of us both. Surely they deserve that after what we have done to them? We've both caused our kids to be tortured and insecure for the rest of their lives. I admit my part in this. You know you share that guilt with me, as you checked out years ago. Let's both set an example for them for once.'

Grace had actually been fine with his little speech – until he had mentioned their kids.

She was someone who set great store by her dignity. Even when she was a full-blown alcoholic, self-medicating sloth, she still deluded herself that nobody else noticed her slurred language or poor timekeeping. Humiliation was a major terror, and she didn't appreciate having her pressure points exposed and prodded in a public place.

So, dabbing her lips with the linen napkin, and with as much elegance as she could summon, she stood up and marched out of St Alban.

Mark was left alone, deserted.

He made the walk of shame towards the exit after asking for the bill. His leaving was made all the more shameful by the patronising sympathetic stare from Dame Judi, Lenny Henry's giggles and David Emin's hand wanker sign, executed even more enthusiastically than when Mark had arrived.

As Mark was about to leave, Mac, the maître d', quipped: 'Bad luck, Mark. Still, she does make a dramatic exit, your missus, doesn't she?'

'Fuck off, fat boy.' It was all the witty banter he could summon up that night.

He fled and hailed a black cab back to Woodford.

The cab driver was the sort that adored a captive audience, and insisted on taking him through the Spurs team and its weakness in mid-field, Ken Livingstone and his speed-hump madness, and the weak gearbox that afflicted his otherwise perfect cab. It was a lecture which lasted for the entire forty-five-minute journey.

Mark had barely uttered a word, with the exception of the odd 'Yeah' or 'Right'. By the time he had reached home he was desperate for the icy silence that no doubt awaited him.

Mark was not to be disappointed. Grace had gone to bed and her door was closed. He brushed his teeth and took a Nytol, Night Nurse and Valium to make sure he went off to sleep quickly.

The next few days were difficult for him. He had no new ideas of how to resume the conversation about winning her support for his political ambitions. He knew that Roger would want solutions and not problems, so that source of counsel was not open to him.

Although he was bereft of inspiration concerning Grace, the PR bandwagon rolled on relentlessly. Unbeknown to Mark, Roger had not been idle, as he still had some belief in his new friend. He had approached Garry Barnett, the programming executive from Sky who had attended the Tory private dinner, with a quiet suggestion.

'How about featuring Mark Cohen on one of your chat shows? He makes ruddy good television. You saw him on the Charlton show – give him a break so he can answer his critics and give his unique spin on the issues of the day.'

The following week Mark received a call inviting him to be a guest on the highly popular live afternoon phone-in/studio audience participation show hosted by Richard Cox and Richard Hampton.

Called *The Dick, Dick Show*, it was produced by Gay-time Television for Sky One.

As a seasoned celebrity these days, Skid had no concerns about microphones, cameras or wearing makeup. He did not even bother to prepare a script of answers to any possible questions which he might face that afternoon.

After the introductions – to a rendition of 'Bad to the Bone', he endured an overly warm greeting from the TV hosts.

The audience clapped and cheered wildly and then the questions began predictably enough.

'What are you most proud of, and what do you regret?' asked Dick Cox.

Dick Hampton interjected: 'Not being able to tell a decent mother-in-law joke for the rest of his life I expect.'

Mark took the banter in good humour and said he regretted nothing, except the pain he had inflicted on those he loved. That and being found out, naturally.

'Are the sins on that list you placed in the papers all true?'

'Yes, those I can remember anyway,' Mark replied. 'I missed most of the 90s being out of my head.' The audience giggled.

Dick Cox came in. 'Okay, let's go over to the phone-lines. They are jam packed with callers. First, questions from Jim in Birmingham.'

'Hello, Mark. Great show, Dick and Dick,' said the thick Brummie accent over the studio speakers.

Dick mouthed a camp 'Thank you', and made a signal for the caller to continue.

'Are you really the Devil?'

'Compared to Mother Theresa or Adolf Hitler?' asked Mark. 'It depends where you set the benchmark. What I will say is that, through experiencing both good and bad extremes, I am able to handle our enemies and defend our values from a better informed perspective. If that makes me a devil then please call me Lucifer.'

Some mild applause of cautious approval followed.

He sat back and purred like a V8 engine that was just ticking over.

That relaxed state of mind was shattered by the next call. He instantly recognised that 'Miss Gina Bucks' was in fact his own daughter, Poppy. Mark's immediate thought was to be grateful that she didn't have the mimicking skills of her brothers, or he would never have known it was her.

She had managed to slip through the programme's vetting net on her mission to broadcast the rehearsed tirade about her mother to as many people as possible. Only Mark had any idea that it was his daughter who had taken control of the airwaves.

Dick Cox jumped in first. 'Hello there, my gorgeous sugar plum. Do you have a question for this deliciously naughty boy Mark Cohen?'

'Yes I have, thanks Dick, so why don't you shut up like a good boy and let me ask it?'

There were gasps from the audience, but Mark kept his composure and remained resolutely expressionless. A shocked Dick obediently sat down, with a look of bewilderment, shrugging his shoulders at the other Dick in a 'What could I do?' kind of way.

'Mr Cohen, the rumours circulating the internet gossip forums suggest your wife is a drunk, vindictive junkie who has abandoned her children. Would you confirm or deny that she is an addict and bad mother? And do you think you have been unfairly cast by the media as the only villain in this piece?'

The Dicks went crimson and made 'Cut' signals, moving their hands across their throats.

Dick Cox suggested: 'I think we should take a break now and…'

Mark said loudly over his panicking host: 'I want to answer those questions if I may.'

Defeated, Dick Cox slumped back down, removing the earpiece from which even the audience could make out a producer having a nervous breakdown.

Back in Woodford, Grace was in her kitchen making herself a cup of tea. The portable TV was on in the background, tuned to *The Dick, Dick Show*. Mark's guest appearance had not even caused her to look up, but Poppy's voice had demanded Grace increase the volume and stare attentively at the screen.

She was crying almost the instant that the vitriol started, humiliated by the handful of cutting words. With baited breath, she awaited her husband's inevitable condemnation and confirmation of her parental neglect and uselessness as a human being.

Mark said quite calmly once the furore had died down: 'Grace is no angel, but she has more love in her than anyone I have ever met. She worships her children and does not deserve to be the subject of gossip columns that I suspect you, "Gina", may also have fuelled with your own uninformed speculation.'

Poppy tried to interrupt. 'But Mr Cohen, surely…'

But Mark held up his hand and spoke loudly over her boisterous words: 'Please pay me the courtesy of letting me answer your questions before jumping in. I want to say for the record that I deserve to be cast as the culprit, not her. She should get a medal for what she has endured. My dear young lady, how old are you? Do you have kids?'

'Gina' answered: 'I am eighteen and, no, I don't have kids but…'

Mark fired back: 'So pipe down for a minute then, please. If only you knew what it is like to bring up three children alone, to sacrifice your own dreams for them and get no help from a selfish egomaniac like me. Maybe then you might have earned the odd glass of wine at the end of a thankless day.

'Live it, before you criticise. Just ask any parent here what that's like. Mothers are incredible and I am in awe of them all.' Dick and Dick were clapping wildly, and the crowd was cheering in the aisles.

'Clearly there are a lotta of mums and dads in today,' said Dick Hampton. 'Mental note to raise the gay quota tomorrow! Let's take that break to get some hankies. Back in five...'

Mark had begun his speech with the sole intention of looking good in front of the electorate. By the end he felt he had to defend Grace to her own children, and to rightly take the brunt of the blame and shame for his own actions. She might have carved him up in the pages of the *Daily Mail*, but Mark knew he had deserved that mauling.

After the show, he retired to the green room for a much needed JD. He took his mobile from his pocket and turned it back on. A text was waiting for him from Poppy, saying simply: *Point taken xxx*.

Back at home Grace was still staring at her TV. She wiped away her tears and felt her now familiar steely resolve slip back into place.

Did Mark really mean all that? Grace pondered. Or is this another brain-ache-in-waiting? She was well aware that the family's future was in the balance; teetering between an utter breakdown and what she now admitted to herself could be the last chance for her to start playing a proper role again in the lives of her children – and to find some way of co-existing with Mark.

Her resolve gave way to anger at the thought that, once again, she found herself wobbling on the edge, wondering if he really was that new man he claimed to be who would stand by her and the kids or if she was simply lining herself up to be drop-kicked back into the abyss, once and for all, by the selfish bastard.

Now furious, she decided then and there that she had to take a leaf from Poppy's book and find a way to ask him some very direct questions when he was at his most vulnerable. She knew a TV chat show wouldn't cut it – he was simply too skilled as a media tart by now. She needed an opportunity where he could not scuttle back to the safety of his rhetoric; where she could find out the truth. And soon.

I need a miracle, she thought before letting out a despairing laugh. Meanwhile, despite his performance on the show, Mark was still dejected. He was also well aware that he needed a miracle too.

As it happened, the miracle that both Grace and Mark were so desperate for turned out to be Julia.

Mark had chosen to ignore the text Julia sent to him on the day his advert appeared in the press because he had wanted to put all his focus on his political career and not be be sidetracked by her text for *a re-hump-tion of sexual relations, Mr future Prime Minister! PS Sorry xx*. However, her second text that had arrived the day after his *Dick, Dick Show* appearance had proven to be a welcome distraction from Mark's despair at having his dreams cut short. It had read: *Don't be shy!. I think you are amazing and I'm truly sorry. Can I see you soon? I WILL make it worth your while! Xxx*

He knew he was ready to let off steam, happy in the knowledge any encounter would be both safe and discreet. And, if his career was dead, what did it matter anyway? He didn't know what to feel about Julia though. Was he angry? Was he flattered? Was he missing her?

He finally admitted to himself that, yes, he had missed her

and that Unfinished Business, as a result of her rejection, had resurfaced between them. So, before the election campaign kicked off aproper, Mark agreed to meet Julia the following night. He added to his reply that she was a 'selfish bitch' and that she had better make her recompense pretty bloody spectacular.

She had said that she had prepared a special treat for him, and he thought he knew what that might mean. 'Better stock up with iodine and Deep-Heat' was his mental note. Sadly he was way off the mark with that prediction.

Julia Hardy-Roberts was an unusual person. A lack of fear of consequences was a recent thing for Mark but, this fearlessness was hardwired into her genes. She had thought long and hard about how to shock and pleasure her man. Sex toys were going to be too tame, especially after his confessions and wild antics.

As he drove to her flat that evening, he was as well prepared as ever and full of anticipation. New boxers, trimmed nasal hairs and ear fur, plus a new set of handcuffs bought from the Eros Centre in Soho.

Once on the Borough doorstep, he rang the bell and was immediately buzzed in. The neighbour's mountain bike was characteristically propped up against the radiator in the hall, and the peeling woodchip paper added to the seedy look. Just as he liked it – rancid squalor.

He climbed the stairs, where the apartment's door was ajar.

'Hello? You there, sweetie? Hello?' Nothing. No reply, only silence. 'Come on, stop freaking me out…'

It was completely dark except for the faint glow of red candles that burned in various corners of the room. There was a sinister feeling to the space, and he wondered what was going on. Then a voice came, interrupting his thoughts which, curiously, had strayed back to the day of Grace and the maggots.

'Come into the dungeon, my slave. You will obey my instructions. I command you.'

'You nutter, Julia,' he breathed but went with the flow, feeling a slight tingle in his black Armani under-shorts.

'Get naked. Say nothing. Lie down on the leather bench and put on the blindfold. NOW...'

He did as he was told.

He waited for a minute. His wrists and ankles were suddenly and roughly bound by straps until he was in a starfish shape and helpless. Then the teasing began. Ice cubes were rubbed around his balls until they ached in agony.

'Owwwwww!'

'Be quiet, or it will be even worse for you.'

His nipples were clamped in metal grips and tweaked as his scrotum was twisted at the same time. Mark bit his lip and remained quiet. Then he felt two sets of lips brush against his body. His toes were sucked simultaneously, then the lips travelled up his calves and to his inner thighs, ending with one pair attached to his erect penis and the other kissing his earlobe. Blimey, a double act? Is it Christmas and my birthday, he thought, lost entirely to this dual pleasure.

It stopped abruptly and there was silence once more. Then, to his right, there was what sounded like a sack of potatoes hitting the floor. He heard the sound of this 'sack' being dragged a short distance before an ominous silence descended. Mark gulped.

Footsteps approached, the sound of high heels getting nearer and nearer.

'Hello, Mark.'

He knew that voice. It wasn't Julia, but he couldn't

comprehend the notion of it being his wife.

'Grace?'

'Hi.'

'Hi.'

Those two words once more, but this time in very different circumstances to when she was in hospital and he was the petrified visitor.

'I think we should talk,' she said in a calm, menacing tone.

'Don't tell me, you have ways of...' said Mark.

Grace interrupted: 'Answer honestly and don't waste words. Before we begin, you should know why I am here. Julia asked me. She thought you still harboured lustful thoughts towards me. Judging from this place, I think this 'encounter' is one weird and screwed-up kick for her anyway. But, frankly, I do not give a flying monkey's about any of that. What I do care about is getting the truth from a serial liar.

'This is my way of discovering if you mean what you say – about that speech you made, wanting us to put things right with the kids. I want to know why you defended me on *The Dick, Dick Show*, and what was the truth and what were the lies throughout our entire marriage. It's my turn to be in charge, so you'd better buckle up – it's going to be brutal.

'So, question one. Did you love me when we first married?' His response came immediately, as it was from his heart and soul and had been rehearsed every night for eighteen years.

'Yes. I loved you then, and I love you now.'

Grace said: 'Shame, it was going so well until that last bit.'

An excruciating pain suddenly shot through his testicles and the air was filled with the smell of burnt flesh and hair as he convulsed and flayed against the leather bench. He screamed so loud and bit down so hard that he dislodged some fillings in his teeth. Must be the electric cattle prod, he thought, trying to fight the pain, the one tool me and Julia never got round to using.

'Naughty boy for making a din,' said Grace, 'but I will let you off that one as it was the first.'

'Well, ta very much,' he said, panting as he caught his breath. 'Where is Julia?'

'She's fine. Incredibly, and against my wishes, I like her. She was very nice about Andrew, whom we both admired.

'I was a bit disappointed you had a thing with her – and still appear to – but I'm not exactly surprised, given my affair. I am pleased it was Julia that you chose and not one of my aunts or uncles, or my sister. But I don't care about any of that anymore; I just want the truth.'

'How gracious, darling,' he said delicately. 'Now, for the love of God, let me go!'

'Not yet, Mark. You always said we should communicate more and get closer. I should open up, you said. Well, here's your bloody chance to "open up". If you're not honest, and don't start spilling your guts, I will spill them for you.'

She took a deep breath before asking: 'Question two. Looking back over two decades, what regrets do you have about us?' Conscious of the cattle prod, he thought for longer before opening his mouth this time.

'I made a mistake. I married you because I believed you were the strong one. You were supposed to bail me out, to prop me up, and to be the rock. Only recently did I take my head from my arse and see you for the person you are – someone in lonely agony and isolation. Working together with you on the Eyes of the World was a genuine attempt to redress that, albeit years too late. It was made for your humanity and creativity. I wanted some forgiveness and redemption for my blindness.'

'Good, that saves me the trouble of blinding you now,' said Grace. The hot tip of the prod came so close to Mark's cheek that he felt the hairs on his face stand up.

'Question three. Who initiated the sordid fling with my mother? Was it you or her? Be very careful how you answer this, I warn you. It might be the last thing you ever utter.'

Mark considered his scrotum and its welfare before answering. 'I went there to tell her about you and Poppy, and we hugged and she comforted me. It just happened. I don't think it was even personal, just her need to feel attractive and my weakness when it comes to being able to reject female affection.'

He sensed the prod now hovering perilously close to his penis, but it was withdrawn as he heard Grace begin to cry. Her sobbing tore Mark's heart out and, surprisingly, he was actually becoming aroused by the danger of this bizarre situation.

'Question four,' she said, holding back her sobs. 'Do you really believe all that stuff you blurted out at St Alban or is it a sales pitch for your own ends as per usual? I am prepared to accept my responsibility for damaging our children, but do you truly believe that we share in that failure?'

Mark simply answered: 'I do.'

Grace's sobbing stopped and he heard her breathe out, relaxing. Or at least he hoped she was calming down, as he felt the heat from the prod return close to his scorched testicles.

'Question five. Do you really need me to help you with your political career? And will it help Poppy, Sam and Max and redeem us in their eyes?'

Mark paused and then said: 'Yes, and all of this is now entirely in your hands. I cannot move without your help. And I want to do good things, beyond just self-interest, truly. Please help us, together, to be worthwhile, for our children's sake. I beg you.'

He felt the prod move away and the tone of her voice became calmer. 'Final question. Do you think my tits are small?'

Without hesitation he replied: 'No.'

And without hesitation, Grace proceeded to push the cattle prod into an orifice that, on a good day, Mark believed the sun shone out of. Thankfully (and much to his relief), Grace had 'disarmed' the instrument before 'taking the plunge' or else the electric shock may well have killed him.

'You deserved that,' she said. 'Now let's go home. Just so you know, I do believe you now and I will help you for the children's sake – they deserve better from both us – but God help you if you make a fool of me again...'

He was released and his blindfold removed. As his eyes cleared, he saw Julia propped up against the side of the wall. Judging from the slight smile fixed across Julia's face, the faraway look in her eyes and the wine glass that lay up-ended next to her, he suspected she'd been heavily drugged courtesy of some of the strongest pharmaceuticals available from Grace's epic collection.

'Never knew you had it in you, wife,' offered a slightly awe-struck Mark. 'That will teach you to underestimate me, you blind, deaf mollusc,' came the reply.

They undressed Julia and put her to bed as one would a sick, sleepy child. They then went home to Woodford, where Mark spent the rest of evening holding bags of frozen peas to his bollocks.

Julia woke with a groggy head, at first angry that she had missed most of what had happened, and that she had been outwitted by another woman. However, as she always did, she buried it deep within her and rapidly moved on. Neither Mark nor Grace ever heard from Julia again.

CHAPTER TWENTY-THREE

A Bedtime Tory

Within the week, Grace was pictured in the *Sun* hugging her husband, smiling happily, the caption celebrating her saint-like forgiveness of him, 'The Scallywag'.

'Behind every devil is a good woman', ran another day's headline.

The dynamic had altered between them. She was as good as her word – by her husband's side throughout the next period of political lobbying and preparation.

The general election campaign fought by Mark was one of the most strenuous and exhausting periods of his life. At the actual time of the election, he was legally restricted to spending only a few thousand pounds on his own promotion, but that was after the millions that had already been lavished on his press advertisements, which had resulted in a multi-media feeding frenzy.

By the time he focused on the good people of Islington,

they already had a better idea of who he was and what he stood for than any official representative of any other party. Ironically, the incumbent Tory MP, Toby Winkworth, had been exposed over a sordid little affair with his secretary, and it was blown up by Winkworth confessing all to a newspaper so it would appear 'important'. When Mark read about it, his initial thought was 'bloody amateur.'

To compound his mistake, Winkworth had blurted out that he had 'fudged' his expenses and had also 'suffered' at the hands of a secret transvestism fetish for many years before 'seeking professional help'. Mark, through good timing, was hailed as a refreshing pioneer; Toby just looked like a sad, sleazy, copy-cat loser.

Thus, Toby Winkworth, MP, was largely discarded by the electorate and party faithful alike. Mark Cohen was on a roll, and his competitor's ineptitude narrowed the gap between them. He had also made it clear that he would become a Conservative if asked, so that no vote would be wasted were he to be elected in place of the 'Winker'.

Using contacts in the studio at BC, he had thousands of posters printed of his smiling face beneath a set of sharp horns. The headline read, 'Mark of the Devil, your humble servant'.

Other posters featured Grace, but with a halo above her head instead of horns. The headline read, 'My husband is the Devil and I trust him – vote Cohen'.

Thousands of red jumpers were knitted with his demonic image and were worn by supporters and colleagues all over town.

In the local press he made sure that he had some form of coverage every day, but always showing his more caring side to balance the satanic show. Picking up on local issues or individual injustices, he demonstrated concern about the little things. Elsewhere, family shots were featured at fetes, charity events and multi-cultural religious festivals. When news was thin, he made it up by writing to powerful world figures about some issue or another and then leaking his letters of outrage to the media.

Grace was regularly interviewed and used the Eyes of the World to further endorse her husband. Apparently 'my Mark' was indispensable to the stricken children and passionate about putting something back into society. She insisted that she had forgiven him and that, for all his talk of the Devil, he had started on a new chapter in his life.

Poppy had been watching her mother suck up to the cameras and pretend to love 'her Mark' with growing irritation. Although a fragile truce had developed between parent and daughter, Poppy's mental wounds had not yet fully healed where her mum was concerned.

'She's sold out,' Poppy complained to her brothers.

'Grow up!' replied Max.

'What do you mean?'

'Dad knows what he's doing,' said Sam. 'He even worked out it was us in the wardrobe filming. He had a quiet word before the election kicked off.'

Poppy was gobsmacked. 'My God, you've sold out as well. Thought we had agreed to lie low? Did he know it was me at the Rookery with my mobile phone camera?'

'Nah, don't panic,' said Sam, 'but we advise you to tell him anyway. He sussed us but we didn't grass you up. He cut us a deal, and he's being really cool about it. I bet he would do the same for you. That's what he's probably done with mum.'

'Better than being bitter and twisted,' added Max. 'Plays

havoc with your skin.'

'I'll think about it,' said Poppy. 'What deal did you do with him?'

Sam replied, 'He got us to spray the Labour Party headquarters yellow and to fill its car park with live chickens.'

Mark's war against dithering, weak politicians was not only a great photo opportunity and funny, it appealed to earthy voters and city types alike.

Sam and Max loved doing their bit for politics and for their infamous father. The tide had turned back in the twins' favour at school – their street cred with classmates was now way off the scale.

Mark's campaign smacked of supreme confidence, which was attracting its own street cred among voters. When campaigning door to door, he was relentless, attentive and witty. Using his contacts, he created a daily ten-minute reality show chronicling his doorstep antics for the entertainment of MTV viewers, and a ripple of PR naturally accompanied it in the gossip weeklies such as *Reveal*, as well as the red-tops.

Poppy did decide to own up that she had snapped the shock Grace and Andrew photo in the Rookery.

'I'm sorry, it was a complete fluke,' she said. 'Never planned it. I never leaked it. Honest.'

'That's okay,' said Mark pragmatically. 'Just do me a couple of favours. Firstly never tell your mother it was you. It would break her heart and she does love you, you know that?' She bit her lip to resist making some cheap jibe, and instead asked, 'And the other favour?'

'Enjoy the limelight for once,' said Mark. 'Have fun and shine like your mum. I think you were born to be centre stage and not a wallflower. Knock yourself out.'

Mark also thought more coverage would be good coverage as far as his campaign was concerned.

Poppy took to the paternal favours like a supermodel possessed. There were interviews in *OK!*, *Heat*, *Cosmopolitan* and *Sugar*, and on Kiss FM and on the daytime Channel 5 show *Trisha*. *Zoo* and *Nuts* took semi-nude pouting shots and she lapped it all up.

Her self-harming scars were talked of as 'badges of honour' in many a magazine profile about her extraordinary young life. She was a guest presenter one weekend on a Channel 4 T4 special with Kelly Osbourne.

Poppy was eclipsing Grace. She loved her daddy for that.

In turn, Mark's cult status grew. The media was hungry for a radical character in a sea of grey, and blessed the Marmite 'Love It or Hate It' debate he sparked across the nation.

He even attached a megaphone to his beloved BMW and, through the sunroof, he stood and shouted his message to the soundtrack of his favourite anthems. Week after week this circus continued, roping in ever more impressive celebrity guests to endorse his credentials.

On the final night, as he stood in the church on Upper Street, Islington, the sound of the cheering crowd seemed muffled and distant to his ears. His main rival, Toby Winkworth, sheepishly arrived on the stage to the jeering and howling of an auditorium shouting in football fashion, 'Loser, loser!' and 'Toby, not even worth a wink.'

It was as if the night was designed just for Mark, and he knew he would win long before the final results were read out to the impatient throng. Utterly calm and deaf to the chanting, he was virtually able to lip read the numbers in sync, as they were openly declared at 10.30pm in the municipal hall.

He was duly elected by a narrow margin of 378 votes.

That vision of him as the shepherd, high above the flock of sheep, came to him, just as it had during his Bar Mitzvah speech some twenty-seven years before. He made an air-guitar-like gesture as if cocking a bazooka and firing a missile into the masses.

His mobile vibrated in his pocket. It was Roger sealing the deal with the Tories' endorsement and an invitation to come on board. 'Look, old chap,' said Roger, 'off the record, we don't stand a cat-in-hell's chance of winning the next general election – but come 2010, we're in like Flynn, I reckon. There's a new wave of Tory cads on the way and you could prove to be invaluable to them with your somewhat "unique" approach. So play your cards right and who knows where it might lead... Now get over here and let's celebrate – and don't forget to bring your chopper for our mutual friend, charlie!'

Roger signed off and Mark took his digital camera from the inside of his jacket pocket one more time, firing off a single shot to record his incredible triumph. Like the photo he took of himself on the evening of Armageddon all those months ago, he wanted to take a picture that recorded what he knew was a pivotal moment in his life.

After more TV interviews, and general back slapping, Mark and his kids were whisked off to Conservative Party HQ in order to join the more elaborate celebrations that were going on there.

A new version of Make My Mark was about to begin.

Poppy, Samuel and Max were now trained and ready to take a role in the family dynasty and continue its legacy of facing unfinished business, fearing nothing to get what they wanted.

A Bedtime Tory

They were the product of an angel and the Devil, equipped to change the world and bend it to their will. They had moved further up the food chain, with all the advantages of a powerful father and mother and unlimited access to anything and everything. A new pact had been made between them.

CHAPTER TWENTY-FOUR

Once, Twice, Three Times an Ironic Lady

Grace was not with them on that triumphal evening, as she had said that she felt unwell.

In fact, she preferred to be at home working on her beloved charity, as she had fulfilled her promise to publicly support her husband. She drew little pride from the experience, but was pleased that Poppy, Sam and Max seemed genuinely excited and proud of what they had done together. And that was the point of the exercise.

The media exposure had not done any harm for fund-raising either. Revenues were going through the roof, pictures were now being auctioned at celebrity events for tens of thousands of pounds, and the footprint for charitable work was expanding across the globe.

So she had stayed in South Woodford with a bottle of Chivas Regal, provided by Mark to celebrate the hoped-for win. She drank it while reflecting on a conversation she had just had with a woman to whom she had never spoken before.

Grace had picked up the phone in the kitchen on her way to retrieve some more ice.

'Hello? Is that Grace Cohen?'

'Yes, it is. Who is this, please?'

'Listen, you don't know me, but I'm a friend.'

Grace was going to hang up, but something in the voice rang true.

'My name's Cherry. I work in the reception at BC, and I know Mark very well. I'm worried about him, or more accurately I'm worried for you, your kids and the entire country, given the election result. I need you to hear this.'

Cherry went on to describe in meticulous and graphic detail all that she had seen in Andrew Bond's office on the day he suffered his fatal heart attack. Grace did not want to absorb Cherry's account of Mark's callous act, but something in her knew it was the truth.

The television in the lounge was still turned on as background noise for her work, and for the first time that evening she looked at the screen. It was the election coverage, and her husband was being interviewed by a reporter. He looked jubilant, and made a strange gesture that resembled firing a machine gun. This struck a chord in her head as she gulped another slug of whisky. His arrogance was incredible.

Her phone rang once more, but she didn't recognise the number displayed. Normally she would not have answered and, given the last call from Cherry she was even more apprehensive than usual about responding.

Yet something made her think, 'What else could happen?'

'Hello, is that Grace Cohen?'

'Yes, it is. Who is this?'

'This is Daniel Martin. I'm an investigative reporter for the

Sunday Mirror. This is not an easy conversation to have – but it has come to our attention, and we have evidence to support this, that your husband has funded his campaign to become an MP, and the charity Eyes of the World foundation that you are involved with, by using money from drugs and racketeering. Do you have any comment, Mrs Cohen?'

The silence was deep and impenetrable. Daniel was cut off instantly.

Grace returned to the lounge and sat down with the bottle of Chivas. A swig was followed by another, and then another, as she glared at the TV.

Mark was now on screen hugging their children as if he were the perfect father. 'Why is your wife Grace not here this evening?' the television interviewer asked him, cutting through this perfectly staged moment of family normality.

'She is exhausted after promoting my election campaign so strenuously. This is for you, Grace,' he boomed, a fist in semi-Nazi salute held aloft for the benefit of yet more cameras and the viewing audience.

In South Woodford the phone rang again.

'For heaven's sake,' she slurred.

'Hello?'

'Hi. Is this Grace Cohen?'

'Yes it is,' she said weakly, feeling as if life were slipping away from her with each second that passed.

'This is Alan Oldfield at the *Daily Express*. I have to inform you that we have received reliable information that your husband has had an affair with a married woman called Sammy Moore. The sources are the employees of a London hotel, and through them we also have the sworn testimonies of several bar and chamber staff members, plus CCTV footage of each of their entrances and exits from the building. We have been sitting on this story for months, and we think that now is the perfect time to release it, given the election result.

'Do you have any comments at this stage before we publish?'

'Yes I do,' said Grace. 'Goodbye.'

She was lost.

In the space of a single night the little that she had thought was solid had melted away. The love of her life, Andrew, had been left to die by Mark. The passion of her life, the Eyes of the World, had been given to and then taken away from her. Funded by dirty money that came from Mark, it was soiled now and, by tomorrow morning, it would be in ruins, courtesy of the Sunday papers.

And, after her own mother had screwed him, her oldest and closest friend had slept with Mark as well – Sammy, who had seduced her into having sex with Derek at that party. Sammy, who had also betrayed her.

Her mind turned to her children – and ultimately the planet.

That smug grin on her husband's arrogant face was still spread wide across the television screen.

It was a case of the Emperor's new clothes, she knew it. Did no one else see him for what he was? Satan. Lucifer. The Devil.

Grace was terrified. But she knew what to do.

The world had no idea what it might be in for over the next few years. A rocket-powered runaway rollercoaster in the hands of the Devil and his demonic children was a daunting prospect for humankind.

That night, however, Mark was at a zenith, and felt that nothing could ever bring him down from his high.

He was invincible.

He was impregnable.

He was a god.

He was God.

Mark had forgotten his Greek mythology, and the danger of flying too close to the sun. But with his characteristic sense of humour and talent for irony, the true God allowed him to enjoy the moment.

As the party subsided and the last glasses of sharp warm wine were drained, the Cohens were driven home in a stretch limo, much to the twins' delight.

'What a night. What an incredible night. Kids, I just want to say that I'm so proud of you, and all you have become. I could not be happier.'

'I'm proud of you too, dad, truly and honestly,' Poppy said, and she smiled and gave him an affectionate peck on the cheek.

'Yeah,' said Max, 'you're not the utter wally I thought you were.'

'Ditto,' added Samuel, 'you're only a half wally.'

'Praise indeed!' said Mark, and for the first time knew he had become not just God but, more importantly, a real man, by being a true father.

CHAPTER TWENTY-FIVE

Mourning has Broken

It was late.

Mark climbed the stairs of their South Woodford home with his three children. He saw them all into their rooms with a kiss and a hug, then tip-toed past Grace's bedroom and headed back down to the lounge.

There, he thumbed through the photo albums, neatly lined up by the wonderful Vicki in chronological order. The last contained the shots of Grace's twiglet leg hanging over the mattress, his own reflection (without horns) in the lounge mirror, and the visits to King George's Hospital.

What a blast, he thought, moving on to the pictures of Jim Smith and Helen Chapman with Bruno at the Primo pitch.

He took a slug of Jack from an opened bottle in the sideboard, set everything back in its place and headed up to bed and the wonderful, contented sleep reserved for the deeply self-satisfied.

As he passed Grace's bedroom, he briefly considered going in to wake her up and seeing if he could have sex with her, but thought better of it. Why risk ruining a perfect day? He really needed some sleep now, and he was hoping that there might be plenty of opportunity for that another day.

He undressed, washed, and slipped gratefully between the crisp, cool sheets.

In his head he recalled the brilliant oratory of his acceptance speech, and dreamed of becoming Prime Minister one day, with Grace at his side and his kids around him.

'King of the World' was the headline in the *Sun* dated 12th May 2015.

As he drifted off, he could just hear the muffled thump of his car boot being shut in the driveway. He registered it, but was already in the twilight zone where such noises rarely cause one to jump into action. At best, they might be recalled for a report of car theft in the morning.

'Too warm, too comfy, too yummy... Anyway, I have the whole of MI5 to sort it out now, if necessary,' Mark silently smirked, sinking into the land of nod.

Deep, deep asleep. Far away from boot lids and thoughts of danger.

If he had stirred, he might have gone to the window and seen his wife, dressed in her pink lacy dressing gown, taking a heavy toolbox from the boot of the BMW M5.

Grace carried it into the darkened hallway, opened it, and looked inside for a spanner. Not just any spanner, but the biggest, heaviest one she could find.

Her face blank and expressionless, the spanner clenched tightly in her right hand, she walked quietly up the stairs towards the spare room, just down the hall from her own. She pushed the door gently, and it swung open over the pale beige carpet.

She approached the bed, the sleeping figure of her husband spread-eagled at its centre under a fine white sheet, snoring softly.

Suddenly she recalled the pictures of her mother in *Readers' Wives* magazine, taken in that very spot with this demon. Then she thought of her beloved Andrew, left to die in his office, the ruined Eyes of the World charity, Sammy...

Grace lifted the heavy spanner above her head and brought it down with full force on Mark's skull. He died dreaming of being that shepherd, watching over his herd of sheep with the bazooka.

The cracking of his skull woke the kids. But Grace kept on pounding it until it was a mass of gristle and purple pulp, and the blood ran in rivulets down the walls and formed puddles on the sheets, particles of grey matter floating like little boats on a lake.

Even as the children ran into the room, she could not stop punishing her dead husband's remains.

'AAAHHHHH!' screamed Max, as they ran for their lives to the neighbours' house, finding refuge with the rodent-tossing Robinsons, who rang the police.

Blue lights and sirens filled the night sky for hours, as did the helicopter news crews covering the spectacle for breakfast television.

The Cohen children became major celebrities within minutes, and were lionised for being so strong and brave despite the horrendous ordeal that they had been through.

Grace was taken away in handcuffs with a blanket over her head, literally stained red with Mark's blood. She never uttered another word except for, 'I killed the Devil...', repeated in a monotone, over and over again.

The yellowing last will and testament of Mark and Grace Cohen, written nearly nineteen years earlier, was found by

Sammy, in a file helpfully labelled 'old crap' by the late Barry. It was duly passed on to the lawyers and executors of the estate.

Under its provisions, the children, though not named because they were not born when it was written, were left in the care of Sammy (and Barry).

So Poppy, Samuel and Max moved into Wattapenis Palace, to live with an astonished Sammy and a thrilled Derek Peterson. At last, he had the love of a woman, and a family. He was now 'The Daddy' and a daddy at the same time.

Mark's funeral was held at the same venue as his dear friend Barry's, where a huge crowd gathered to pay their latest respects. Mavis and Sid were crushed by the loss of their miracle child, and their tears never stopped. Denise was inconsolable, too. Kerry Goldstein and Gene were there, and even Patrick Craze blew his nose once or twice.

The gravestone was erected a year later and was carefully chosen by Poppy, who missed her daddy very much. She understood what it needed to be, and what the eulogy should say.

It was a simple stone in polished black granite, with bold gold lettering. It said:

'Here lies Mark Cohen.

Do not mourn or shed a tear for him.

His flame burned hot and bright, but for all too short a time for those of us that love and miss him.

Rest now, dear Mark, you must be exhausted.'

EPILOGUE

All is Fair in Love and War

The sun was setting, and it was magnificent. It was a molten orb, its shape no longer a true sphere.

The horizon was a limitless panorama, lilac and purple, magenta and crimson.

The sea was almost flat, rolling gently like the Atlantic, its surface reflecting a wide beam of light from the sun as it sunk into the west, like a glimmering pathway to heaven.

Mark was a spirit, a disembodied presence, walking along this shaft of light as though it were the yellow brick road. He had no idea how the road came to be there. He did know that he had died, but he was excited, even exhilarated, at the notion that whatever constituted the essence of Mark Cohen stubbornly continued to exist.

'But where am I?'

He continued strolling along the path, and was startled to see a bright blue neon sign to his left.

It read, 'God's Bar'.

Mark thought a drink sounded like a fine idea, so he took a characteristically sharp left swerve and found himself in a bar that Carlsberg ('If Carlsberg made bars, they would probably be the best bars in the world...') would be proud of.

It was made of pure glass, every surface reflecting the vivid reds, purples and indigos of the sky. Numerous bottles of Jack Daniels (evidently God's favourite tipple), Bombay Sapphire Gin and Absolut were lined up on the shelves.

This is surely heaven, Mark thought with a smile.

As he turned to survey the scene, he became aware that he was not alone. Seated in a booth of plump violet velvet, were three men.

Barry stood up with arms outstretched, inviting Mark to join them.

Next to him was Andrew Bond, cool and smiling with a twinkle in his eye.

The third chap was familiar, but Mark knew they had not met before. Then the penny dropped.

It was Eric Cantona.

Barry spoke first. 'Skid, let me introduce you to someone. Mark this is God, God this is my old wanker, Skid.'

'Pour me a large Jack, Baz,' said Mark, 'I think I really, really need one.'

God watched indulgently for a few moments as Mark poured down the brown nectar. With its help, Mark found nothing strange in the fact that he was sitting in a bar with two dead people and Eric Cantona, who was not dead at all, but was apparently God. Secretly he had always suspected that the former Manchester United centre forward, was too much of a genius; the mixture of poet and athlete more than any mortal could aspire to.

Of course, he was God, and could exist in many dimensions

at the same time.

It was just a shame that he turned out to be French. Their arrogance was not misplaced after all. Les bastards.

The discussion went on for what seemed like an eternity but, as they had all the time in the world it really didn't matter. The three dead men had all shared a love of life, and that was why they had a place at the bar with God.

Back on earth, the results of their deliberations were quickly felt, and shaped the lives of those being judged.

Grace was sent to an asylum, where she became a dribbling old woman nestled in a wheelchair under a chequered blanket, unable to recognise even her own children, had they ever visited her. This was precisely the fate Mark had feared that day in that King George's hospital ward, and it surely came to pass. At least the money that remained from the Derek 'bonus' was usefully spent on her care when the medical insurance eventually ran out.

Mark took no real satisfaction in her plight, though he was relieved that he had been spared his own role in this living hell, the Sunday spoon-feeding sessions, as he was dead.

It was through their daughter, Poppy, that Grace's best qualities were allowed to blossom. Poppy, aged twenty-two, went off to Ethiopia and became an aid worker and teacher to the children of that impoverished country. She was happy, a ray of sunshine to all those around her, exuding boundless energy.

When she was thirty, she returned to Britain and took up a roving ambassadorial role at the Eyes of the World. It had survived the drugs-funding scandal, mostly through the efforts of Karen Phillips, who had become its full-time CEO in place of Grace. Under her stewardship, it had gone from strength to strength.

In her forties, Poppy set out on another distinguished

career, this time in film and on the stage as a character actress. After stealing the headlines during Mark's election campaign so many years before, she was stealing them again, but this time in the entertainment sections of magazines.

She had no fear – just like her father hadn't during the last year of his life.

Poor Grace did not fulfil her earthly potential, but she did become an angel when her time came, many years later. Redemption and peace were finally hers, the pain in her tortured soul quelled at last.

Derek, in typical style, managed to avoid being traced to any drug-sourced funding of Mark's political or charitable activities. Instead, when police investigations were initiated, it was loyal Colin Black who volunteered to be the fall-guy. He was still grateful to Del for his earlier kindness, and decided to do the bird with dignity for the man who granted his knees their reprieve.

The twins took like ducks to water to the role of Essex rascal Derek Peterson's true sons. They devised a new online gaming product linked to sex sites, and cleaned up in their own right. Then, in their late twenties, they took on the Las Vegas casino scene and won. They moved to Nevada and never looked back.

'That's my boys,' Del would say, the proudest step-dad in the world.

Less happily, Sammy and Denise died just eight years after the Cohen kids arrived at Wattapenis Palace. One bleak December evening, Sammy took Derek's brand new bright orange Maserati for a spin with her friend and an alcohol blood level equivalent to rocket fuel. They were subsequently scraped off the trunk of an ancient oak tree beside the Epping New Road. The joint in Sammy's lips was still smouldering in her mouth and, as ever, she was wearing no knickers.

Sammy's life may have been cut short but she had at least known what it was like to be utterly loved and cherished by another human being. She had no demons at the end, and so was blessed.

Denise died with her mouth open, which was not a blessing but was at least appropriate.

As though the history of Grace and Mark was repeating itself, it was the unlikely rock of Derek who stepped up to the plate and became a father to Poppy and the twins. Mother figures had always been in short supply to the Cohen children, and always would be.

Fat Dave was never convicted of his crimes, but left the employment of his mentor when the twins took his place at the King's side.

He opened a butcher's shop in Dagenham, selling speciality meats and sausages. Endangered species were his unique selling point, and Dave thought nothing of flogging white tiger or dolphin to a curious public on the black market. He died some years later, choking on a piece of fatty gristle from the blow hole of a sperm whale.

Sid Cohen died quite soon after Mark, quietly and peacefully in his sleep. Mavis took some of the money that Mark had discreetly left her, together with Sid's life insurance, and sailed the seven seas on ocean liners. This floating catered-for experience was an excellent tonic for the lovely lady and she became, in time, a happy globe-trotting grandma. Mavis never remarried, but began to look after herself for the first time in her life.

Julia Hardy-Roberts rose to be Chief Executive of the Inter Public Group, one of the largest advertising networks in the world. She moved to an apartment in Fulham, had a villa in

Jamaica, and a chalet in St Moritz. She kept the Borough dungeon as well. It was the perfect place to teach some of the young male account handlers the meaning of obedience and discipline. 'After all,' she would say, 'no pain, no point,' as she connected yet another poor underling to the mains supply.

She never married, and never missed it, fulfilling her life in other ways. She negotiated the purchase of BC for IPG and had the joy of firing Patrick Craze from his role as non-Executive Chairman during a brief thirty-second phone call. That felt very good indeed to Julia – while officially he was only in an advisory role, some of the BC's old school could still be manipulated by the ad world's original Devil when he felt like causing mischief. Julia also took ownership of a yellow Lamborghini Reventón after outbidding Patrick for it on eBay.

Indeed, it was Julia who turned out to be his true successor in the snake pit of corporate advertising. As for Patrick, his BC shareholding was safe in her manicured hands and he was finally completely free to go forth and multiply his millions in the city without being distracted by BC. With no Andrew to prick his conscience, or to hold Julia back from making ruthless decisions, he was secretly thrilled to be let go.

'Let loose, more like,' he said after hanging up on Julia.

As for Mark, Barry and Andrew, they sit there still, drinking in God's Bar at the end of time, sharing their love of life and Jack Daniels on the rocks, with no intention of coming back to haunt anyone or anywhere on planet Earth.